HAVE BRIDES,
WILL TRAVEL

Look for these exciting Western series
from bestselling authors
William W. Johnstone and J.A. Johnstone

The Mountain Man

Preacher: The First Mountain Man

Luke Jensen: Bounty Hunter

Those Jensen Boys!

The Jensen Brand

MacCallister

Flintlock

Perley Gates

The Kerrigans: A Texas Dynasty

Sixkiller: US Marshal

Texas John Slaughter

Will Tanner, Deputy U.S. Marshall

The Frontiersman

Savage Texas

The Trail West

The Chuckwagon Trail

Rattlesnake Wells, Wyoming

HAVE BRIDES, WILL TRAVEL

WILLIAM W. JOHNSTONE
and
J.A. JOHNSTONE

KENSINGTON BOOKS
www.kensingtonbooks.com

All Kensington titles, imprints, and distributed lines are available at special quantity discounts for bulk purchases for sales promotion, premiums, fund-raising, educational, or institutional use.

Special book excerpts or customized printings can also be created to fit specific needs. For details, write or phone the office of the Kensington Special Sales Manager: Attn. Special Sales Department. Kensington Publishing Corp, 119 West 40th Street, New York, NY 10018. Phone: 1-800-221-2647.

Library of Congress Card Catalogue Number: 2018912508

ISBN-13: 978-1-4967-1848-8
ISBN-10: 1-4967-1848-8
First Kensington Hardcover Edition: April 2019

10 9 8 7 6 5 4 3 2 1

Printed in the United States of America

Chapter 1

The two men reined their horses to a halt. Below them to the left, at the bottom of a green, grassy bluff, a river meandered along between steep banks. Ahead of them, perched atop the bluff, were the buildings of a good-sized town, dominated by a big stone courthouse at the north end.

"Fort Worth," Scratch Morton said as he leaned on his saddle horn. "Reckon we'll see the panther?"

"I'm not sure there's any truth to that story," Bo Creel replied. "And even if there was, Fort Worth isn't a sleepy enough place anymore for a panther to curl up in the middle of Main Street and go to sleep."

That was true. Even from a distance, Bo and Scratch could see that the town was bustling. Off to the northwest, on the other side of the Trinity River, lay a broad stretch of cattle pens, over which hung a faint haze of dust. Fort Worth was no longer just a stopover on the cattle trails that led north. It was an important shipping point in its own right these days.

Scratch grinned. Like Bo, who had been his best friend for more years than either of them liked to count, he was at the upper edge of middle age. He was far from being ready for a rocking chair on a shady porch, though, as he would emphatically tell anybody who even hinted at such a thing.

"Next thing, you're gonna be tellin' me there's no such place as Hell's Half Acre," Scratch said.

"No, it's real enough, I reckon. We've been there, remember?"

"Oh, yeah. Well, it's been a while, and last time we were in Fort Worth, we didn't really have a chance to enjoy ourselves. We were on our way somewhere else, weren't we?"

"Yeah," Bo said, "but I disremember where."

"With a couple of fiddle-footed hombres like us, I ain't sure it matters." Scratch straightened in the saddle and heeled his horse into motion again. "Come on."

The two of them were the same age and about the same size, but that was where any resemblance ended. Scratch was the more eye-catching of the duo, with silver hair under a big cream-colored Stetson; a ruggedly handsome, deeply tanned face that usually sported a grin; a fringed buckskin jacket over brown whipcord trousers and high-topped brown boots; and a pair of ivory-handled Remington revolvers in fancy tooled-leather holsters attached to an equally fancy gunbelt.

Folks always noticed Scratch first, which was just fine with Bo, who never craved attention. He wore a flat-crowned black hat on his graying dark brown hair. The hat matched the long coat and trousers he wore. He'd been accused more than once of looking like a circuit-riding preacher, but not many preachers carried a Colt revolver with such well-worn walnut grips.

They had become friends as boys during the Texas Revolution, in what came to be known as the Runaway Scrape, when the Mexican dictator Santa Anna and his army chased thousands of Texican settlers eastward after the fall of the Alamo.

Yeah, Santa Anna chased them, all right . . . until they came to a place called San Jacinto, where they rallied under General Sam Houston's leadership, turned around, waded into battle against overwhelming odds, and whipped that Mexican army up one way and down the other.

That was the birth of the Republic of Texas, which eventually became part of the United States, and now, more than forty years after that history-making day, Bo and Scratch were both still proud they had fought side by side in that battle, despite their youth.

They had remained friends ever since. They had gone through tragedy and heartbreak, danger and hardship, and for a big chunk of that time, they had ridden together, drifting from the Mississippi River to the Pacific Ocean, from the Rio Grande—sometimes *below* the Rio Grande—to the Canadian border. They had seen mountains and deserts and forests and plains.

But despite all that, something still drove them onward in search of new places to see and new things to do.

If they ever stopped moving, Bo had reflected more than once, they might just wither away to nothing.

In recent times, a visit to the ranches where they had been raised down in South Texas, after the revolution, had gotten prolonged to the point where it seemed like they might actually settle down and live out their lives there. It would have been easy enough to do. They had friends and relatives and special ladies who would have been glad to settle down with them there.

Then one morning Scratch had shown up, trailing a loaded packhorse behind his mount, and had said to Bo, "You ready?"

"I am," Bo had replied without hesitation as he reached for his hat and his gun.

That was how they had come to be riding into Fort Worth on this warm late spring day. Any thoughts of putting down roots were far behind them and could stay there, as far as the two pards were concerned.

They rode along the top of the bluff until the trail they were on became an actual street that followed a tree-lined course between rows of big, impressive houses where the leading citizens of Fort Worth lived. They took that street to the part of town known as Hell's Half Acre, which was famous—or notorious—for its saloons, gambling dens, dance halls, and houses of ill repute. Most of those enterprises were clustered within an area of just a few blocks, and businesses that were more legitimate thrived all around them.

At the moment, Bo and Scratch weren't interested in legitimate businesses. They needed something to cut the trail dust from their throats.

Scratch looked along the street, pointed, and laughed.

"There you go, Bo," he said. "That's the perfect place for us to do our drinkin'."

Bo's eyes followed his friend's pointing finger and saw on the front of a building a sign that read THE LUCKY CUSS SALOON.

"We're lucky cusses if anybody ever was," Scratch continued. He angled his horse in that direction. "Let's try the place out."

"I expect one place is as good as another," Bo said as he followed Scratch's lead.

The hitch rail in front of the Lucky Cuss was full, and while Bo and Scratch might have been able to wedge their horses in with the others tied there, neither of them wanted to do that. Horses could get skittish and start to fight when they were forced up against other horses they didn't know.

Instead, they swung down from their saddles and looped the reins around the rail in front of the business next to the saloon, which, according to a cardboard sign propped up in the window, was Strickland's Domino Parlor. Judging by the horses tied up there, it wasn't as busy as the Lucky Cuss.

Bo and Scratch had to walk past the mouth of an alley to reach the saloon, and as they did so, Bo heard something that made him pause.

"What was that?" he asked Scratch.

"What was what?" the silver-haired Texan wanted to know.

"Sounded like somebody yelling for help back there in that alley somewhere."

Scratch cocked his head to the side in a listening attitude, then, after a moment, said, "I don't hear a thing."

"Well, it stopped kind of short, like somebody *made* it stop."

Scratch frowned and said, "What you heard was most likely a cat yowlin'. There may not be panthers sleepin' in the streets of Fort Worth anymore, but I'd bet a hatful of pesos there are still plenty of cats in the alleys."

"This wasn't a cat," Bo said as he turned and started toward the narrow passage between the domino parlor and the saloon.

"What it ain't," Scratch said as he followed, "is any of our business. We don't know anybody in Fort Worth."

"That doesn't matter. We're not in the habit of turning our backs on folks in trouble."

"Yeah, and that's how come *we* wind up in trouble more often than you'd expect for such peaceable hombres. Don't forget, there are beers with our names on 'em waitin' for us inside that saloon—"

A cry of pain from somewhere not far off interrupted him. It was on the high-pitched side, but definitely human, not feline.

"Shoot," Scratch said. "That sounded like a woman, or maybe a little kid."

"I know," Bo said as he increased his pace. He didn't see anything ahead of them in the alley except a rain barrel and a few pieces of trash. The cry had come from somewhere past the end of the alley He and Scratch were both trotting by the time they got there.

Both of them were still keen eyed in spite of their age. As soon as they emerged from the back end of the alley, they spotted several men to their right, in a dusty open area between the rear of the Lucky Cuss and the back of the buildings on the next street over.

Four men, Bo noted after a quick count, had surrounded a fifth man. The four hombres were roughly dressed in range clothes. From what Bo could see of their faces, they were cruel and beard stubbled.

The fifth man was dressed in a black suit and had a derby on his head. A fringe of mostly gray hair ran around his ears. Spectacles perched on his nose, and judging by the way they made his eyes look bigger, they had to be pretty thick. He was short, a little on the stocky side, and clearly no physical threat to anybody.

In a high-pitched voice, he said, "I'm telling you I don't have any money other than what I already gave you. Please, just leave me alone—"

"Two dollars," said one of the men surrounding him. "Two measly dollars. You're lyin', mister. Fancily dressed little pissant like you's got to have more dinero than that."

The man in the derby shook his head and said, "I swear I don't." He flinched as one of his assailants reached for him. "Please don't hurt me again."

"Mister, we ain't even *started* hurtin' you yet."

They shoved the little man roughly back and forth, so hard that his head jerked from side to side. He made another mewling sound, confirming that the noises Bo and Scratch had heard hadn't come from a woman or a child or a cat, but from this unfortunate victim of these would-be robbers.

"Well, this just puts a burr under my saddle," Scratch said quietly.

"Mine too," Bo agreed. "We taking cards?"

"Damn straight."

At that moment, one of the men roughing up the little fella in the derby hat noticed them and stopped what he was doing. He said, "Hey, Birch, look there."

The man called Birch turned and saw Bo and Scratch standing about ten yards away. He laughed and said, "You old geezers go on and get outta here now. This ain't none o' your business."

He turned back to the others, as if confident that Bo and Scratch would do what he had told them, and motioned to two of his companions.

"We've wasted enough time," he went on. "Grab his arms and hang on to him. I'll wallop him a few times, and he'll stop bein' so stubborn."

Bo raised his voice and said, "Hold on a minute."

Two of the robbers had grabbed the little man's arms, like Birch had told them to. They hung on, and the fourth man stood just off to the side as Birch swung around again with a look of annoyance on his scraggily bearded face.

"Are you still here?" he said. "I told you to skedaddle!"

Bo ignored him and said to the man in the derby, "Mister, what's your name?"

"M-Me?" the man managed to say.

"That's right."

"I . . . I'm Cyrus Keegan."

"Well, I have a question for you, Mr. Keegan," Bo said.

Birch glared and said, "I didn't tell you, you could ask any damn questions! I'm fast losin' my patience with you, you mangy old pelican—"

Bo held up an open hand to stop him. "Mr. Keegan, who's the law in Fort Worth these days?"

"The . . . the law? Why, M-Marshal Jim Courtright."

Bo nodded solemnly and said, "All right. When Marshal Courtright shows up here in a little while, you just tell him the truth about how these fellas tried to rob you. Can you do that?"

"I . . . I . . . Sure, I guess so—"

Birch yelled, "Now hold on! Nobody's gonna be talkin' to the damn law. If anybody's got anything to say, it's gonna be us."

"You boys won't be doin' any talkin'," Scratch said.

"Oh?" Birch put his hands on his waist and demanded, "Why the hell not?"

"Because if you don't let go of that fella and get the hell out of here right now, you're gonna be dead," Scratch said. "That's why not."

Birch stared at him for a couple of heartbeats, as if he couldn't quite comprehend what he had just heard.

Then, howling a curse, he stabbed his hand toward the gun on his hip.

Chapter 2

Bo and Scratch had been in enough gunfights over the years that they didn't have to talk about what they were going to do or even exchange a glance. They just knew instinctively how to proceed in this deadly confrontation.

Bo went left and Scratch went right, splitting apart to make themselves more difficult targets.

The Colt leaped into Bo's hand as if by magic. Scratch was just a hair slower hauling out the Remingtons but faster on the draw than most men.

Birch and one of his companions cleared leather before the other two would-be thieves, so they were the biggest danger. Bo targeted Birch. They fired at almost the same time, the reports coming so close together, they sounded like one shot.

Bo felt as much as heard the wind-rip as Birch's slug passed within a couple of inches of his ear. It missed because a shaved fraction of an instant earlier, Bo's bullet had slammed into Birch's chest and had caused him to jerk his hand slightly.

Birch took a step back and swayed a little as he gazed down in horror at the blood bubbling from the hole in his chest.

Then he folded up like an empty paper sack being crumpled in a giant hand.

A few yards away, Scratch fired while on the move. Both long-barreled, ivory-handled Remingtons roared and bucked in his hands.

The man he targeted got a shot off, too, but it went wide to Scratch's left, passing harmlessly between him and Bo. Meanwhile, the two .44 slugs from Scratch's revolvers pounded into the man's body, one striking him in the chest while the other ripped into his Adam's apple.

The man went over backward, crimson fountaining from his bullet-torn throat.

The other two had managed to get their guns out by now, but seeing what had happened to their companions unnerved them. One yelled a curse and fired, but his shot didn't come anywhere close to either Bo or Scratch.

With more time to aim, Bo drilled the third man through the shoulder, shattering bone and spinning him halfway around. The man cried out in pain and dropped his gun, then clutched his wounded shoulder with his other hand as he fell to his knees. Blood welled redly between his fingers.

If he was lucky, he might be able to use his right arm again, at least a little, but it would take a long time for him to recover that much. He was out of the fight now, that was for sure.

The fourth and final man who had been trying to rob Cyrus Keegan saw Scratch's revolvers swinging rapidly toward him. He dropped his gun so vehemently that it flew a good six feet in front of him before it thudded to the ground.

"Don't shoot!" he cried as he thrust both hands into the air. "For God's sake, don't kill me!"

Scratch's thumbs had both hammers drawn back. He held them there and said, "Don't move, hombre. If you do, I'll let daylight through you, sure as hell."

"I . . . I won't. I swear! I don't want any trouble!"

"Could've fooled me," Bo said. "It looked to me like you and your pards were trying to rough up and rob this fella."

"We . . . we were just gonna take his money. You didn't have to kill Birch and Sadler!"

"They shouldn't have thrown down on us," Scratch drawled. "That's the reason they're dead."

Bo motioned with his gun and said, "Back away, mister, but don't try to run off." He looked at the intended victim. "Are you all right, Mr. Keegan?"

Cyrus Keegan had stood stock-still while the shooting was going on. He was pale and wide eyed but still composed. He nodded and said, "I think so. They hadn't gotten around to really trying to hurt me yet. But they would have."

"More than likely," Bo agreed. "Step off to the side over there, just in case either of these varmints gets any more ideas."

That seemed pretty unlikely. The wounded man was still on his knees, clutching his shoulder and whimpering, while the man who had surrendered still had his hands in the air and looked too scared to try anything.

The gun thunder had been enough to attract plenty of attention. Bo heard shouts from the street, then running footsteps. A couple of men carrying shotguns burst into the alley from the passage beside the saloon.

Seeing law badges pinned to the newcomers' shirts, Bo and Scratch pouched their irons and stood easy, hands in plain sight. Making a man holding a scattergun nervous was never a good idea.

The deputies pointed the weapons at Bo and Scratch. One of them demanded, "What in blazes is goin' on here?"

"Gentlemen," Keegan said as he moved forward a little, "I can explain everything."

One of the deputies swung his shotgun toward Keegan and snapped, "Hold it right there."

Keegan stopped and hastily thrust his hands up, too.

"I'm unarmed," he said. With a nod toward Bo and Scratch, he added, "And these two men haven't done anything wrong. They kept me from being robbed, and they may well have saved my life."

"Are those fellas dead?" the second deputy asked as he stared at the robbers called Birch and Sadler, who lay motionless in slowly spreading pools of blood.

"If they ain't, they're doin' a mighty good imitation of it," the first deputy responded with a note of impatience in his voice. "Of course they're dead!"

"I'd be glad to explain everything," Keegan said again.

"Save it for the marshal." The first deputy glanced over his shoulder. "Here he comes now."

Indeed, another man had entered the alley behind the buildings. He strolled unhurriedly toward the scene of the shootings, but Bo noted that the lawman kept his hand on the butt of the gun at his hip, just in case he needed it. Such caution was common among men who packed a star.

This man was well built, a little taller than average, wearing a brown suit and vest and hat. His badge was pinned to his coat lapel. A luxuriant mustache adorned his upper lip, and thick, wavy hair came down over his ears and touched his collar. He was a handsome man and obviously a bit of a dandy.

The deputies spread out a little so the marshal could step up between them. He came to a stop and said, "Mr. Keegan, is that you?"

"Yes, Marshal," Keegan replied, putting his hands down.

With an amused smile on his face, despite the carnage in the alley, the marshal said, "For a man in your line of work, you seem to find yourself in the middle of trouble fairly often."

"I know, and I can't explain it, Marshal. You know what a peaceable man I am."

The lawman just grunted and said, "Tell me what happened here."

"These men"—Keegan waved a hand to indicate the two bodies, the wounded man, and the one with his hands still in the air—"grabbed me off the street, brought me back here, and were going to assault and rob me. I was quite in fear of losing my life, not just my money and valuables, when these two gentlemen came along and intervened on my behalf."

Coolly, the marshal regarded Bo and Scratch, then asked, "And who might you be?"

"Bo Creel," Bo said, introducing himself.

"Scratch Morton," Scratch added.

The marshal appeared to consider for a moment before saying, "I don't recognize the names from any wanted posters."

"That's because there ain't any dodgers out on us," Scratch said.

That might be stretching the truth just a little, Bo thought. He and Scratch had run afoul of lawmen—usually, but not always, crooked ones—in the past, and a few, mostly spurious, charges had been levied against them here and there. Nothing serious enough to have bounty hunters tracking them down, but there were areas in the West where rewards were still posted on them.

As far as they knew, however, they weren't wanted in Texas, so there was no need to bring up any of those other places.

"You killed those two men?" the marshal asked as he nodded toward Birch and Sadler.

"We gave them a chance to walk away," Bo said.

"They weren't of a mind to," Scratch said. "They drew first."

Keegan said, "That's very true, Marshal, and I'll testify to it if I need to."

"You'll need to," the marshal said. "There'll have to be an inquest on these deaths."

He relaxed and hooked his thumbs in his vest pockets as he looked at Bo and Scratch.

"But I don't doubt that they'll be ruled justifiable killings. Because of that, I'm not going to take you two gents into custody. In fact, you may have the thanks of the community coming to you. There's been a rash of such violent robberies recently. A couple of the victims have been beaten so badly they died. So there's a good chance you just rid Fort Worth of a pair of murderers and will be responsible for two more being locked up."

The robber who had surrendered blurted out, "I never killed nobody, Marshal. That was all Birch's doin'. If anybody tried to put up a fight, he'd get mad and hit 'em too much and too hard."

The lawman smiled and said, "We'll be sure that's entered into the record at your trial."

He turned to his deputies. "Get the prisoners out of here. That one's shoulder will need patching up, but you can send for the doctor once you've got them behind bars, where they belong. And get the undertaker back here, too."

To Bo and Scratch, he said, "As I said, you're not under arrest, but don't leave town until after the inquest is held."

"We weren't plannin' to, Marshal," Scratch said. "We just got here."

"And found yourselves up to your necks in a shooting scrape almost right away," the lawman mused. "Does trouble seem to follow you around?"

"It's sort of stubborn that way, all right," Bo said.

Chapter 3

Bo and Scratch stood with Cyrus Keegan while the marshal ambled off and the deputies took charge of the two prisoners. The wounded man had to be helped to his feet, and one of the deputies took his left arm to steady him as he stumbled out of the alley.

"So that was Jim Courtright, eh?" Bo said to Keegan. "The famous gunfighting marshal?"

"That's right. He's gone a long way toward cleaning up Fort Worth. Certain unsavory elements hate him, though. I certainly wouldn't want his job."

"Neither would I," Scratch said. "Bo and me have packed stars before, now and again, but it ain't somethin' I'm overfond of."

"That's because you're too fiddle footed to stay in one place for very long," Bo said with a smile.

Scratch chuckled and said, "There's an old sayin' about the pot callin' the kettle black."

Keegan looked at them and shook his head. He said, "You were just involved in a desperate gun battle that could have cost your lives. You killed two men and badly wounded another mere minutes ago, and yet now you appear as cool and calm as can be."

"Well, the shootin's over, ain't it? And we're all still breathin'." Scratch shrugged. "No reason to be upset."

"You remind me of two young men I met a while back. They were quite levelheaded and handy with their guns, as well."

"It's a good quality to have," Bo said. "Otherwise we might not have stayed alive as long as we have."

Scratch laughed and said, "I guaran-damn-tee we wouldn't have."

"What brings you to Fort Worth?" Keegan asked. "Are you here on business?"

"We don't really have any business," Bo said, "except for seeing what's on the other side of the next hill."

"Right now, though, we were fixin' to have a drink," Scratch said.

"Then let me buy it for you," Keegan said without hesitation. "It's the least I can do." He glanced at the bodies nearby, which had already started to attract flies. The buzzing was loud in the warm afternoon air. "And I'd just as soon go somewhere that's not quite so, ah, grim."

"The Lucky Cuss is right here," Scratch responded with a grin.

A few minutes later, the three of them were sitting at a table in the saloon, which was a busy place full of cowboys, railroad workers, and townsmen drinking and gambling.

Cyrus Keegan looked around curiously and said, "I've never been in here."

He had stopped at the bar and gotten three mugs of beer for them while Bo and Scratch had claimed the empty table.

"This wasn't where you were headin' when those scoundrels jumped you?" Scratch asked.

"Goodness, no," Keegan said as he slid full mugs of cold, foaming beer in front of his companions. "I was just passing by. It's not that I don't enjoy a drink now and then." A sheepish look came over his face. "In fact, in the past I had a tendency to, ah, overindulge from time to time. But a mishap that involved a broken leg convinced me that it would be wise to hew more closely to the straight and narrow. So since then I've avoided getting carried away."

"I can drink that beer for you if it's too much of a temptation," Scratch offered.

"No, no, that won't be necessary. Whiskey is my weakness. An occasional beer is perfectly fine."

As if to demonstrate, Keegan lifted the mug and took a long, healthy swallow. When he lowered it, he licked foam off his upper lip and then sighed in satisfaction.

"Ah," he said. "To be honest, after everything that's happened, I needed a bit of a bracer to fortify my nerves, and that did the job quite nicely."

Bo drank some of his beer and agreed that it was pretty good. He said, "Mr. Keegan—"

"Please, call me Cyrus," the little man interrupted in his high-pitched voice.

"All right, Cyrus," Bo went on. "Something Marshal Courtright said made it sound like you'd been mixed up in some ruckuses before."

"I'm afraid so," Keegan said with a solemn nod. "It had to do with those two young men I told you about who were handy with their guns."

"The marshal mentioned your line of work, too. What is that, if you don't mind me asking?"

"Not at all. After you risked your lives to save me, you have the right to ask anything you want. I'm a matrimonial agent."

"A matri-what?" Scratch said. "I don't much like the sound of that. Too much like *matrimony*."

"Well, of course it is. A matrimonial agent arranges marriages. Or to be more specific, in my case, provides brides for prospective grooms."

"Mail-order brides," Bo said.

Keegan nodded and said, "That's the commonly accepted term, yes. I think it sounds a bit mercenary . . . but it *is* the way I make my living, so I suppose that's accurate."

"I can't for the life of me figure out why somebody would be so desperate for a wife that he'd send off for one," Scratch commented, shaking his head. "Seems to me it's hard enough to avoid gettin' saddled with some gal, without goin' out lookin' for trouble."

"We're fine ones to talk about not looking for trouble," Bo pointed out.

"Yeah, but there's trouble . . . and then there's *trouble*."

Keegan chuckled and said, "I'm glad not every man feels like you, Mr. Morton, or I'd be out of business."

"Mr. Morton's my pa. I'm Scratch."

"And I'm Bo. That sounds like mighty interesting work you do, Cyrus, but I don't think we'll need to avail ourselves of your services."

"All right," Keegan said, "but if you ever change your minds, I maintain a file of eligible ladies, mostly from the East and Midwest, who are all refined, intelligent, and domestically skilled. If you think any of them might be to your liking, you can correspond with them and get to know them better."

Scratch said, "You didn't mention anything about 'em bein' good-lookin'."

"Well . . . beauty is in the eye of the beholder, isn't it?"

They sat there for a while, nursing the beers and talking. Keegan was very interested in the adventures the two drifters had had, and while Bo wasn't the type to talk much about such things, such modesty didn't make up any part of Scratch's personality. He spun a few yarns, and when he embellished things to make the tales sound ever wilder and woollier to the rapt Cyrus Keegan, Bo didn't point that out. Scratch and Keegan both seemed to be enjoying themselves, so Bo didn't see what a few whoppers would hurt.

Finally, Keegan suggested, "Why don't the two of you come back to the office with me?"

"We told you, Cyrus," Scratch began, "we ain't in the market for no brides—"

"No, no, that's not what I had in mind. I need to pick up some papers there, and then I thought perhaps you'd like to accompany me to my home and have supper with me. My housekeeper, Lantana, is an excellent cook. I daresay you won't find a better meal in Fort Worth. I'd like to repay you for coming to my rescue with more than just a beer."

"That's not necessary," Bo said. "We weren't looking for any repayment."

"We just don't like to see anybody gettin' picked on," Scratch said.

"Please," Keegan insisted. "I'll be insulted if you don't accept my hospitality."

Being Texans, born and raised, Bo and Scratch both understood that sentiment. They looked at each other and nodded.

Scratch said, "Sure. I reckon we can do that, Cyrus."

"Excellent," the little man replied, beaming.

Bo said, "We need to stable our horses and find a hotel room, so why don't you tell us where your office is and we'll meet you there in a little while?"

"All right. It's over on Rusk Street. That's four blocks east of here. Just go to Fourth Street, here at the corner, and walk straight over to Rusk. Then turn left, and the office will be halfway up the block, on the left." Keegan drained the last of his beer. "I'll wait there until you arrive."

"We'll try not to be too long," Bo promised. "Do you know a good livery stable around here?"

"As a matter of fact, I do. Patterson's Livery is on your way. You'll see it. And there's a good hotel close by, too."

Keegan left the Lucky Cuss. Armed with the information he had given them, Bo and Scratch reclaimed their horses from the hitch rail and walked toward the stable.

"Seems like we've made ourselves a friend," Scratch commented with a smile.

"He's just grateful to us for helping him out," Bo said. "We'll have supper with him, and I reckon that'll be the end of it."

They turned their horses over to the proprietor of the stable, a friendly, stocky man with a close-cropped, rust-colored beard. When Bo mentioned that Cyrus Keegan had recommended the place, the stableman chuckled and said, "Yeah, he keeps his wagon and team here. He's quite a character. Used to come in drunk as a lord, but he seems to have straightened up lately."

"He said as much to us. Mentioned some sort of accident that got him a broken leg," Bo said.

"A mule kicked him," Patterson said, "because he was drunk and stumbling around and trying to hitch up the team himself. Reckon that taught him a lesson."

"Mule kicks have a way of doin' that," Scratch said.

They found the hotel less than a block away, made arrangements to rent a room for a few nights, and then walked on toward Rusk Street and Keegan's office. Wagons rattled through the streets, and people crowded the sidewalks. Fort Worth wasn't exactly a boomtown, but it seemed to be thriving.

They turned when they reached Rusk Street. Up ahead, halfway along the block, as Keegan had indicated, a sign stuck out over a door, with lettering on it that read KEEGAN MATRIMONIAL AGENCY.

"It still seems loco to me that somebody would pay to get a wife," Scratch said. "Don't the poor varmints realize they're gonna be payin' for the rest o' their lives?"

"I guess they just look at things differently than fellas like you and I do," Bo said.

"Damn right it's different," Scratch muttered. "Loco."

Bo noticed several men coming along the street from the opposite direction. One man strode purposefully in front of the rest of the group. He wore range clothes like the others, but the garb was of good quality and didn't show any signs of wear, as if he didn't actually work in it like the rest of the men worked in their clothes.

That was enough to give Bo a hunch that the man was a successful rancher and the other men were cowhands who worked for him.

The man in the lead was in his thirties, tall and broad shouldered, with a tanned, handsome face dominated by a strong jaw and a cleft chin. Curly brown hair showed under his expensive Stetson. His walk had more than a touch of arrogance to it, as if he expected everyone he encountered to step aside and get out of his way.

Bo and Scratch weren't in the habit of stepping aside for folks, no matter who they were, and since they were headed in the opposite direction, this might be a little trouble in the making, Bo thought.

But it didn't come to that, because the man in the lead of the bunch suddenly turned in when he reached a door and his companions stopped to lounge along the sidewalk.

Problem was, the man yanked open the door under Cyrus Keegan's sign and stalked into the office of the matrimonial agency.

"Did you see that?" Scratch asked under his breath.

"Yeah," Bo replied, "and I'm not sure I liked the looks of it . . ."

The next moment, he was sure he didn't like it, because the man had left the office door open, and as Bo and Scratch came closer, they had no trouble hearing the loud, angry voice that came from inside.

Chapter 4

From where they were, Bo and Scratch couldn't make out the words, but there was no mistaking the tone. The deep voice didn't belong to Keegan, so it had to be coming from the man who had just gone in there.

"We'd better see what's goin' on," Scratch said.

Bo's only reply was an increase in the speed of his walk. Scratch kept pace with him.

As they approached the open door, the cowhands who had accompanied the well-dressed man saw them coming and moved to block their path.

"Where do you fellas think you're goin'?" one of the cowboys demanded.

"In there," Bo replied, with a nod toward the door of the matrimonial agency. "And we'd be obliged if you'd get out of the way."

"You don't look like you got any business here," another man drawled. "Couple of old geezers like you don't have no need of wives."

A third cowboy snickered and said, "Reckon they even remember what to do with wives?"

Scratch responded angrily, "I've forgotten more about women than you'll ever know, you young pup."

"Yeah, that's just my point, old-timer. You've *forgotten* all of it."

Bo heard Cyrus Keegan's unmistakable high-pitched voice coming from the office now. The other man's angry response overrode it.

Bo said, "We're going in there, whether you fellas like it or not."

That challenge had an instant effect. The amused attitude fell away from the cowboys. They straightened from their casual poses and glared at Bo and Scratch.

"We gave you a chance to move on," one of them said. "Keep pushing, and you're gonna be sorry. There are four of us, and we're a hell of a lot younger than you are."

"One thing you need to remember, sonny," Scratch said. "Old men got a lot less to lose. *You* keep pushin' *us*, and you're liable to get hurt."

The cowboy who had taken over the role of spokesman for the group sneered. "If you think you're scarin' us, Gramps—"

A sudden loud crash from inside the office interrupted him. All four cowhands turned quickly in that direction. It was a natural enough reaction, but it was also a mistake. Bo's Colt came out of leather swiftly and he leveled the revolver at them, his hand steady as a rock.

"Get out of the way," he snapped. "I won't tell you again."

"And I'll just let these Remingtons do my talkin'," Scratch added as he filled his hands, as well.

With three revolvers pointed at them, the cowboys had no choice except to back off. Bo strode through the open door. Scratch backed into the office behind his friend, keeping the Remingtons trained on the cowhands as he did so.

Inside the office, Bo spotted Cyrus Keegan standing behind a desk, with the other man in front of the desk, glaring and clenching his fists. A chair that must have normally sat in front of the desk was a few feet away, on its side. That explained the crash. The visitor had knocked it over in his anger.

The man looked over his shoulder at Bo and burst out, "What the hell! Put that gun away and get out of here. Keegan's busy."

The arrogance in his voice and the impatient expression on his face made it clear that he was accustomed to being obeyed whenever he gave an order.

"Mister, you're not the boss here," Bo said. "This is Mr. Keegan's office."

"And Keegan works for me!"

Bo glanced at the clearly shaken matrimonial agent and asked, "Is that true?"

"Mr. Craddock is *not* my employer," Keegan said as he pulled a handkerchief from his pocket and mopped sweat off his forehead. "But he *is* a client, so you could say I work for him in the sense that I'm trying to provide a service for him."

"And doing a mighty piss-poor job of it," Craddock said.

"You're hardly being fair—"

"I've got eyes, don't I? I can see just fine! I know what sort of inferior goods you're trying to pawn off on me."

For the first time, Bo saw anger on Cyrus Keegan's face. The little man slapped a hand down on the desk with a sharp crack and said, "Sir! I'll not have you speak that way about another human being. Miss Hampshire is hardly 'inferior goods.' She's a fine, morally upstanding young woman—"

"I don't know about her morals," Craddock broke in, "but she sure as hell isn't young." He turned to Bo and Scratch. "I don't usually explain myself, but listen to what Keegan is trying to pull. He sent me a picture of a dewy-eyed young girl—"

"A photograph that Miss Hampshire provided," Keegan interrupted. "I can hardly be blamed for that."

"And when I get here to pick her up, she turns out to be a forty-year-old . . . old maid!" Craddock leveled an accusing finger across the desk at Keegan. "He had to know that, and he still expects me to marry her and pay the rest of his fee."

"It's true the photograph is a bit out of date," Keegan said, "but the lady is not forty years old. I doubt if she's much over thirty-five."

Craddock snorted and said, "Have you asked her?"

Keegan drew himself up as straight and tall as he could and replied, "A lady may volunteer her age, but it can hardly be demanded of her."

"Well, I don't care. You're trying to pull a fast one, and I won't put up with it. You make things right, Keegan, or you'll be sorry."

"At this point, what would you have me do?" Keegan asked as he spread his hands.

"Find me a good-looking young woman to marry, like I paid you to!"

Bo and Scratch were both watching the argument now, and they were interested enough in the back-and-forth between Keegan and Craddock that they had lowered their guns.

The men they had left outside on the sidewalk must have been waiting for an opportunity like that, because one of them shouted from the doorway, "Rush 'em, boys!" and all four of the cowboys burst into the office to charge at Bo and Scratch.

Opening fire on thieves who were throwing down on *them* was one thing. Blasting unarmed punchers who were just sticking up for their boss was another. Bo and Scratch both hesitated instead of firing, and in that moment's delay, the attackers swarmed them.

One man knocked the Colt out of Bo's hand, while another slammed a fist to his face, which knocked him back against Keegan's desk.

Keegan yelped in alarm. Bo caught himself, got his left arm up in time to block another blow, then shot out a powerful straight right of his own that landed on the assailant's nose and rocked his head back.

A few feet away, two of the cowboys had hold of Scratch's arms so he couldn't lift the Remingtons. They drove him back against the wall with bone-jarring force, which caused the ivory-handled revolvers to slip from his fingers. As the guns thudded to the floor, the men started whaling away at Scratch.

Bo couldn't go to his friend's assistance, because he had his own hands full. The punch he'd landed had caused one man to fall back, but the other one continued the attack.

A hard fist landed in Bo's belly and puffed air from his lungs. He gasped and bent forward, and the man got him with a left hook. Bo would have gone down if the desk hadn't been there to catch him again.

He shoved off from the desk and bent low to let a round-house go right over his head. The cowboy's midsection was wide open right in front of him. He drove three swift punches into it, left, right, left, which put the man in position for a right uppercut that Bo lifted from the floor. The man's teeth clicked together loudly as the punch landed on his chin. His eyes rolled up, and his knees buckled.

The man Bo had hit in the nose was still on his feet, though, and bulled in furiously as blood welled from the injured member in the middle of his face. Bo had to give ground as a flurry of punches hammered him.

Meanwhile, Scratch had gotten his back against the wall in a corner, so the two men he was battling couldn't attack him effectively at the same time.

One of them said, "I'll take care of this old pelican!" and bored in confidently.

With decades of experience in bare-knuckles brawling, Scratch blocked most of the man's punches and snapped several blows of his own to the hombre's face. Blood leaked from smashed lips, and the man's eyes began to swell. This damage just made him angrier.

And the anger made him careless. Suddenly, Scratch leaned back against the wall and brought his right foot up in a kick that landed his boot toe squarely in the man's groin.

The man's mouth opened wide, and so did his eyes. A bleat of agony came from him. As he stopped short and tottered there, he gasped, "You . . . you kicked me . . . in the *balls*."

"Told you not to crowd an old man," Scratch rasped. "He'll hurt you."

The cowboy clutched himself, fell to the floor, and curled up. His companion advanced on Scratch and said, "I'm gonna kill you for what you did to him, you bastard."

Over by the desk, Bo's remaining opponent let overconfidence get the best of him, too. He ventured too close, and Bo was able to drop low, grab him around the knees, and heave upward. With a startled yell, the cowboy went over backward and crashed down on his back with bone-jarring force.

The man was too stunned to get up right away, which gave Bo the time he needed to scoop up his Colt, which he had dropped when the fight started. With the gun in his hand again, he stepped back beside the desk and pointed the Colt at the man who was about to attack Scratch again.

"That's enough," Bo said. His voice wasn't loud, but it was hard as flint.

Craddock had backed off and hadn't taken part in the fight. More than likely, he had expected his men to make short work of the two drifters. None of them realized just how much bark Bo and Scratch had left on them, though.

Now Craddock said, "Put that gun away, you old fool. If you shoot one of my men, I'll see that you hang for it."

Cyrus Keegan said, "Do you really think you can convince a jury it wasn't self-defense? I mean, four burly young cowboys attacking two elderly gentlemen—"

"I don't cotton much to that word *elderly*," Scratch said. "Makes it sound like my best days are behind me." He grinned rakishly. "I feel like I'm just gettin' started."

His hat had been knocked off in the fracas, like Bo's, and he had a few bloody scrapes on his face, also like Bo. His silver hair was askew. But he looked like he was enjoying himself, which was true. There were few things Scratch Morton liked better than a good fight.

Bo was a more peace-loving sort, but he had to admit, it felt pretty good knowing that he and Scratch were still on their feet while three of their opponents were down and the fourth one had Bo's gun pointed at him.

"I don't plan on shooting anybody," he told Craddock, "as long as your boys don't do anything *else* foolish. If I were you, I'd gather them up and get out of here. Go on back to wherever you came from."

"This doesn't change a damned thing," Craddock argued. "Keegan's still trying to cheat me. I'm not going to marry that old maid."

Keegan said, "I can't force anyone to marry against their will. I think it's a terrible thing you're doing to Miss Hampshire, though. She came all the way here from Vermont in good faith."

Craddock shook his head. "I don't call it good faith when she's twenty years older than how she looks in that picture."

Through clenched teeth, Keegan said, "Because of the misunderstanding, I won't insist that you pay me the remainder of the fee."

"How about what I already paid you? I ought to get that back!"

"I'm giving it to Miss Hampshire to cover her expenses and get her back to where she came from. That seems only fair."

Craddock snorted and said, "After you put some of it in your pocket, you mean."

"Not a penny, sir. Not one blasted penny."

On the floor, the man who'd been kicked in the groin moaned and said, "Boss, can . . . can we get outta here? I'm hurtin' mighty bad—"

"You ought to hurt," Craddock said, "letting an old man get

the best of you that way." He jerked a hand in a curt gesture and snarled at the others, "Get him up on his feet. We're leaving."

With groans and curses, the cowboys stumbled out of the office. Craddock followed, but he paused in the doorway to level a finger at Keegan and say, "This isn't over. Mark my words, mister."

"If I see you again, I'm filing a complaint with Marshal Courtright," Keegan responded.

"I don't care, you little pip-squeak." The rancher glared at Bo and Scratch. "I'll see you two geezers again, too."

Scratch had picked up his Remingtons but had not holstered them yet. His tanned, supple fingers spun each revolver effortlessly for a second before he slid the guns back into leather.

"Better be careful you don't get what you wish for, Craddock," he said.

Chapter 5

Craddock sneered and stalked after his men, who had disappeared along the sidewalk.

When they were gone, Cyrus Keegan sighed and sank down into the chair behind his desk.

"I'm so sorry," he said to Bo and Scratch. "I knew Mr. Craddock was displeased with the way things had worked out, but I never dreamed he would cause such a fuss over it. Are you gentlemen all right?"

Bo holstered his gun. His hat had fallen on Keegan's desk. He picked it up, brushed it off a little, and put it on his head.

"Bunged up a mite, but nothing to worry about," he said.

"Yeah," Scratch agreed. "We've hurt ourselves a heap worse'n this just fallin' out of bed in the mornin'."

"You can go see the marshal and file assault charges against them . . . ," Keegan began.

Bo shook his head and said, "We don't run to the law to handle things."

"Always been the sort to stomp our own snakes," Scratch added. He found his hat on the floor and put it on.

Bo picked up the chair that had been turned over, set it in front of the desk, and said, "Who is Craddock, anyway?"

"Hugh Craddock has a big spread southwest of here, down in Erath County. His father was one of the first settlers in that area and built up a successful ranch, but Craddock has made it even bigger. He's accustomed to success and getting what he wants." Keegan shook his head solemnly. "Unfortunately, that didn't do him a bit of good when his first wife died in child-birth about fifteen years ago. The infant didn't survive, either."

Bo felt a pang inside. He had lost a wife and children, too, although not in the same way. And even though many, many years had passed since then, the pain of that loss had never gone away completely. He knew it never would.

"Ever since that happened," Keegan continued, "Craddock has devoted himself to his ranch, but he's decided that enough time has passed and he ought to take another wife."

"Hold on a minute," Scratch said. "No offense, Cyrus, but a fella like him, no older than he is and obviously well to do, shouldn't have to hire a matrimonial agency to find him a wife. Seems to me like all the eligible gals in this part of the country would be linin' up for a chance to convince him to pick them."

"Yes, you'd think so," Keegan agreed. "But that's not what he wants. He made up his mind that he should marry a refined lady from back East."

Scratch snorted and said, "So he's puttin' on airs."

"I think it's more a case of him not wanting a Texas girl, be-cause she might remind him too much of the one he lost."

"I can understand that," Bo said with a nod, without ex-plaining why he understood. "But the one you picked for him didn't work out."

Keegan held up a hand, as if to stop him. "I don't pick. I of-fered Mr. Craddock several choices, and he corresponded with more than one of the ladies. Ultimately, he was the one who settled on Miss Hampshire and made arrangements for her to travel here to Fort Worth so they could meet."

"And she's a whole heap older than she pretended to be, right?" Scratch said.

Keegan made a face. He opened a drawer in the desk and took out a piece of paper.

"This is a copy of the photograph she provided," he said as he turned the picture on the desk so Bo and Scratch could see it.

The dark-haired young woman in the photograph was very attractive and appeared to be about twenty years old.

Bo nodded and said, "She's a looker, all right."

"She still is, in my opinion," Keegan said. "And she's approximately the same age as Hugh Craddock. I'm convinced it would have been a good match, except . . ."

"Except for the fact that he still wants to have children," Bo said, guessing that was the problem.

"And this Miss Hampshire's gettin' a mite long in the tooth for that," Scratch added.

"It's certainly not beyond the realm of possibility," Keegan said with a shrug, "but I suppose I can't deny that most women bear their young at an earlier age. Still . . ." A note of exasperation came into his voice. "It wouldn't have hurt him to try."

Bo rubbed his chin and asked, "What do you think he'll do? Is he likely to make more trouble?"

"My hope is that he'll come to his senses and either give Miss Hampshire a second chance or at least allow her to return to Vermont with her dignity intact."

"Might be hard goin' home without a husband when you set out to get one," Scratch said.

"Yes, well, there's nothing I can do about that."

"Do things like this happen often?" Bo asked curiously.

Keegan smiled and said, "It's a surprisingly exciting profession. I suppose that's what happens when you're dealing with people's emotions, though. Naturally, they can get quite, ah, passionate about such things."

He got to his feet and went on, "Don't concern yourselves about that, however. I've dealt with problems like this before. I appreciate you stepping in to help me yet again, and now I have more reason than ever to want to repay you with a good home-cooked meal. Come along, gentlemen. I sent word to Lantana that we'd be having guests for dinner, and if I know her, she's prepared a feast!"

Cyrus Keegan's housekeeper and cook was a heavyset middle-aged black woman, and as Keegan had promised, the meal she prepared was delicious. Roast beef, potatoes, gravy, greens, corn on the cob, and some of the fluffiest biscuits Bo and Scratch had ever eaten, followed by peach pie, all washed down with strong coffee flavored with chicory, New Orleans style.

"Lantana, you've outdone yourself," Keegan praised her as she topped off their coffee cups following the meal.

"Ma'am, food like this is almost enough to make me think twice about my wanderin' ways," Scratch chimed in.

Lantana laughed and said, "Go on with you, Mister Scratch. I ain't knowed you and Mister Bo but for a little while. I can tell, though, that you fellas ain't the sort to ever let grass grow under your feet."

Keegan said, "Certainly, at some point, age will dictate that you stop your continual drifting."

"You mean when we get old?" Bo asked with a smile.

"I reckon that wagon train's already rollin'," Scratch said.

Keegan looked a little embarrassed as he went on, "I just meant that there comes a time when we all have to slow down, whether we want to or not. The mind and the body can only do so much, you know, before they wear out."

"Maybe we'll reach that point," Bo said, "or maybe we won't."

"As much as we've knocked around, chances are we're livin' on borrowed time already," Scratch added. "The odds'll catch up to us one of these days."

"Well, now, that's not what I meant," Keegan said, clearly flustered.

Scratch laughed and said, "Don't worry about it, Cyrus. Bo and me understand. We just learned a long time ago to take life one day at a time and deal with what it brings us as best we can."

"And that's a mighty good way to be," Lantana said.

Later, the three men sat on the porch of Keegan's neat little house on Bluff Street, overlooking the winding Trinity River below, and smoked cigars that the matrimonial agent had handed out. Dusk had settled over the rolling Texas plains to the west, although an arch of red and gold remained in the sky, a lingering reminder of the sun, which had set a while earlier.

"A beautiful time of day," Keegan mused.

"That it is," Bo agreed. "Thank you for inviting us this evening."

"Yeah, we're much obliged to you, Cyrus," Scratch put in. "And to Miss Lantana for that fine feed."

Keegan puffed on his cigar for a moment, then took it out of his mouth and said, "Actually, I had another motive for inviting you gentlemen here tonight, over and above my genuine gratitude for your assistance."

"Uh-oh," Scratch said. "That sounds a mite ominous."

"Oh, no, it's not, I assure you," Keegan said hastily. "I just want to issue another invitation. I'd like for both of you to come to my office tomorrow morning."

"If you're thinkin' about openin' up your files and tryin' to find prospective brides for us as a way of thankin' us, we've already told you we ain't interested."

"No, no, nothing like that. I have a business proposition for you."

Bo said, "I don't think Scratch and I are really cut out to be matrimonial agents, Cyrus."

"Yeah, we'd be more likely to go into business tellin' fellas how to *avoid* gettin' hitched!"

"Believe me, I understand," Keegan said. "But it's nothing like that. If you'll just stop by the office in the morning, I'll explain everything."

Bo puffed on his cigar and frowned in thought for a moment, then said, "I don't suppose we have anywhere else we need to be. Unless, of course, Marshal Courtright summons us to the inquest for those robbers we shot."

"If you have to attend that, then I will, too," Keegan pointed out, "and we can go back to the office later."

"All right, Cyrus," Scratch said. "I reckon that meal we had tonight more than squares up any debt you owed us, so we'll play along with you."

"Thank you," Keegan said with what sounded like heartfelt relief. "I was really hoping you'd agree."

Bo warned him, "We haven't agreed to anything yet, except that we'll come by the office and see what it is you've got on your mind."

A few minutes later, they finished their cigars and said their good nights.

"Tell Miss Lantana again how much we appreciate that grub," Scratch said. "Maybe you should find *her* a husband, Cyrus."

"And give up that cooking?" Keegan exclaimed. "I should say not!"

As the evening deepened, Bo and Scratch walked along tree-lined Bluff Street, back toward downtown, half a mile away.

"Should've brought the horses," Scratch commented. "Cyrus may be used to makin' this walk, but we ain't."

"We'll be all right," Bo said. "It doesn't hurt us to stretch our legs a little once in a while."

"Maybe not, but that don't mean we ought to risk it."

A few moments of silence went by, and then Scratch asked, "What in blazes do you think ol' Cyrus has got on his mind?"

Bo shook his head. "I don't know. I can't think of any sort of business that would involve us with a matrimonial agency, but then, I don't know anything about running an operation like that, either."

"What's there to know about it? You pair up lonely old maids with fool bachelors who ain't got a lick of sense. Most times when somebody wants to hire us for anything, it's because we're handy with trouble . . . and with our guns. How could that have anything to do with a bunch of mail-order brides?"

"I suppose we'll find out," Bo said.

Chapter 6

They were approaching Cyrus Keegan's office on Rusk Street the next morning when the door swung open and Marshal Jim Courtright stepped out onto the sidewalk.

"There you are," the dapper lawman said. "I asked Keegan to pass this information along to you, but since you're here, I'll just tell you myself. The inquest on those would-be bandits you killed yesterday will be held at ten o'clock over there at the courthouse."

He nodded toward the imposing structure visible over the roofs of the nearby buildings and went on. "I wouldn't worry too much about the verdict. The one we have in custody whose name is Max Bartell has been singing his fool head off, blaming the other three for everything under the sun, including those earlier killings, in the hope that he won't wind up climbing onto the gallows himself. So there's not much doubt about the inquest's outcome."

"That's good to hear, Marshal," Bo said. "We'll be there."

Courtright nodded and walked off. Bo and Scratch went on into the office and found Cyrus Keegan sitting behind the desk.

Keegan smiled and said, "Good morning, gentlemen. Did you sleep well?"

"Sure did," Scratch replied. "Hard not to after a fine meal like the one we had yesterday evenin'."

"Did you happen to run into Marshal Courtright outside? He just left here."

"We talked to him," Bo said. "He told us about the inquest."

"Good. We can walk over to the courthouse together, if you'd like. But until then, we have time to discuss the proposition I have for you. Please, sit down..."

A second chair was in the corner. Scratch pulled it over, and he and Bo sat down in front of the desk.

"Would you care for a cigar?" Keegan asked.

Bo said, "I reckon we'd rather hear about this idea you've got percolating around in your head, Cyrus."

"Yeah, you've got us plumb curious," Scratch added.

Keegan leaned forward, clasped pudgy hands together on the desk in front of him, and said, "Simply put, I find myself in a situation where I need help. I have five ladies bound for a town in New Mexico Territory called Silverhill, and I'm reluctant to send them out there, into unknown waters, so to speak, unaccompanied. In the past I always made such trips myself, but honestly, after that broken leg I suffered a while back, I'm just not up to it anymore."

From what Bo had seen of Keegan so far, he didn't think the man would have been capable of handling much trouble to start with, even when he was younger and sprier. Some men were cut out for such things, but Cyrus Keegan wasn't one of them.

Keegan went on, "I was able to make arrangements with the two young men I mentioned before... those Jensen boys... to deliver a group of prospective brides to San Angelo for me, but they've moved on and never came back to Fort Worth, so I can't hire them again. You two remind me of them in many ways, so I hoped I might convince you to take up the challenge."

"You want us to escort a group of young women all the way to New Mexico Territory?" Scratch asked with a frown.

"I thought you might be interested in the job since you like to travel," Keegan said. "And frankly, I'm a bit worried about sending young men along on a trip with young, unmarried women, as I did before . . ."

Bo smiled and said, "But since Scratch and I are old geezers, you figured it'd be safe enough for us to go along with these ladies."

"I wouldn't go so far as to call you old geezers, but to be blunt, I did think that any interest you took in the ladies would be more avuncular in nature."

"More what?" Scratch asked.

"He means we'd be like uncles to them," Bo explained.

Scratch snorted and said, "More like grandpas."

"That would work, too," Keegan said. "At the same time, no matter what age you are, you're quite competent when it comes to dealing with trouble. I've seen ample evidence of that with my own eyes, twice now."

"Are you *expecting* trouble on this trip?" Bo wanted to know.

Keegan unclasped his hands and spread them on the desk. "Not at all," he said. "But from what I've read about it, this Silverhill is a mining town and has grown a great deal in the past year, following the discovery of several rich silver veins in the nearby mountains."

"It's a boomtown, in other words," Bo said.

"I think you could call it that."

Scratch said, "Some of those boomtowns can be mighty rough. Are you sure you should even be sendin' gals into a place like that?"

Keegan looked a little defensive as he said, "They've been

fully informed as to where they'll be going. And the gentlemen from Silverhill who engaged my services all seem like fine, upstanding businessmen."

"If they're telling the truth," Bo said. "Don't you ever run across fellas who lie?"

Keegan sighed. "It's an occupational hazard in my line of work," he admitted. "When it comes to establishing romantic relationships, many people, ah, shade the truth to a certain extent. But over the years I've developed a pretty good feeling for such things. I can weed out the ones who are blatant liars, men and women both. I believe everything in this particular arrangement is on the up-and-up, but still, Silverhill is a long way out there, and I'd prefer that the ladies not make the trip alone. What do you say, gentlemen? I'll pay all your expenses, of course, plus a reasonable fee."

Bo and Scratch looked at each other.

Scratch shrugged and said, "You know I've always figured you ought to do most of the thinkin', Bo. You ain't really steered us wrong yet."

Bo was still hesitating, frowning in thought, when the office door opened again. Keegan looked up to see who was there. A smile broke out across his face as he said, "Perhaps this will help you make up your mind, fellows. Here are the ladies now."

Bo and Scratch looked around and then came quickly to their feet as five young women in their twenties filed into the office. The two drifters took their hats off and held them politely in front of them.

The leader of the group, or at least the first one into the office, was a tall, slender young brunette dressed in a dark blue suit and a matching hat that was free of adornment. She had high cheekbones and blue eyes almost the same shade as the traveling outfit she wore.

The next prospective bride was shorter, but not by much,

and had an athletic spring in her step. Thick blond hair was piled up under the green hat, which went with her dress.

The third young woman had raven hair and eyes almost as dark. Right behind her was a tall, chestnut-haired beauty, and lastly, another blonde, this one with curls that gave her a bit of a Southern belle look.

Each of them was undeniably pretty. Scratch's rapt gaze was proof of that.

Their presence in the office meant that the room was a little cramped, too.

The slender brunette, who had come in first, said, "If you're busy, Mr. Keegan, we can come back later . . ."

Keegan was on his feet, too. He held up both hands, palms out, and said, "No, that's quite all right, Miss Spaulding. I'm very glad you and your friends are here. I'd like you to meet Mr. Creel and Mr. Morton."

Five pairs of eyes swung toward Bo and Scratch.

The curly-haired blonde said, "You're not two of the men from Silverhill who sent for us, are you?"

The faint note of dismay in her voice made Bo smile. He said, "No, ma'am. You can put those worries to rest. Scratch and I aren't in the market for brides."

"Scratch?" the other blonde repeated.

"That's me, ma'am," the silver-haired Texan said. "Scratch Morton. This here's my pard, Bo Creel."

Bo nodded politely and said, "Ladies."

"Let me complete the introductions," Keegan said. "This is Miss Cecilia Spaulding."

The cool, reserved brunette, who had led the way into the room, nodded to Bo and Scratch but didn't say anything to them.

"Miss Beth Macy."

That was the fresh-faced, athletic blonde. She said, "Hello," prompting Scratch to nod to her and say, "Ma'am. I mean, miss."

"Miss Luella Tolman," Keegan went on.

Luella Tolman was the young woman with hair black as midnight and a sultry, somewhat exotic look about her. In a low, throaty voice that probably sent shivers along the spine of most men, she murmured, "Gentlemen."

"Miss Rose Winston," Keegan said.

That was the coltish, wholesome chestnut-haired young woman. She looked like she ought to be a preacher's daughter, Bo thought as she smiled at them and said, "Hello."

That left the curly-haired blonde, and Keegan introduced her as Miss Jean Parker.

Scratch told her, "It's a pleasure to meet you, miss. A plumb pleasure."

Jean Parker was all business, though, as she asked, "Mr. Keegan, what do these two men have to do with us?"

"I'm trying to persuade them to provide you with an escort on your journey to Silverhill," Keegan explained.

Cecilia Spaulding said, "I thought you told us we'd be taking the train. We shouldn't have any real need of an escort."

"The train will take you only as far as El Paso. Silverhill is still a significant distance over in New Mexico Territory from there. You'll have to use some other form of transportation for that part of the trip, probably a wagon."

"I can drive a wagon if I need to," Rose Winston said. "I spent a lot of time on a farm when I was growing up."

"I can handle a team, too," Beth Macy added. "I drove my father's buggy all the time."

Handling a buggy horse was considerably different from getting a team of sometimes balky mules or draft horses to do what you wanted, Bo thought. But a lot of it was just putting in the effort and being willing to learn, so he didn't argue with Miss Macy's claim.

Keegan said, "I just believe it would be safer for you ladies if you had a couple of men along to handle any, ah, unexpected difficulties. As you know from your correspondence with the gentlemen who live there, Silverhill is a mining town, and those can be rather . . . boisterous."

"You wouldn't send us to a place where it's not safe, would you, Mr. Keegan?" Cecilia Spaulding asked.

"Of course not! I'm sure that once you're there and you've met the men you're supposed to meet, everything will be fine. I'd just feel better if Mr. Creel and Mr. Morton went along to make sure there are no problems."

"Scratch and I haven't said we'd sign on for this yet," Bo pointed out.

"Bo, can I talk to you for a minute?" Scratch asked. "Outside?"

Bo had seen the way his old friend had been looking at the young women, and he had a pretty good hunch he knew what Scratch was going to say. Still, given their history, it was only right that he listen.

"All right," he said. He put his hat on and added, "If you ladies will excuse us . . ."

"Of course," Cecilia said. She moved over so Bo and Scratch could get to the door, and the others followed suit, scooting up close together on one side of the room.

Once they were on the sidewalk and the door was closed behind them, Bo took out his pocket watch and flipped it open to check the time. It was still a little while before they had to be at the courthouse for the inquest.

Before Bo could say anything, Scratch said, "We've got to take this job, Bo. We can't let those poor defenseless women set out all the way to New Mexico Territory by themselves."

"I don't know how defenseless they are. Miss Macy and Miss Winston look like they could give a pretty good account of themselves."

"Maybe, but you know what boomtowns are like."

"Even if we went with them, our responsibility would end as soon as we got them to Silverhill. Then it would be up to the men who are supposed to marry them to look out for them."

"Yeah, but there's a lot of wild country betwixt here and there. You heard what Cyrus said. The train'll take 'em only as far as El Paso. After that you've got Apaches and Mexican bandits and who knows what all else to worry about."

"Most of the Apaches are either south of the border or farther to the west, in Arizona Territory," Bo said.

"Well, what about the bandidos?"

Bo didn't say anything for a moment. Although he hadn't heard any reports of border raids recently, bandits who ventured across the line from time to time represented an actual danger, as anyone who lived in the southern part of the territory knew. Bo wasn't sure exactly where Silverhill was located, but he assumed it was in that area, since as far as he knew, that was where all the silver strikes had occurred.

"You know I'm right," Scratch went on, without waiting for Bo to answer. "Anyway, dang it, you saw those gals! Did you ever lay eyes on a prettier bunch, all in one place like this?"

"You know good and well none of those women would ever have the least bit of interest in us. Not that way. You said yourself we're old enough to be their grandpas."

"Well . . . maybe Cyrus had it right when he said we'd be more like uncles—"

"That still doesn't make any difference."

"You're right," Scratch said, nodding. "But answer me this. Don't you enjoy bein' around young, pretty gals, even if there *ain't* any chance anything'd ever happen between you and them? And be honest now, Bo."

Bo frowned at Scratch for a couple of seconds and then said, "All right, blast it. You've got a point. They're mighty easy on the eyes, and just being in their company for a trip like that would be a pure pleasure, as long as no trouble cropped up."

"And if it did, it'd be a good thing we were there to give 'em a hand with it, wouldn't it? Plus, you got to remember, Cyrus said he'd pay us. We could use some extra funds to keep us in provisions for a while."

"When did you become so doggone persuasive when it comes to arguing?" Bo asked.

"About the same time I laid eyes on those gals," Scratch replied with a grin.

"All right, let's go back inside and talk to Cyrus."

They stepped into the office. The young women had been talking about something, but they fell silent as Bo and Scratch came in. Keegan looked expectantly at them, and the other five pairs of eyes swung their way, as well.

"All right," Bo said. "I reckon we'll take the job."

A big smile broke out on Keegan's face. "That's splendid!" he said. "The train leaves this afternoon. I'll make arrangements right away to purchase tickets for the two of you."

"Haven't you forgotten something?" Bo asked. "We have an inquest we need to get to, all three of us."

"Oh, yes, of course. Well, I'll get those tickets as soon as I can after that's over—"

"Wait a minute," Cecilia Spaulding said. "What's this about an inquest?"

"It's nothing you need concern yourselves with . . . ," Keegan began.

"We had to shoot a few fellas yesterday afternoon, is all," Scratch said, "and now the coroner's jury's got to make up their minds whether or not they was justifiable killin's. No question they were, though. Those varmints were about to rob Cyrus and rough him up, maybe even kill him, and he'll testify to that."

Scratch made it sound so commonplace, Bo thought, but the

way the five young women were gaping at them told him they regarded the situation as anything but.

They might have registered their alarm about that, but at that moment a footstep sounded in the doorway. Bo and Scratch looked around and saw Hugh Craddock standing there.

Judging by the expression on the rancher's face, he was ready for another fight.

Chapter 7

Bo and Scratch turned and squared up to block Craddock's path if he tried to get to Keegan.

Craddock raised his hands, though, and held them palm out as he said, "I'm not looking for any trouble."

"Then what *are* you lookin' for?" Scratch asked.

Cecilia Spaulding said, "Is this man a friend of the men you shot yesterday?"

Craddock's eyebrows rose in obvious surprise. He said, "You shot somebody yesterday?"

"Just three would-be robbers," Bo said. "That doesn't concern you, Craddock."

"But him and some fellas who work for him caused a ruckus here," Scratch put in, explaining the situation to Cecilia Spaulding. "Lucky for them, it *didn't* come down to shootin'."

Cecilia's chin lifted as she said to Craddock, "Then please, sir, allow us to finish conducting our business with Mr. Keegan, and then you can speak with him."

Craddock's face had been dark with anger when he came into the office, but now he just looked a mite befuddled. The natural chivalry and good manners of a Westerner, born and raised, took over, causing him to reach up and jerk his hat from his head.

He said, "My apologies for busting in on you like this, ladies. I didn't know Keegan was occupied this morning."

"Very well," Cecilia said coolly. "No harm done."

Craddock backed out of the room. Bo was a little surprised by him giving up that easily, but like most decent Texans, when a lady made a direct request of him, it was difficult for him not to honor it. Cecilia turned back to Keegan and went on, "So everything is arranged? We'll depart for El Paso on the train this afternoon, as planned?"

"That's right. And once you get there, Mr. Creel and Mr. Morton can make arrangements for whatever form of transportation seems appropriate for the rest of the journey."

"One more thing, Cyrus," Bo said. "We'll want to ship our horses on the train, too, because even if we hire a wagon for the ladies, Scratch and I will need our mounts."

Keegan nodded and said, "Of course." He looked around the room. "Are there any other details we need to attend to?"

"I don't believe so," Cecilia said. "Shall we go back to the hotel and finish packing, ladies?"

She led the others out of the office, just as she had led them in.

That was one gal who was used to being in charge, Bo thought.

As soon as the young women were gone, Craddock loomed in the doorway, so Bo, Scratch, and Keegan didn't have a chance to talk among themselves any.

Keegan said, "What do you want, Mr. Craddock? Have you decided to give Miss Hampshire another chance?"

"That old maid?" Craddock shook his head. "Hell, no." He drew in a deep breath and went on, "But I've come to apologize to you, Keegan. I reckon I was out of line yesterday. It's not your fault that woman pulled the wool over our eyes. She lied to both of us."

Keegan waggled a hand in front of him and said, "A lie of omission, perhaps—"

"Is still a lie," Craddock said. "But no matter. That's over and done with."

"Well, I'm glad you're being reasonable on that point, at least. I accept your apology, Mr. Craddock. Now, if you'll excuse us, my friends and I have somewhere we need to be . . ."

Craddock shook his head and said, "Not yet. I've got some more business to do with you."

"I fail to see what that could be," Keegan said with a puzzled frown.

"Those women who were just here, they're mail-order brides?"

"I'm not really fond of that term, but yes—"

"Good," Craddock said. "I'll take one of them. That tall brunette, the one who spoke to me."

Keegan still looked confused. He said, "What?"

"That girl in the dark blue traveling outfit. I'll marry *her*, instead of the one you brought here for me, and we'll call it all square between us. Hell, I'll even pay you the rest of the fee I owe you."

Keegan's mouth opened and closed a couple of times before he was able to say, "But . . . but . . . that's impossible."

Bo said, "That young lady is spoken for, Craddock."

The rancher glared at him and said, "I don't think this is any of your business, mister."

"Reckon it is our business," Scratch drawled. "We just went to work for Cyrus here, didn't we, Bo?"

"That's right," Bo said. "And we've given you the straight of it. Miss Spaulding already has a prospective bridegroom picked out and waiting for her."

"Spaulding, eh?" Craddock repeated. "So that's her name. Well, I plan on changing it to mine, once we're hitched."

Keegan shook his head and said, "Please, sir, have you not

listened to anything we've told you? It's utterly impossible for you to marry the young lady."

"People told my pa it was impossible to start a ranch on the other side of the Brazos, too. They said the Comanche would have his scalp before he was there a year. But the Diamond C is still there, bigger and better than ever, and it always will be. There'll come a time when my sons and grandsons will run it, just the way it was supposed to be all along!"

Even though Craddock's arrogance rubbed him the wrong way, Bo couldn't help but understand how the man felt. He had been the same way himself once, bound and determined to build a legacy that his descendants would carry on.

That wasn't the way things had worked out, of course. Any small legacy Bo had was that of a footloose adventurer . . . but he remembered what those other dreams were like.

Despite that, Craddock was barking up the wrong tree, and Bo told him as much, bluntly.

"You're just going to have to find somebody else, mister," he said. "Miss Spaulding's not available."

Craddock sneered and snapped, "That's not for you to say. Looked to me like she's a grown woman. She can make up her own mind."

"She already has. You'd better leave that lady alone," Keegan warned. "If you bother her or any of those other young women, I'll have the marshal on you!"

"You think I'm scared of Longhair Jim?" Craddock shook his head. "He's just another tin badge."

"You may find out differently when he comes to arrest you."

Scratch hooked his thumbs in his gunbelt and said, "Court-right ain't the only one you have to worry about, neither. Like we told you, we work for Cyrus now, and that job includes makin' sure nothin' happens to the ladies in his charge."

Craddock laughed and said, "You're full of hot air, old man."

Bo took out his watch and checked the time again. "We have to go," he said. "Otherwise the marshal is going to come looking for *us*. Move along, Craddock."

"Are you threatening me?"

Bo put his hand on the butt of his Colt and said, "Just telling you to move along."

"You'll be sorry about this," Craddock blustered. "And this isn't over, Keegan. Not by a long shot!"

"You keep sayin' that," Scratch said, "but that don't make you right about it."

Craddock glared darkly, turned on his heel, and stalked out of the office. The door slammed hard behind him.

Keegan blew out a breath and said, "Good Lord, if I had known what a stubborn, unpleasant individual that man is, I never would have entered into a business arrangement with him in the first place."

"We'd best go," Bo said, "or we're liable to find out how unpleasant the coroner and the marshal can be."

They made it to the courthouse in time for the inquest—barely.

Marshal Courtright had been correct, though. The proceedings were simple and relatively short. Cyrus Keegan was called to testify first, then Bo and Scratch. Finally, the marshal himself took the stand and repeated everything the surviving robbers had told him, all of which backed up the testimony Bo, Scratch, and Keegan had given.

The jury didn't even have to leave the room to deliberate before delivering a verdict stating that the deceased had died in the commission of a crime and had been killed, justifiably so, by Bo Creel and Scratch Morton. They also recommended that no charges be brought against said Creel and Morton.

Even though that was the outcome Bo and Scratch had expected, it was always good to hear such a verdict entered into the official record.

Courtright confirmed it after the affair was adjourned by telling the drifters, "You fellows are free to go. I'll appreciate it, though, if you don't kill anybody else while you're in Fort Worth. And if you do, please make sure you've got a mighty good reason."

"They're going to be here for only a few more hours, Marshal," Keegan said.

Courtright cocked an eyebrow and said, "Oh?"

"They're accompanying a group of my young ladies to New Mexico Territory. They'll all be leaving on the afternoon westbound."

"You sounded a little like a whoremonger there, Cyrus," Courtright said with a smile.

Keegan flushed a deep red and said, "You know it's nothing of the sort, Marshal. Everything is perfectly legitimate, and the ladies involved are of the highest moral character—"

"I'm just joshing you," Courtright said. "I know you run an honest business."

He looked at Bo and Scratch and added, "I can't say I'm sorry to hear that you're leaving town, though. And it's nice to know the young ladies will have some protection on their trip. Where'd you say they were heading?"

"Silverhill, New Mexico," Keegan replied.

Courtright raised his eyebrows again. "Seems like I've heard of that place," he said. "Boomtown, isn't it?"

"That's right," Bo said.

"Watch your step when you get there, and keep an eye on those ladies until you're sure they're safe."

"We know how to do our job, Marshal," Scratch said.

"Oh? You've escorted mail-order brides before?"

"Well . . . no. But we've rode shotgun on some mighty precious cargoes, and I can't think of none more precious than five fine young ladies."

Courtright nodded and ambled away.

Keegan said, "We'd better get started making arrangements for you and your horses. I don't want that train leaving without you."

"Hold on a minute, Cyrus," Bo said. "I've been thinking about something. Craddock heard Miss Spaulding's name, and he knows they have rooms at a hotel. It wouldn't be that hard for him to scout around and find the place where they're staying."

A look of alarm appeared on Keegan's face. He said, "Good Lord. You don't think he'd try to locate them, do you? And . . . and kidnap Miss Spaulding?"

"I think it might be smart to keep an eye on the ladies until they're ready to leave this afternoon. One of us can go to the hotel and stand guard while the other gets the horses and our gear ready to go."

"That's an excellent idea," Keegan agreed.

"I'll go to the hotel," Scratch volunteered, which didn't surprise Bo at all. Standing guard meant that much more time he would spend around the five young women, even though he'd be down in the lobby and they would be up in their rooms.

Bo didn't have a good reason not to go along with the suggestion, though, so he nodded and said, "I'll get everything ready, then join you at the hotel. Where are they staying, Cyrus?"

Keegan gave them the name of the establishment and told them how to find it. The hotel was only a few blocks from the courthouse.

"I hope Craddock doesn't cause any more trouble," he said worriedly. "I swear, when I started this business, I never dreamed such things would happen."

"That's why you've got us around now," Scratch told him. "To make sure they don't."

Chapter 8

It was midday before Bo reached the hotel where the five young women were staying. He found Scratch in the lobby, sitting in an armchair next to a potted palm. He stood up as Bo approached.

"No sign of Craddock or any of those cowhands who were with him yesterday," Scratch reported. "But there's been plenty of other fellas in and out who might work for him that I ain't ever seen before."

"We can't help that," Bo said. "What about the girls?"

Scratch grinned and pointed up with a thumb. "They've got rooms on the third floor. I went up when I got here, and spoke to each of 'em through the doors to make sure they're all right. They're all fine. Nobody's bothered 'em. You reckon maybe Craddock decided to back off, after all?"

"He didn't strike me as the sort who backs off from much of anything once he's got his mind made up," Bo answered. "But all we can do is keep our eyes open and deal with any problems that come up."

"I'll tell you what's come up—my appetite. It's about time to eat, Bo, and they've got a dinin' room in this hotel."

Bo smiled and said, "Go ahead and get some dinner. I'll spell you out here. Then you can come back and I'll get something to eat."

"A mighty fine plan," Scratch agreed. He hurried off toward the arched entrance to the dining room on the other side of the lobby.

Bo sat down in the same chair, thumbed his hat back on his head, and looked around. As Scratch had said, people were coming and going, but none of them looked threatening.

A quarter of an hour later, Cyrus Keegan walked in from the street.

"I thought I might find you here," he said as he came over to Bo. "Any trouble?"

"Not a bit. Scratch has gone to eat dinner."

"A good idea." Keegan reached inside his coat and brought out two rectangular pieces of pasteboard. "Here are your tickets. The ladies have compartments, but I'm afraid all I could get for you and Scratch are regular seats."

"That'll be fine," Bo assured him as he took the tickets and tucked them away in his own inside coat pocket. "We've slept sitting up on a train many a time. And we're only talking about one night. I reckon the train gets into El Paso tomorrow?"

"Around noon," Keegan confirmed. "Have you seen the young ladies?"

"No, but Scratch talked to all of them and said they were all right."

A worried frown creased Keegan's forehead. "I just find it hard to believe that Craddock isn't going to show up and cause more trouble," he said.

"Even the most annoying hombre decides to back off every now and then. One thing I've learned, Cyrus, is to take any luck you can, where and when it comes to you."

"Words to live by," Keegan muttered.

A few minutes later, Scratch returned from the dining room. He grinned and rubbed his belly as he said, "Mighty good grub, Bo. I left you a little, so you'd best go get it. Howdy, Cyrus. Everything all right?"

"Yes. I just gave Bo your tickets for the train. I also paid to have your horses shipped in one of the stock cars. The train arrives at one forty-five and leaves at two."

"We'll be ready," Bo promised.

"And I'll be on hand to make sure the ladies are situated properly," Keegan added.

"Why don't you come have dinner with me?"

Keegan smiled and said, "Lantana always packs my lunch for me. Today I have roast beef sandwiches from last night's leftovers. No offense, Bo, but I don't think I want to miss that."

"None taken," Bo assured him with a grin in return. "I wouldn't want to, either!"

Bo left the hotel at 1:30 p.m. to get the horses and take them to the railroad station at the southern end of downtown. It was a long walk from the livery stable to the station, so he swung up into the saddle and rode.

His and Scratch's visit to Fort Worth had been eventful, he thought as he headed down Main Street. It hadn't been quite twenty-four hours since they'd ridden in, and in that time they had been involved in a shoot-out and a brawl, had made some new friends—and possibly some enemies—and had been introduced to five of the prettiest young women he'd seen in a long time. Not only that, but they were also on the verge of spending the next several days in the company of those beauties.

He didn't think either of them could have predicted those things when they left South Texas to drift in this direction. Well, the shoot-out and the brawl, maybe, because things like that always seemed to happen sooner or later wherever he and Scratch were . . . but not the other things.

The train's whistle sounded as Bo approached the huge brick depot building. He saw puffs of smoke rising into the air on the other side of the building and knew they came from the loco-motive's smokestack.

A carriage with bags piled on top of it had pulled up in front of the station. It must have just come to a stop, because Scratch was still on the seat beside the driver. As he climbed down, Cyrus Keegan emerged from the vehicle and stood beside the door to help each of the young women out in turn.

Bo pinched his hat brim as he nodded to the women and said, "Looks like we've got good timing, ladies. I'll see about getting these horses loaded."

"And I'll supervise the baggage handlin'," Scratch said.

"While I escort the ladies to their compartments," Keegan put in. He waved a hand. "Right this way."

Porters came out to load the bags onto carts. As soon as that was done, the hired carriage driver flicked the reins against the backs of his team and drove off.

By then, Bo had circled the depot with the horses to a live-stock loading area at the eastern end of the building. Keegan had also given him the sheet of paper authorizing him to have the horses loaded into one of the stock cars.

"Take good care of them," he told the men who tended to the animals.

"We will, mister," one of them promised. "Looks like a fine pair of horses."

"They've traveled a lot of long, hard trails," Bo said.

Sort of like him and Scratch, he thought.

With that taken care of, he walked along the tracks to the steps leading up to the station platform. As he did that, his eyes scanned the crowds around the train.

He wasn't convinced that Hugh Craddock had given up.

Sure, the rancher's declaration that the matter wasn't finished yet had contained a certain amount of bluster. But even taking that into account, Bo believed that Craddock meant what he said.

And even though it was ridiculous that Craddock thought he could marry Cecilia Spaulding after having laid eyes on her once, that was what he'd said he intended to do, and his pride would make him carry through on the promise. Or try to, anyway.

So Bo more than halfway expected to see Craddock or some of the rancher's men lurking around the depot. However, he didn't spot any of them. Maybe he was wrong and Craddock had some sense in his head.

Just to make sure, though, he went up the steps into the rearmost passenger car and began working his way toward the front of the train, checking each car for familiar faces and signs of potential trouble.

The car where the Pullman compartments were located was the first one behind the engine and tender. The compartments weren't made up in the middle of the day like this, of course. Bo found the ladies sitting on comfortable benches. Scratch and Keegan stood nearby.

Keegan had his bowler hat in his hand. He bent forward almost in a bow and said, "It's been a pleasure to have met you ladies, and please, once you've settled into your new homes, I really hope you'll write to me and let me know how you're doing."

"Why, sure we will, Mr. Keegan," Rose Winston said. "Won't we, girls?"

The others murmured agreement.

"I wish you the best of luck," Keegan went on. "If you ever find yourselves back in Fort Worth, drop in to see me." He put his hat on and smiled solemnly. "Good-bye."

They said their farewells. Keegan lifted a hand in response and left the car, stepping out into the vestibule, then going down the steps to the platform.

"Stay here," Bo told Scratch. "I'll be back in a minute."

"Don't let the train go off and leave you," Scratch warned.

"Don't worry. I won't."

Bo swung down to the platform, where Keegan had stopped to stand and dab at his eyes with a handkerchief. He put it away quickly when he saw Bo.

"I wasn't crying," he said. "It's the smoke from the locomotive, you know. It irritates my eyes."

"It can sure do that, all right," Bo agreed.

"I realize it's foolish. I barely know those girls. And yet a part of me almost feels like they're my daughters. You know? I don't have any children of my own, so I suppose I . . ." Keegan's voice trailed off. Then he added, "So I suppose I'm a foolish old man."

"Not hardly," Bo said. "I just wanted to let you know that I checked through the other cars and didn't see any sign of Craddock or his men. I sort of thought he might show up and start more trouble."

"So did I. In fact, I worried about it quite a bit. I'm glad you made sure he's not here. That really eases my mind."

"Of course, there could be other problems along the way . . ."

Keegan smiled and said, "I know. But that's why you and Scratch are going along. I'm confident that whatever happens, you'll be able to handle it."

"That's the plan," Bo said.

The conductor was moving along the observation platform beside the train now, bellowing, "*All aboooard!*"

Bo held out his hand to Keegan and said, "So long, Cyrus. I'll wire you when we get to El Paso to let you know we made it that far safely, and if there's a telegraph in Silverhill, I'll do the same when we get there."

"There's supposed to be a telegraph," Keegan said as he shook Bo's hand. "I'm looking forward to hearing from you."

Steam billowed from the engine. The whistle shrilled. As the drivers engaged on the rails, Bo stepped up onto the platform at the back of the car and lifted a hand in farewell. Keegan was still standing on the station platform, watching, as the train rolled out, heading westbound.

Five minutes later, a tall, rangy figure bounded from the station lobby onto the platform, looked around, and uttered a heartfelt "Damnation!"

One of the porters passing by paused and asked, "Something wrong, sir?"

"The westbound train headed for El Paso, it's already gone?"

"Yes, sir. Pulled out just a few minutes ago, right on time. We try to keep to the schedule here. Stationmaster won't have it no other way."

Hugh Craddock cursed again. If it hadn't taken him so long to discover where the five young women were going . . . if he hadn't had to visit several hotels and grease a dozen palms to find out what he needed to know . . . he might have gotten here in time to plead his case again.

He could make Cecilia Spaulding see the light if she would just give him a chance. He knew he could.

"Mister," the porter said, frowning, "are you all right?"

Craddock got control of his anger and frustration and asked, "Did five ladies get on the train?"

"There were quite a few passengers boardin' today. I expect more'n five of 'em were ladies."

Craddock started to snap impatiently at the man but stopped himself in time. Forcing himself to stay calm, he said, "If you happened to see the ladies I'm looking for, you'd remember them. You'd never forget them. They're all young and beautiful, especially this slender, dark-haired one . . ."

Craddock's voice trailed off as Cecilia Spaulding's image filled his mind. He couldn't have said why he was so drawn to her, but the attraction she held for him was undeniable. She was like a lodestone, and he was nothing more than a crude chunk of iron, caught by unfathomable forces.

The porter scratched his head and said, "Well, I *might* know who you're talkin' about, sir."

Craddock bit back another curse, reached into his pocket, and pulled out a silver dollar. The porter's open palm appeared as if by magic. Craddock slapped the coin into it.

"Five young women, like you said. All mighty fine lookin', if I can be so bold as to say so, sir. I saw 'em get on the train, all right."

"You're not telling *me* anything I didn't already mention to *you*," Craddock snapped.

"There was two older fellas with 'em," the porter replied. "Looked sort of like cowboys, they did. And you didn't say nothin' about *them*."

No, he hadn't, Craddock thought. If the porter had seen Creel and Morton with the young women, then he was still on the right trail. He was sure of that.

"So they got on the train for El Paso."

"Yes, sir. Fact is, I helped load their bags in the baggage car."

Craddock nodded and asked, "When's the next west-bound?"

The porter cleared his throat meaningfully.

"For God's sake," Craddock said. "I can go back in the station and look at the damned schedule board!"

The porter shrugged and said, "There's a westbound at eight o'clock this evenin'."

Eight o'clock. Craddock knew the delay would gnaw at his guts.

But the train would reach El Paso in less than twenty-four hours. Any other way he tried to make the journey would take a week or more. By that time, the ladies and their annoying escorts would have reached Silverhill, their ultimate destination in New Mexico Territory.

No, like it or not, Craddock knew that if he was ever going to catch up to Cecilia and make her understand that they were meant to be together, he had to catch that eight o'clock train. At least he'd have plenty of time to round up the men he had brought with him from the ranch, he told himself.

The porter broke into his thoughts by asking, "Anything else you want to know, mister?"

Craddock shook his head and said, "No. Not a damned thing."

Cecilia Spaulding thought she could get away from him, but he wasn't going to allow that.

Whatever it took, she was going to be his wife.

Chapter 9

Bo rejoined Scratch and the five young women in the railroad car. Scratch was sitting on one of the benches, between Beth Macy and Rose Winston, and seemed to be having the time of his life. He had a big grin on his face, that was for sure, Bo noted.

"Well, we're on our way," he said as he thumbed back his hat and leaned against the wall. "By this time tomorrow, you ladies will be in El Paso."

"Have you been there before, Mr. Creel?" Cecilia Spaulding asked.

Scratch answered the question before Bo could, saying, "Why, sure we've been there. Bo and I have visited El Paso plenty of times."

"What's it like?" Cecilia wanted to know.

"It's a border town," Bo said, as if that answered the question all by itself.

Still grinning, Scratch said, "What Bo means is that it can be a mite rambunctious at times. Cuidad Juárez, the Mexican town right across the Rio Grande, is pretty much wide open. Fellas from both sides of the border go there to cut loose their wolf. El Paso itself, on our side of the river, has tamed down some over the years because there's been a Ranger post there for a long time. But it can still get to be quite a fandango now and then."

"I love listening to you talk, Mr. Morton," Luella Tolman said. "You're so . . . colorful."

"Yeah, he's that, all right," Bo commented dryly. "Don't let what he's saying spook you, though, ladies. There's a good chance you'll be in El Paso for only one night, and we'll find a decent, comfortable hotel where you can stay. I'm hoping that by day after tomorrow, we'll be ready to set out for Silverhill."

"By wagon?" Cecilia asked.

Bo nodded and said, "That's probably the best way. There'll be room for all you ladies and your bags. The other alternative would be to go by stagecoach, and I don't know how often—or even if—they run to Silverhill."

"Bein' as it's a mining town, there's a good chance there's a stage line," Scratch said.

"We'll see. The ladies might be more comfortable traveling by wagon, though."

"Yeah, those old Concords can be a mite rough," Scratch agreed.

"Why not buy horses?" Beth suggested. "All of us know how to ride."

"You're sure of that?" Scratch asked.

"Of course. We're all from the same town. Four Corners, Iowa."

"We've known each other all our lives," Rose added.

Bo raked a thumbnail along his jawline, tugged at his right earlobe, and said, "Silverhill is more than a hundred miles from El Paso. I don't imagine any of you ladies are used to riding that far on horseback."

"That's true," Cecilia said. "I've never done more than ride around the park in our hometown on a Sunday afternoon."

"Plus, we'd still have to have a wagon of some sort for your bags," Bo said. "It makes more sense just to get one big enough to carry everything."

Cecilia smiled. "We'll bow to your better judgment, Mr. Creel," she said. "You and Mr. Morton are the ones with the experience out here in the West, after all."

"Why don't you call him Bo and me Scratch?" the silver-haired Texan said.

"That seems disrespectful," Jean Parker said. "You're both so much older than us."

"We ain't ever been the sort of fellas to stand on ceremony. Ain't that right, Bo?"

Bo said, "You ladies just call us whatever you're comfortable calling us."

"As long as it ain't late for supper," Scratch added.

Rose frowned and shook her head, then said, "I don't understand."

"Don't call us late for supper. It's, uh, a joke, I reckon."

"Oh," Rose said, although she still nodded doubtfully. "And a very amusing one."

The distance was considerable between Fort Worth and El Paso. Crossing most of Texas was like traveling across several normal states.

Of course, there was nothing normal about Texas as far as Bo and Scratch were concerned. As sons of the Lone Star State since before it even existed, they knew good and well that everything about Texas was better than normal and always would be.

Even if the train were able to run at top speed all the way, without stopping, it would take ten or twelve hours to reach El Paso. As it was, since the train had to make stops in numerous towns along the way, the journey would take almost twice that long. By evening, the train had reached Abilene, a settlement with the same name as the more notorious cow town in Kansas. There was no dining car on this run, but while they were stopped in Abilene, a boy pushing a cart came around and sold sandwiches and fruit. Bo and Scratch had known from experience that supper on the train was liable not to amount to much. That was why they had eaten good midday meals at the hotel in Fort Worth.

Cecilia and Luella bought just apples and oranges, but Beth, Rose, and Jean gnawed on tough roast beef sandwiches.

After a while, Rose said, "My, you really need strong teeth to eat these, don't you?"

"We need to get you some jerky," Scratch said. "That'll either make your teeth good and strong or bust 'em right out of your head."

Without looking up from the orange she was peeling, Cecilia said, "Neither of those sounds like a very appealing option, Mr. Morton."

"That's one thing about the frontier. Sometimes you don't have a whole lot of choice about what you eat. You take what's there, or you do without."

"Sort of like husbands," Jean said. "Once we realized we weren't likely to find any good ones in Four Corners, we decided to try another approach."

"Like becoming mail-order brides," Bo said. He had taken a folding knife from his pocket and was cutting an apple up into pieces.

"Like contacting a matrimonial agency," Cecilia corrected him. "Calling us mail-order brides sounds so . . . crass."

"Like we're for sale," Jean added. "It's nothing like that. All the arrangements were completely proper and aboveboard."

Bo nodded and said, "I'm sure they were."

"It ain't like fellas can order you from a Monkey Wards catalog," Scratch put in.

Beth looked at the remaining half of the sandwich in her hand and sighed. "Would you like what's left of this, Mr. Morton?" she asked. "I think I've had all I want."

"Why, sure," Scratch said, reaching for the slab of roast beef between two hunks of bread. "That's another thing about the frontier. You never let food go to waste."

Bo heard the locomotive's whistle blow, and a moment later, with a faint lurch of the floor underneath them, the train got under way again. Slowly, it began to pick up steam as it pulled away from the depot in Abilene. The next stop would be in Sweetwater.

The conductor came around not long after that and asked, "Is everything all right so far, ladies?"

"It's been fine," Cecilia assured him. "We look forward to the rest of the trip."

"A porter will be around to make up the compartments in just a little while." The conductor pinched the stiff black bill of the cap he wore as he nodded to them; then he moved on.

Bo finished the apple he was eating and opened a window to toss the core out into the gathering darkness that rushed by outside. He said, "I'm going to take a walk up and down the passenger cars before you ladies turn in, just to have a look around."

"You think Craddock might've slipped on board at the last minute?" Scratch asked.

"I don't think it's likely, but I'd rather be sure."

Cecilia said, "Wait a minute. Are you talking about the man who barged into Mr. Keegan's office this morning?"

"That's right," Bo said.

"Why would he be on the train?"

Bo and Scratch exchanged glances. They hadn't told Cecilia about how Craddock had gotten the loco notion of marrying her, as soon as he first laid eyes on her. They hadn't wanted to worry her or any of the other young ladies.

On the other hand, she probably had a right to know, especially if there was a chance Craddock might come after her. Scratch must have been thinking the same thing, because he nodded to indicate that Bo should go ahead and explain.

"That fella is one of Cyrus's clients," Bo said. "He has a

ranch southwest of Fort Worth and is a widower looking for a new wife. Cyrus arranged for him to correspond with a lady from back East, and she came to Fort Worth, expecting to marry Hugh Craddock. But he changed his mind."

"He decided not to marry her after she'd come all that way?" Beth said.

Bo nodded and said, "Yeah, I'm afraid so."

"That's terrible!" Luella said.

"Seems like a pretty sorry thing to us, too," Scratch put in.

Cecilia frowned slightly and asked, "Why did Mr. Craddock decide to go back on the agreement?"

"Well . . . he says the lady isn't quite as young as he believed she was." Bo didn't go into detail about the photograph of Miss Hampshire that Craddock had seen.

"She's older than him?" Cecilia asked sharply.

"Not exactly. They're about the same age, I think."

Cecilia sniffed in obvious disgust and shook her head. "What a dreadful man."

Jean said, "It's all right for us to marry men who are considerably older than us, but this rancher is too good to marry a woman his own age?"

"He's a pretty sorry rascal," Scratch drawled.

Cecilia was still looking at Bo as she said, "None of that explains why you believe Craddock may be on this train with us."

Having come this far in the explanation, Bo figured he didn't have any choice but to plunge ahead with it.

"After he saw you there in Cyrus's office, he asked about you. He wanted to know if all of you were . . ."

"Mail-order brides," Cecilia said, finishing for him, as a disapproving frown creased her forehead.

"Well, yeah. And he was especially interested in you, Miss Spaulding."

That caused Cecilia's finely arched eyebrows to go back up. She said, "He was interested in me? How exactly do you mean that, Mr. Creel?"

"He told Cyrus that instead of the woman who came out here to meet him, he would marry you."

The blunt statement surprised the other young women and, judging by the smiles that they tried to hide, amused them, as well.

"That would make you a replacement mail-order bride, Cecilia," Jean said.

Cecilia had gone back to frowning. She said to Bo, "You mean he wanted to . . . to court me?"

"No. He seemed to figure the two of you would just go ahead and get hitched right away, because that's the way he wanted it to be. He wasn't interested in any sort of courtship."

"That's outrageous!" Cecilia's face wore a full-fledged glare now. "As if he wanted to . . . to return a piece of merchandise and exchange it for something else!"

Bo nodded and said, "He did seem to regard it as more of a business transaction."

"Well, I hope Mr. Keegan set him straight, in no uncertain terms."

Scratch said, "All three of us did. We told the varmint you was already spoken for, Miss Cecilia."

"He was stubborn about it, though," Bo said. "That's why I searched the train real good before we left Fort Worth. I wanted to make sure Craddock hadn't found out where we're going and decided to come after us. After you, I should say."

Cecilia's already pale face whitened a little more as she thought about Bo's words.

"You mean you believe he might try to . . . to kidnap me?" she asked in a soft, shocked voice.

"I don't think it's very likely," Bo told her. He tried to make his voice reassuring, but Cecilia still looked pretty worried— and angry, to boot. "From what I know of him, he's not an outlaw or anything, just an honest rancher who's too accustomed to getting his own way."

"Well, he's not getting his way in this matter, I can tell you that," Cecilia said.

"No, ma'am, we never figured he would," Scratch said.

"So it's really just for everybody's peace of mind that I thought I'd take another look around," Bo said. "It's not likely, but Craddock *could* have sneaked on board right at the very last minute."

"What are you going to do if you find him?" Rose asked. She leaned forward eagerly. "Are you going to shoot him?"

The question surprised Bo a little. He said, "No, I can't just haul off and shoot him. It's not against the law to ride a train. But if we know he's around, we can keep an eye out for him and be ready if he does try anything."

Cecilia nodded and said, "Yes, I think that's wise." She opened the small handbag she carried and slipped her hand into it. "I'm not totally unprepared, though, in case of trouble."

She pulled out a pistol and held it up where Bo and Scratch could see it.

Chapter 10

The gun was a little Smith & Wesson pocket pistol, a seven-shot weapon in .22 caliber with a bird's-head grip and, like all the small-caliber S&Ws, no trigger guard. Little more than a kid's popgun, really, but under the right circumstances, it could be dangerous.

Scratch sat up straighter and said, "Uh, ma'am, is that thing loaded?"

"Of course it is," Cecilia answered. "What good would it be if it wasn't?"

"Well," Bo said, "given that it's a twenty-two, unless you're a really good shot, you could probably do more damage to a fella by throwing it at him instead of shooting him."

Clearly offended, she said, "Are you insulting my choice of firearm, Mr. Creel?"

"He's just sayin' it likely won't stop any hombre who's bound and determined to do you harm," Scratch explained. "Not unless you, say, shoot him in the eye."

"And you'd have to be pretty close to do that," Bo added, "since at any range more than ten feet, that gun's not going to be very accurate."

"Well, then, perhaps we should practice," Cecilia said.

"We?" Bo and Scratch responded in unison.

The other four young women reached into their handbags and hauled out pistols identical to the one Cecilia held.

"We went and bought these together," Beth said.

"We didn't think it would be a good idea to venture into the Wild West without being able to defend ourselves if necessary," Jean said.

Scratch was on his feet now. He made gentle patting motions with both hands and said, "Ladies, put those hoglegs away. You don't want to go to shootin' here on the train. Innocent folks could get hurt."

Yeah, innocent folks like him and Scratch, Bo thought. He said, "It's just not a good idea to start waving guns around if you don't need to."

"You and Scratch carry guns," Rose said.

"And from what we've heard, you're quite proficient with them," Cecilia put in. "I remember hearing something about an inquest . . ."

Bo sighed and nodded. "Scratch and I can handle our guns all right. We're not fast-draw artists, like Smoke Jensen or Falcon MacCallister—"

"The dime-novel heroes," Rose said with a bright smile.

"Yeah, but they're real fellas, too, not just in books."

"Really?" Rose's eyes widened.

She must be a reader of those lurid yellowback tales, Bo thought.

"Do you know them?" she asked.

"Never crossed trails with either of 'em," Scratch said. "But the point is, if you ain't used to handlin' guns, you got to be mighty careful with 'em. You ought to be careful even if you *are* used to 'em."

"We're going to be on the trail between El Paso and Silverhill for several days, aren't we?" Cecilia said.

"We are," Bo replied.

"Then I still believe it would be an excellent idea for my friends and me to get in some target practice along the way. I assume we'll be passing through some sparsely populated areas, where no one would be in any real danger if we did some shooting."

Bo thought about how empty a lot of southern New Mexico Territory was and said, "You're right about that."

"It's settled, then." Cecilia slipped the pistol back in her bag. The others followed suit. She looked up at Bo and added, "You can go search the rest of the train now and make certain that man Craddock isn't on board. And if he should happen to show up here while you're gone, I daresay he'll find us pre-pared to put up more of a defense than he expects. Isn't that right, girls?"

The others all nodded solemnly.

Bo and Scratch looked at each other.

Scratch said weakly, "Just go. I'll keep an eye on things here."

"Yeah," Bo said. Trying not to shake his head, he went to the rear of the car and stepped out onto the observation platform.

Full night had fallen, and the air had a hint of coolness, which felt good as Bo paused. It would be even more refreshing if he didn't have to smell the smoke from the engine, but a fella couldn't have everything. He stood there for a moment, then stepped across to the front platform of the next car back and opened the door to its vestibule.

For the next ten minutes, Bo walked through the rest of the passenger cars without seeing any sign of Hugh Craddock or any of the men who had been with Craddock the day before. There was still a slim chance that one of Craddock's men was on board, one Bo hadn't seen before, but Bo considered that so unlikely it wasn't worth worrying about.

Equally unlikely was the possibility that Craddock was back in one of the freight or stock or baggage cars. Hell, the man might be riding on top of one of the cars, but Bo didn't think there was much chance of that!

Only one other possibility remained, and when Bo found the conductor in the last passenger car, he asked the man, "You don't happen to have a passenger riding back in the caboose, do you?"

The conductor frowned in what appeared to be genuine surprise and said, "The company doesn't allow that, mister."

"Yeah, but I know that sometimes there are special circumstances."

He was talking about a bribe.

The conductor may have realized that. He drew himself up straighter and said, "There aren't any circumstances special enough for the rules to be broken on this train. Not on *my* train."

"That's good to know," Bo said, nodding. "I didn't figure there would be."

The blue-uniformed man looked suspiciously at him and asked sharply, "Is there going to be trouble that I don't know about?"

Satisfied that Hugh Craddock wasn't aboard the train, Bo shook his head. "Nope. I think the rest of the trip to El Paso will go mighty smooth."

"It'll go smooth all the way to California," the conductor said. "I intend to see to it."

"Yes, sir." Bo pinched the brim of his hat and nodded. "Good night."

The conductor still regarded him with a narrow-eyed frown as he started back toward the front of the train.

Bo had walked through two of the passenger cars and was about to step out onto the front platform of the second one when he almost bumped into someone entering from that platform. He caught himself and stopped just before he ran into the person, who also came to an abrupt halt.

Then Bo reached up and took off his hat as he said, "I'm sorry, ma'am. I didn't mean to be so clumsy."

"No harm done, sir," the woman replied with a smile. "Although neither one of us was moving very fast, so even if we *had* collided, I doubt if there would have been any real damage."

"Likely not," Bo agreed. He started to step aside. "Let me get out of your way . . ."

"I'm in no hurry. I was just out on the platform, getting a breath of fresh air. Relatively fresh air, I should say."

"Yeah, it's got some smoke and the occasional cinder in it. The cars can get stuffy, though."

The woman inclined her head toward the platform and asked, "Would you care to join me for a few minutes? I realize I'm being very forward by asking such a thing, but I assure you, I'm not a brazen woman."

"Uh, no, ma'am, that thought never crossed my mind," Bo said.

He was telling her the truth. He had been around a lot of soiled doves in his life. Not that he'd ever made a habit of patronizing them very often, but they were to be found in many of the saloons he and Scratch had wandered into over the years. Not only was this woman older than most of them, but she also lacked the subtle—and some not so subtle—signs of dissipation that most doves acquired.

She was pretty enough that she would have been popular, though, with thick dark hair pinned up under her hat and a face that was lovely in the light spilling through the railroad car's open door. The years had left a few lines around her eyes and mouth, but as far as Bo was concerned, that just gave her character.

"So, would you like to join me?" she asked again.

"I suppose I could keep you company for a few minutes," Bo said. "It would be my pleasure."

"Please, go ahead and put your hat back on," she told him as she moved back out onto the platform.

Bo settled the hat on his head as he followed her. He hesitated for a second before closing the door but then pulled it shut behind him.

The woman was already standing at the railing on the side of the platform, with her hands resting on it. Bo moved alongside her. In this particular spot, the smell of smoke from the locomotive's diamond-shaped stack wasn't too bad.

With the door closed, there wasn't as much light on the platform, although some still came through the small window in the door. Bo could see her fairly well as she stood beside him, once his eyes had adjusted to it. A few strands of dark hair had escaped from the careful arrangement under the hat. The wind blew them around.

From where they stood, they were gazing northward across the West Texas plains. Enough silvery glow from the moon and stars washed over the landscape that they were able to see the occasional clump of trees around an isolated ranch house. Bo spotted a few distant low patches of darkness, which he figured were mesas. The train was moving into that part of the country. Soon they would reach the Caprock, the eroded but still significant escarpment that ran for hundreds of miles across Texas and marked the eastern edge of the Staked Plains.

"It's beautiful, isn't it?" the woman murmured.

Bo said, "It's probably a mite prettier like this, in the moonlight and starlight, than it is during the day. When the sun's out, you can see how hot and dry and dusty it is."

She laughed and said, "You sound like you don't care for it here."

"Oh, don't get me wrong," Bo responded quickly. "I'm a Texan, born, bred, and forever, and Texas is still the best place on the face of the earth. But there's no disputing that some parts of it are more hospitable than others. This country here"—he waved a hand at the landscape rolling past their eyes—"it was good for the buffalo and the Comanche a few years back, and it's good for the cattlemen now. Some people say that if they can figure out how to get enough water to it, it'll even be good farmland."

"I'm not from here," the woman said. That came as no surprise to Bo, who already knew that because of her accent. "I'm quite impressed with this country, though. It's so . . . big. Is the rest of the West like this?"

"Well, not as big as Texas, of course. But there's a lot of country west of the Mississippi. I should know. I've seen most of it."

She looked over at him and said, "You travel in your line of work?"

"You could say that," Bo replied. Actually, drifting from place to place *was* his line of work, his and Scratch's, but he didn't feel like confessing to this attractive new acquaintance that he was just a rootless saddle tramp.

"I've never traveled much," she said. She turned and extended a gloved hand toward him. "I'm Susan, by the way."

He felt a little embarrassed that he hadn't introduced himself before now. He took her hand and said, "My name's Bo."

"Short for Beauregard?"

"No, ma'am. Just b-o, Bo."

"Well, it's nice to meet you, Bo," she said as she pressed his hand with hers.

"The pleasure's all mine, Miss Susan."

Of course, he didn't know she was a miss, he reminded himself. She might be married, on her way to join her husband, and just enjoying a little harmless flirtation.

She pointed to a faint yellow glow in the distance. "What's that?" she asked.

"A light in some ranch house, more than likely."

"It looks so lonely, just a tiny spot of light in all this vast darkness."

"From out here it does," he said. "Inside, though, with a fella's family around, it probably seems nice and cozy."

She laughed and said, "I'll bet it does. That's a nice thought, anyway." She paused. "I suppose I'd better be getting back to my seat, and I'll let you get on to wherever you were bound when we bumped into each other."

"Almost bumped into each other," Bo reminded her. "We never actually, uh, bumped."

"Well, that's fortunate in one way," Susan said, "and perhaps unfortunate in another."

With that, she stepped back into the car, leaving Bo to stand there for a moment before he chuckled, shook his head, and went back to rejoin Scratch and the five young women.

Chapter 11

The train arrived in El Paso at eleven thirty the next morning. The night had passed quietly, and when it had, Bo and Scratch were more convinced than ever that they didn't have to worry about Hugh Craddock anymore. The arrogant rancher either was back in Fort Worth, hundreds of miles behind them, or else had returned to his home.

"Who knows?" Scratch had commented over breakfast, which consisted of biscuits and preserves bought from another cart that rolled through the train cars during one of the stops, this time by a little girl. "Maybe Craddock decided to give that Miss Hampshire gal a chance, after all."

"I doubt it," Bo had said. "He didn't strike me as the sort of hombre given to changing his mind."

"A stubborn jackass, in other words."

"Exactly."

The two Texans had taken turns standing guard in the narrow aisle outside the Pullman compartments, once the curtains had been closed and the young ladies had turned in for the night. They hadn't wanted to take any chances, and besides, despite what Bo had told Cyrus Keegan, sleeping sitting up on a hard bench seat in a jolting, rattling train car was just barely better than not sleeping at all.

As Bo had rolled his shoulders that morning to try to get some of the stiffness out of them, he had pondered the idea that maybe it wasn't *any* better.

To judge by their attitudes, the prospective brides had slept just fine. They laughed and chattered among themselves all morning, and—thankfully, as far as Bo was concerned—they didn't wave those pistols around again.

As the train rolled through some spectacular scenery, with rugged mountains rising to the south, they gathered at the windows on that side of the train to look out.

"You see those mountains over yonder, ladies?" Scratch asked them. "Those are in Mexico."

They turned their heads to look over their shoulders at him, and Jean exclaimed, "What? Surely not."

"Yep," Scratch said with a solemn nod. "See that darker line of vegetation between here and there? That's where the Rio Grande runs. Everything on the other side of it is in old Mexico."

"I've never been this close to a foreign country before," Rose said.

"I have." That came from Cecilia. "My father took our whole family to Canada one summer, remember? We saw Niagara Falls and took a boat across the river and ate dinner at a restaurant in Canada. It was quite a thrilling experience."

"I remember you telling us about that," Beth said. She looked at Bo and Scratch. "Will we have to cross over into Mexico to get where we're going?"

"Let's hope not," Bo said. "If we wind up in Mexico, it'll mean that something's really gone wrong."

Now, as the train pulled into the station in El Paso, they were even closer to Mexico, since the river was only a few blocks away and Juárez lay on the other side of the bridge.

As the young women gathered their belongings and got ready to leave the train, Cecilia said to Bo, "Is there really any need to stay here overnight? Couldn't we go ahead and start for Silverhill today?"

"We don't know how long it'll take to round up a suitable wagon and a team," he explained. "Also, we'll need to buy quite a few supplies to take with us, and that'll take some time, as well. It's already the middle of the day, and I think by the time we get everything done, it'll be too late to cover more than a few miles, if that much. Better to get a good night's sleep and start off fresh first thing in the morning."

"I suppose when you put it that way, it makes sense," she said.

Beth smiled and said to Cecilia, "You're just eager to get where we're going and meet your new beau, aren't you?" Then she added, "Oh, I mean 'beau,' as in suitor, of course, Mr. Creel, not your name."

"Yeah, he's the old Bo, not the new one," Scratch said with a grin.

Bo just chuckled. He was used to Scratch's joshing.

In a bustle of activity, he saw to it that the ladies' bags were unloaded and placed on a cart, while Scratch made sure their horses made it out of the stock car and down the ramp. He would take the animals to a livery stable and then would meet Bo and the young women later at the hotel.

Bo gave the Mexican porter a couple of silver dollars to insure that the bags would be delivered to the hotel, as well; then he and the ladies set out for their destination on foot. The Pacific Hotel, which the conductor had recommended to Bo as a comfortable hostelry, was only a couple of blocks away.

All five of the young women were wide eyed at the colorful crowds surrounding them. Cowboys and their sombrero-wearing vaquero counterparts from across the river, fancy-dressed tinhorn gamblers, stuffy businessmen, sedately gowned white women, señoritas in brightly colored beaded skirts and heavy bracelets, American cavalrymen in blue, all those and more walked the streets of El Paso in the midday heat.

Just north of the city loomed the Franklin Mountains, with their rugged pine-covered slopes. The valley formed by the Rio Grande provided a natural route between those mountains and the ones farther south, in Mexico. Travelers through the area had been using it for centuries, maybe even longer, and when the Spanish had first come here, they had called the gap El Paso del Norte—the Pass of the North.

The hotel, built in the Spanish style with white stucco walls and red tile roof, was two stories tall and had a balcony bordered by a wrought-iron railing along the front of the second floor. The porch underneath that balcony was shady and relatively cool, with wicker chairs and decorative cactus and other plants in pots. The double doors at the entrance were heavy and ornately carved wood, made even sturdier by the addition of iron straps.

"This place is built like a fort," Beth said as the group went inside.

"You know about forts?" Scratch asked.

"Well, no, not really. But my father was in the army when he was young, and told stories about the posts where he served." Beth looked around a little nervously and asked, "The Indians aren't going to attack, are they? Not a big town like this?"

Bo said, "There are still some Apaches running wild down in the Big Bend and across the line in Mexico, but it's peaceful around here these days."

"I thought all the Apaches were out in Arizona Territory," Cecilia said. "That's what I've read in the newspapers."

"That's where most of them are, and naturally enough, it's the troublemakers you hear the most about. But the Apaches used to roam all over Texas, too, until the Comanche drifted down from the north and pushed them all the way out here, in West Texas."

"And this is about as far west as you can go and still be in Texas," Scratch added.

They arranged for rooms for the ladies, and while they were doing that, a couple of porters from the railroad station showed up with the bags. Once those had been taken up to the rooms on the second floor, Bo, Scratch, and the young women adjourned to the hotel dining room for some lunch.

The ladies wanted to try Mexican food, since they were so close to that country. Bo and Scratch were used to the spicy nature of those dishes, but their five companions were gasping and reaching for glasses of water before the meal was over. The Texans smiled but managed not to laugh at their discomfort.

When the meal was over, Jean said, "Goodness, I think I need to rest for a while after that."

"So do I," Luella agreed.

"If all you ladies want to go up to your rooms and take it easy for a spell," Scratch said, "Bo and I will go and see about hirin' a wagon and team."

"Just be sure to lock your doors," Bo added.

Cecilia said, "I thought Westerners prided themselves on their honesty and hospitality and didn't worry about locking doors."

"In some places, that's true enough, but this is a big city, and not everybody can be trusted." Bo paused and then added with a smile, "Too many Yankees have moved in."

For a second, Cecilia looked like she might take offense at Bo's comment—which was only half joking—but then she nodded in acceptance of the explanation and led the others upstairs. Although there was no real hierarchy among them as far as Bo could tell, more often than not the other young ladies did whatever Cecilia did. She seemed to just naturally take charge, and they accepted that.

A few blocks away, Bo and Scratch found a wagon yard and freight company owned by a man named Alberto Garcia. His wagons traveled back and forth between El Paso and Silverhill on a fairly regular basis, anyway, so he was happy to rent one of them for the journey, along with a team of horses to pull it.

"There's talk of running a spur line down there to Silverhill in the next year or so," Garcia told Bo and Scratch. "The hombres who run the railroad want to wait awhile and see if the strike is going to play out. If the mines stop producing, Silverhill will dry up and blow away in no time, and then they'd be left with a railroad to nowhere."

"Is there a stage line that runs that way?" Bo asked.

Garcia nodded and said, "It makes two round trips a week. One left yesterday."

That information confirmed Bo's hunch that it would be better to rent the wagon instead of waiting for the stagecoach. The ladies would be more comfortable, could travel at their own pace, and they wouldn't have to sit around in El Paso, doing nothing for several days.

Scratch said, "We'll be pickin' up some supplies and havin' 'em delivered over here. Can you tell the fellas who bring 'em to load 'em in the wagon?"

He took a silver dollar from his pocket, which Garcia made disappear with all the deftness of a stage magician.

"Sure," the wagon-yard owner said. Then he asked, "Just what sort of freight are you fellas hauling to Silverhill, anyway?"

"I don't reckon you'd believe us if we told you, señor!" Scratch replied with a grin.

Chapter 12

When Bo and Scratch met the ladies in the hotel dining room for breakfast the next morning, Bo had a good-sized wrapped-up bundle with him. He placed it on the floor beside the table and said, "You'll want to take this with you when you go upstairs to get ready to leave."

"What is it?" Beth asked.

"Some sort of present?" Luella said.

"Well, not exactly. We got some hats for you."

Cecilia arched an eyebrow and asked coolly, "*You* bought hats for *us*?"

"Yes, ma'am," Scratch said. "Broad-brimmed hats, which will do a good job of shadin' you from the sun so it don't burn your delicate skin."

"You'll need different clothes, too," Bo said. "Dresses that'll hold up better and be more comfortable."

"Not that there's anything wrong with what you've been wearin'," Scratch added quickly. "They're mighty nice-lookin' outfits, no doubt about that."

"But they're not really suitable for days of traveling in a wagon," Bo said.

Jean looked dismayed as she said, "You make it sound as if we'll be dressed like . . . like farm women working in the fields!"

"Well, Miss Jean, you'll appreciate it once we get out there on the trail," Scratch assured her.

Cecilia said, "I suppose we'll have to bow to your judgment, since you two gentlemen know more about what we're doing and where we're going. But I hope you'll allow us to fix ourselves up a little before we reach Silverhill and meet the men we intend to marry."

"Yes, ma'am," Bo said, nodding. "I reckon you'll be pretty as pictures when we roll into town."

Garcia had delivered the wagon, now loaded with supplies, to the hotel early that morning. The two leaders in the six-horse hitch were tied to a streetlamp post in front of the hotel. Bo and Scratch's saddle mounts were tied to the same post.

The Texans were eager to get on the trail, but they didn't want to rush the ladies. They forced themselves to wait patiently after breakfast while the young women went across the street to a ladies' clothing store to buy more suitable outfits, such as Bo had described.

As they waited on the boardwalk in front of the establishment, Scratch said, "I heard some fellas in the lobby talkin' while you were out checkin' over the wagon and the team. They were saying that Jaime Mendoza has been pretty active along the border lately. They figure it's only a matter of time until he starts raidin' on our side of the line again."

"Mendoza . . . ," Bo repeated. "That's the bandit the *Rurales* chased all over Chihuahua and Sonora last year and never caught?"

"Yep. I remember readin' about him in the newspapers. Seems like one of the papers even sent a fella down there to live with the bandits and write about 'em and send back dispatches."

"Yeah, I believe I recall that, too," Bo said. "Are you thinking we might run into him on the way to Silverhill?"

"Well, the odds are against it, I reckon," Scratch said with a
shrug. "But it'll be somethin' to keep in mind." He paused.
"Best not to say anything about it to the ladies, though. No
need in gettin' 'em all worked up about somethin' when it's
more likely nothin' will happen."

Bo agreed. The trip would be taxing enough on the young
women without extra worries.

Besides, that was why he and Scratch had come along. It was
their job to be concerned about such things—and to deal with
them if they came up.

A few minutes later, Cecilia Spaulding appeared in the store's
doorway. She wore a gray dress and a pair of those sturdy shoes
Bo had mentioned. Her dark hair was pulled back and tied behind her head under the broad-brimmed black felt hat she
wore.

"You look mighty nice, Miss Cecilia," Scratch told her.

"Don't be ridiculous," she responded. "I look like a share-
cropper."

"Plenty of fine folks have worked for shares," Bo said. "It's
nothing to be ashamed of."

"Of course not," Cecilia said. "I meant no offense. It's just
that I'm not accustomed to such garb." She fingered the stiff
fabric of the dress. "I can see what you mean about it holding
up better, though."

"Yes, ma'am, and if you ever have to walk very much, you'll
be grateful for those shoes."

"Lots of rocks and cactus where we're goin'," Scratch said.
"Them slippers of yours are pretty, but they'd have you hob-
blin' in a hurry."

"Well, the others are ready to go, too," Cecilia said, "so I
suppose we might as well depart."

The other four young ladies emerged from the store, dressed

in varying shades of gray, brown, and blue, in brown or black hats.

"A family of Quakers came through Four Corners once," Jean said with a note of dismay in her voice. "That's what we look like."

Cecilia said, "We'll get used to it. Come on."

Bo lowered the wagon's tailgate, and he and Scratch helped the ladies climb inside. The supply crates had been arranged to form seats for four of them, and room remained for blankets to be spread out for sleeping.

"Am I going to drive the team?" Rose asked, excitement and anticipation in her voice. She was the only one of the young women who hadn't gotten into the wagon.

"No, I'll handle the horses starting out," Bo said, "but you can ride on the seat beside me."

"You don't think I'm capable of doing it?"

"I never said that. But I think it would be a better idea to wait until we're out of town before you take the reins. We don't know these horses yet. Señor Garcia uses them with his wagons, so they're probably pretty easy to handle, but they might spook."

"All right," Rose said, with grudging acceptance. "At least I get to ride up front."

"I'm sure you'll all take turns doing that," Bo said as he took her hand and helped her climb onto the high driver's box.

Scratch had already untied his mount's reins and swung up into the saddle. Bo closed the tailgate and fastened his horse at the back of the wagon, then pulled himself up onto the seat next to Rose.

"Are you ladies ready to go?" he asked as he took hold of the team's reins.

"More than ready," Cecilia answered from inside the wagon, underneath the arching canvas cover.

"Let's head out, then."

Bo hauled the team around and started the wagon rolling in the direction of Silverhill.

The four young women riding in the wagon bed clustered around the opening in the front so they could look out past Bo and Rose and see where they were going. The road followed the Rio Grande for a while, then turned west and crossed the river on a wooden bridge.

"I thought you said we weren't going into Mexico," Cecilia said as she peered over Bo's right shoulder.

"We didn't," he said. With his left thumb, he pointed back to the south. "The Mexican border's half a mile or so that way. After it reaches that point, it doesn't follow the river anymore. We're in New Mexico Territory now. The Rio Grande runs on north through the territory to its source in the San Juan Mountains in southern Colorado."

"You know a lot about such things, don't you?" Rose asked.

Bo shrugged and said, "I ought to. Scratch and I have wandered around out here for a lot of years."

"But you're from Texas," Rose said. "Why have you been so many other places?"

"It's a long story," Bo said. "Maybe I'll tell it to you ladies sometime."

In truth, though, he had no intention of doing that. Some things a man was better off keeping to himself. The history he and Scratch shared had a lot of tragedy in it, as well as plenty of incidents that proper young ladies didn't have any business hearing about.

The day was a beautiful one, although Bo knew it would be plenty hot before the afternoon was over. Right now, at their location in the valley of the Rio Grande, a hint of coolness lingered in the breeze that swept over the semiarid plains. The sky was a breathtaking blue, dotted with white, puffy clouds.

A number of places in the West were called Big Sky Country,

and those descriptions were accurate. The sky and the land-scape in front of them seemed to go on forever. Scratch rode about a hundred yards in front of the wagon, scouting the trail for any signs of trouble.

Bo knew they could cover twenty miles a day without push-ing the team too hard. When he estimated they had put half that distance behind them, the sun was almost directly overhead. During the morning, he had stopped a couple of times to let the horses rest, but this time as he reined the team to a halt, he said, "We'll stop here for a while and eat some lunch."

"It'll feel good to get out and stretch our . . . limbs," Cecilia said, carefully choosing the more decorous word.

Bo wouldn't have been offended if she'd said, "Legs." He knew perfectly well that women had them just like men did. But if Cecilia wanted to maintain a sense of propriety, that was fine.

Scratch trotted back to join them and dismounted. So far they hadn't seen anyone else on the trail, but Bo didn't expect that to last. With Silverhill being a mining boomtown, more people were bound to be on the way there.

"Want me to rustle up enough wood for a fire, so we can boil a pot of coffee?" Scratch asked.

Bo looked around. Trees were scarce, almost to the point of nonexistence, in this area, but he saw plenty of mesquite bushes and knew Scratch could find enough broken branches to fuel a small fire.

"Sure, go ahead," he told his friend. "I'll fry up some bacon, too."

They could take their time, he thought. After all, they didn't have to arrive in Silverhill on any certain day. The young women had given their intended bridegrooms a rough window of when they would arrive, but a day or two either way wouldn't make any difference.

The meal was simple but good and filling. Bo and Scratch were hunkered beside the dying fire, enjoying the last of the coffee in their tin cups, when Cecilia went to the wagon and came back with that little Smith & Wesson revolver in her hand.

"No one is anywhere around," she said. "I think it's time for some target practice."

Chapter 13

Bo and Scratch traded dubious glances. The other four young women weren't the least bit hesitant, though.

Rose said, "Yes, let's!" and hurried toward the wagon. The other three followed her, obviously bent on retrieving their pistols.

Scratch said, "I suppose it wouldn't hurt to make sure they know what they're doin'. The last thing we want is for those gals to start throwin' lead around without ever firin' a gun before."

Bo nodded and said, "You're right." He drank the last of his coffee. "But I don't have to be enthusiastic about it."

A grin stretched across Scratch's face as he said, "Aw, come on. It might be fun."

"We'll see," Bo said.

He and Scratch stood up and waited as the five young women gathered around them, each holding one of the identical little revolvers.

"First thing," Bo said. "Have any of you ever shot a gun before?"

"I have," Rose said. "My father tried to show me how to shoot. He wasn't very good at it, though."

"Fathers are never good at teaching daughters anything," Jean said. "They're too impatient."

She got nods of agreement from Beth and Luella.

Jean went on, "My father doesn't even know I have this gun. He wouldn't have approved, and my mother certainly wouldn't have. She'd insist that a lady has no business even being anywhere around a firearm, let alone shooting one."

Scratch said, "There's an old sayin' about how God created all men, but Colonel Sam Colt is the one who made 'em equal. That applies to ladies, too. Remember, a gun don't know who's holdin' it or whose finger is on the trigger. You get good enough with a hogleg, you don't have to worry about whether there's a fella around. You can take care of yourself." The silver-haired Texan chuckled. "Although I reckon it'd be a stretch to call them things hoglegs. They ain't even as big as a hog's foot."

"Are they all loaded?" Bo asked.

Cecilia held up her pistol and said, "Of course. As we discussed before, what good is an unloaded weapon?"

"Let me see it."

Bo held out his hand, and with a bit of reluctance, Cecilia placed the Smith & Wesson in it. He unlatched the barrel and pivoted it up, removed the cylinder, used the rammer pin under the barrel to poke one of the .22 cartridges out of it, then replaced the cylinder and closed the gun. He turned the cylinder until the empty chamber was under the hammer.

"That's the way you want to carry a revolver," he told the young women. "Unless you know you're going to be doing a lot of shooting right away, keep the hammer resting on an empty chamber. That way it won't go off by accident if you drop it."

"Can that really happen?" Rose asked.

"Sure," Scratch said. "I've seen it happen more than once. Came close to havin' a slug part my hair because of it, too."

"Why don't all of you go ahead and do that, like I just showed you?" Bo said. He handed the pistol he had used for the demonstration back to Cecilia, along with the bullet he had taken out of the cylinder. She dropped it in a pocket of her dress.

Jean and Luella struggled with the mechanism on their guns, but Rose and Beth took to it more easily. Bo and Scratch worked with them until they all had the guns loaded properly.

"These are single-action revolvers," Bo went on. "That means you have to pull the hammer back to cock it before you squeeze the trigger to fire. Line up there beside the wagon, facing away from it, with about three feet between each of you."

He waited until they had arranged themselves satisfactorily, then said, "All right, use your thumb to pull the hammer back, but keep the gun pointed toward the ground in front of you when you do. You'll see that when you cock it, the cylinder turns so there's a live round where the hammer's going to fall. So *don't* pull the trigger. In fact, keep your finger away from it."

"We can't shoot if we don't put our finger on the trigger," Cecilia said.

"You're not going to shoot just yet," Bo told her. "You're just cocking the gun."

"This seems awfully slow," Rose said. "In the dime novels, Smoke Jensen never takes this long to get his gun out and start shooting."

Scratch said, "Generally speakin', them dime novels are written by fellas who don't know their . . . uh . . . elbows from a hole in the ground. I've heard that they're mostly drunk while they're writin' 'em, too."

"See those three clumps of prickly pear about fifteen feet from the edge of the trail?" Bo asked. "I want you to raise your guns, aim at any of those clumps, and whenever you're ready, go ahead and shoot."

"Should we hold the gun with one hand or two?" Luella asked.

"However you're most comfortable."

Luella nodded and steadied her grip by using both hands. So did Jean and Cecilia. Rose and Beth each used one hand. The young women stood there and pointed the little revolvers at the clumps of prickly pear cactus as long seconds dragged by.

"Well?" Rose finally said. "Is anybody going to shoot or not?"

No sooner were the words out of her mouth than the gun in Jean's hand cracked and jumped. Jean screamed and jumped. More shots blasted as the sounds made the other young women jerk their triggers.

Bo was watching the cactus. No bits of the spiny flesh leaped into the air. He saw a few spurts of dust well beyond the cactus, though.

"What happened?" Rose cried. "Did we hit it?"

"I think we all missed," Cecilia said with a note of disgust in her voice.

"You did," Bo said, "but don't feel too bad about that. Like I told you, those guns aren't very accurate at more than ten feet. Rose, you take a few steps in front of the others. The rest of you, point your guns at the ground again and leave them that way."

"Should we cock them again?" Beth asked.

"Not just yet," Scratch told her. "Leave the hammers down."

Rose moved forward until Bo told her to stop. She was approximately ten feet away from one of the cactus clumps. Bo told her to cock the gun and aim at one of the plants.

"Take your time. When you're ready to shoot, take a breath and hold it. Then squeeze the trigger. Don't jerk it."

A few more seconds went by. Bo watched Rose this time, so he knew when she took that breath and held it. A heartbeat later, the gun cracked.

Bo had switched his gaze to the cactus. He saw pulp and juice fly from the very top of one of the pads.

"I hit it!" Rose exclaimed, sounding like she couldn't believe it. "I hit it! I *did* hit it, didn't I?"

"You sure did," Scratch told her. "See if you can hit it again, just like you did that time."

Rose repeated the process. Her next shot drilled the cactus pad a couple of inches down from the top.

"That's good," Bo said. "Somebody else step up and give it a try."

Rose looked like she would have preferred to keep shooting, but she stepped back to let the others have a turn.

They all hesitated, but after a moment, Beth said, "Oh, all right. I'll see what I can do."

Her first two shots missed, but the third nicked the side of a pad. That seemed to please her immensely.

The others were getting into the spirit of it. Luella said, "I'm next!" and stepped up to aim two-handed at the cactus. When she fired, one of the pads split in two as the bullet struck it. Luella stared at it in disbelief for a second, then squealed and did a little dance of delight.

Scratch wore a wide grin as he said, "That was good shootin'."

"She was just lucky!" Rose protested. "I can do better than that."

"You had several tries, and you *didn't* do better," Luella said.

"Well, let me back up there—"

"Hold on, hold on," Bo said. "Miss Jean and Miss Cecilia haven't taken a turn yet."

Jean looked at the revolver in her hand and said, "I'm not sure I want to. I think getting a gun may have been a mistake—"

"Nonsense," Cecilia said briskly. "Mr. Morton is right about Colonel Colt making men—and women—equal. If we become proficient in the use of firearms, that can only be a good thing."

She strode forward a couple of steps, lifted the revolver, and steadied it with both hands as she squinted over the barrel. Her first shot kicked up dirt right in front of one of the prickly pear clumps. Cecilia took a deep breath, cocked the gun, and aimed again. This shot knocked a chunk from one of the pads into the air.

"See?" she said to Jean as she turned around. "If I can do this, so can you."

"Well . . . maybe."

Unfortunately, Jean couldn't, at least not today. Every one of her shots missed, even though she emptied the revolver, and when she was done, she just shook her head in despair.

"Don't worry about it," Beth said as she patted her on the shoulder. "You'll get the hang of it."

"There are so many more important things for a young woman to know," Jean muttered.

Bo wasn't sure about that, not when the young women in question were heading for a mining boomtown. But they all had prospective husbands waiting for them, he reminded himself. It would be up to those hombres to make sure nothing happened to their new brides.

The only responsibility he and Scratch had was making sure that they got there safely.

"The horses have rested long enough," he said. "Let's climb back in the wagon and get started again. Probably be a good idea if you all reloaded those pistols. You saw how to do it. Just remember, make sure the hammer's resting on an empty chamber. We don't need any accidents along the way."

Chapter 14

For the next two days, the wagon rolled at a steady pace across the hot landscape. These were the upper reaches of the Sonoran Desert. The flat, sandy, arid terrain was broken up by small ranges of hills here and there, but those didn't present any obstacles. They were scattered enough that it was no trouble to go around them.

Bo kept his word and let Rose Winston handle the team much of the time, spelling her only when she got worn out. Beth took a few turns at driving, as well, and having spent time on a farm as a girl, she seemed to know what she was doing.

Whenever one of the young women had the reins, Bo saddled his horse and rode ahead with Scratch. That gave them a chance to talk without being overheard.

"What do you think of them?" Bo asked his old friend.

"The ladies? Why, they're just about the prettiest bunch of fillies—"

"I know they're easy on the eyes," Bo said. "Do you think they can make it in Silverhill?"

Scratch pursed his lips and didn't say anything for a moment. Bo knew he was thinking about the question.

"Some of 'em can," Scratch finally said. "I'd bet a hat full of pesos on that. That Miss Rose, she's a tomboy, and she's capable of handlin' 'most anything life throws at her. Miss Beth ain't far behind her when it comes to that. And Miss Cecilia . . ." Scratch glanced over his shoulder toward the wagon and grinned. "Miss Cecilia's so durn stubborn, she ain't gonna let anything get the best of her if there's anything in the world that she can do about it."

"That's the way I have them sized up, too," Bo agreed. "But what about Miss Luella and Miss Jean?"

"Well . . . I reckon both of 'em have been sort of protected and pampered all their lives because of how pretty they are. They never had to learn how to do much, so they didn't. I'd say that Miss Luella is a mite more capable than Miss Jean is."

Bo nodded and said, "Jean's the one I'm the most worried about. I hope the fella who marries her figures out pretty quick that it's going to be a big job keeping her happy . . . and that he's willing to work at it."

"He'll have to be," Scratch said. "Otherwise he's in for a whole heap o' trouble."

"Have they said anything to you about the men they intend to marry?"

"Nope. Didn't figure it was really any of my business."

"Mine either," Bo said. "I'm curious, though."

Scratch chuckled and said, "You always have been. You like to know what makes folks tick. I'm happy just to take 'em however they appear to be."

"People aren't always what they appear."

"No," Scratch said, "but sooner or later, you find out about that. Their true nature comes out. Snakes got to bite, and scorpions got to sting. It's the way of the world."

Bo nodded, knowing his old friend was right.

That evening around the campfire, Bo indulged his curiosity. He said, "Why don't you ladies tell us about the men you're going to marry?"

"They all have successful mining claims," Cecilia said. "They're substantial men."

Jean added, "We wouldn't have agreed to marry them otherwise."

"We all talked it over," Luella said. "You might say we made the decisions together."

"Of course, we didn't share *everything* that was in the letters we exchanged with our gentlemen," Jean said. "That wouldn't have been proper." She blushed prettily in the firelight.

Cecilia said, "The important thing is that they're all in a position to support a wife and family. None of us would have agreed to their proposals if we didn't believe that."

"You make it sound like we're just marrying them for their money," Rose said with a frown.

"Not at all. But it's important to be practical in life. Going into something as significant as marriage all starry eyed can lead to a great deal of hardship and heartbreak."

"So can having cold water in your veins instead of blood."

Cecilia's lips tightened. Bo could tell she was about to make some angry retort to Rose's blunt comment, so he said quickly, "I was thinking that tomorrow morning we might have some more target practice before we pull out."

"Oh, I'd like that," Rose said. She looked at Luella. "I want another chance to show everybody that I'm a better shot than *some* people around here."

Luella sniffed and said, "It's results that count, not words."

"And we'll see what the results are next time. That's all I'm saying."

To head off any further wrangling, Scratch said, "I reckon it's about time to turn in."

"Why don't you let us stand guard tonight?" Beth suggested. "The two of you probably need a good night's sleep by now."

Bo and Scratch had split the guard duty at night so far. If they were by themselves, they would rely on their horses to warn them if any sort of threatening presence came around, but with the added responsibility of the ladies' safety, they weren't going to take that chance.

Bo said, "That's all right. We're used to it."

"Yeah, we've rode many a night herd in our time," Scratch said. "We get a fair amount of sleep."

"And that's part of what we're getting paid for," Bo added.

"But it's not fair," Beth said, "and it's not necessary, either. Rose and I are perfectly capable of standing guard. We can split up the duty, just like the two of you do."

"What about the rest of us?" Cecilia wanted to know. "We're not capable of keeping our eyes and ears open?"

"I was just thinking that if there *were* any trouble, Rose and I are the best shots—"

"No, I am," Luella said.

"I keep telling you, that was just luck," Rose objected.

"You don't know that."

"Yes I do."

Bo said, "Ladies, there's no point in arguing about it. Scratch and I will keep on standing guard like we have been. But if things get to where we feel like we need help, we'll let you know. You have my word on that."

"All right," Beth said grudgingly. "But we really don't mind helping."

"You help a lot just takin' turns drivin' the wagon," Scratch told her.

The rest of that night passed peacefully, and in the morning, after breakfast, Bo assembled the young women alongside the wagon, as he had before. They had their pistols and were ready for more practice, although Jean looked a little like she wished she was doing something else.

Bo had them take turns, as they had before. Luella was eager to go first this time. They didn't have any cactus to shoot at, so Scratch stuck a mesquite branch in the ground and put an empty airtight on it.

"That can's a smaller target," Bo warned Luella as she took aim.

"I can hit it," Luella said. She took a deep breath and squeezed the trigger.

The can didn't move, and there was no sound of the bullet striking it.

Rose said, "Evidently, you can't."

Luella glared back at her over her shoulder and then said, "Let me try again."

"Go ahead," Bo told her.

Luella frowned in intense concentration. She took her time about aiming but finally squeezed the trigger again.

The empty can still didn't move.

"All right, let me do it," Rose said as she strode forward. Luella looked like she wanted to argue, but Bo motioned for her to step back.

Rose lifted her pistol and peered over the barrel. She made a face and said under her breath, "It really is smaller, isn't it?"

"I don't think you can hit it, either," Luella said in a surly tone.

"Just wait," Rose snapped. She drew a bead on the airtight and finally squeezed the trigger. The can jumped and spun so hard that it came off the mesquite branch.

Rose cried out in triumph and said, "I told you I could do it!"

"Luck," Luella said.

"Ha!"

Scratch said, "Point the gun at the ground, and I'll go put the can back on the stick."

He did so. Since Rose had already hit the can once, Bo told her to step back and let someone else have a turn. Beth went next, and although it took her two shots, she hit the can.

Cecilia stepped up to the mark, aimed, and missed with three shots.

"This is ridiculous," she declared. "I'd say that it's an impossible shot—"

"But you saw Beth and me make it," Rose said.

Cecilia looked over at Bo and said, "One more try?"

"Go ahead," he told her.

Cecilia took several deep breaths before she even started aiming. When she finally pressed the trigger, the gun barely jumped in her hand as the shot cracked.

If nothing else, she was learning how to control the recoil, Bo thought.

And this time, the can spun on the branch.

Scratch grinned and said, "It's got a new hole in it. I can see it from here."

Cecilia sighed and looked relieved. She said to Bo, "I'll never be a good shot."

"Only the very best are good starting out," he told her. "Handling a gun is like anything else. You've got to work at it."

That left Jean, and once again she burned through all six rounds in her cylinder without once coming close to the target, as far as Bo could tell. She didn't look as despairing this time, because that was the result she seemed to have been expecting.

With that done, the ladies turned toward the wagon, obviously thinking that it was time for them to get started on their journey again.

But Bo said, "Hold on a minute."

They stopped and looked around at him.

Cecilia asked, "What is it?"

Scratch appeared puzzled, too.

"I want to try something else," Bo said. He walked to his horse, which was already saddled and ready to ride. He reached up, took hold of the Winchester, and pulled it out of its saddle sheath. He worked the rifle's lever and went on, "Let's see how you do with a long gun."

Chapter 15

"I've shot a rifle before," Beth said as she came toward Bo. "It was just an old single-shot rifle my brothers used for hunting squirrels, though."

"This is a Winchester seventy-three, forty-four–forty caliber. Shoots the same round as my pistol, so I only have to have one kind of ammunition. It holds fifteen rounds. The finest rifle ever made so far, in my opinion." Bo held it out to her. "Be careful. It's heavy, especially if you're not used to it."

Beth took the weapon from him. Her hands sagged a little when Bo let go of it.

"You weren't joking. It *is* heavy. And long."

"They make a carbine with a shorter barrel, but Scratch and I have always preferred this version. We've found it to be just a hair more accurate."

"And sometimes a hair can make a difference," Scratch put in.

"Can I shoot it?" Beth asked.

"That's the idea," Bo told her. "You need to aim for something farther out, though." He looked around, then pointed. "See that little rock, sitting on top of a bigger rock, about twenty yards out? Try to hit it."

Cecilia said, "That's too far. No one could ever hit a target like that."

Bo and Scratch glanced at each other. Either of them could knock that little rock off the bigger one with a single swift shot . . . but they'd had decades of practice.

"I'll try," Beth said. "The worst I can do is miss."

She struggled to raise the rifle to her shoulder and hold it steady. The barrel wobbled back and forth wildly.

"Hold on," Bo said. He took a couple of pieces of wadded-up cloth from his pocket and put one in each ear. He had thought the young women might have trouble holding the rifle, so he was prepared.

He walked in front of Beth, being careful not to get in a direct line with the Winchester's muzzle, then bent over a little and braced his hands against his thighs.

"Rest the barrel on my shoulder."

"Won't that hurt you?"

"It'll be fine," Bo said.

"But it'll be loud."

"That's why I put those plugs in my ears. Those twenty-two pistols aren't loud enough to hurt your hearing, but if you do much shooting with the rifles, you'll need to fix something to put in your ears, too."

Jean said, "Now I *really* don't want to do it."

"I do," Rose said. "I can't wait for my turn."

"Well, you'll have to," Beth said as she carefully placed the rifle's barrel on Bo's shoulder. "I'm doing this now."

"It's ready to shoot," Bo said. "When I worked the lever, that threw a round in the chamber and cocked the hammer. So just line up both sets of sights and squeeze the trigger, like you would with the pistol."

The rifle was a lot steadier in Beth's grip with the barrel resting on Bo's shoulder. He waited patiently while she aimed, and then he heard her breathe, "All right." The next instant, the whipcrack of the shot sounded right over his shoulder, painfully loud despite the wadded-up cloth in his ears.

"Darn it!" Beth said. "The rock's still there. I didn't hit it."

Scratch said, "You were only a few inches off, though, judgin' by where the bullet hit on the other side of the rocks."

"How do you know where it hit?"

"I saw it kick up dust."

"So did I," Cecilia said. "I think Mr. Morton is right."

Beth moved the barrel from Bo's shoulder, giving him the chance to straighten up again.

"Work the lever," he told her. "Push it all the way down, and then bring it back up sharply. It'll probably seem a little stiff to you, but you can do it."

With a small grunt of effort, Beth did so. Then Bo leaned over again to provide a rest for the Winchester. She drew a bead and fired, and this time the slug whanged off the side of the bigger rock underneath the smaller one.

"That's better," Bo said. "Try it again."

The lesson continued. It took Beth three more shots, which got closer each time, and finally, the smaller rock leaped in the air and fell out of sight behind the bigger one as a bullet struck it. Beth was excited beyond words.

Rose pushed forward, saying, "All right, you hit it. It's my turn now. Somebody go out there and put that little rock back on the big one."

"I'll do it," Luella volunteered. She walked briskly out to the spot where the rocks were, rounded the bigger one, which came up almost to her waist, and suddenly stopped short as a frightened cry came from her lips.

"What is it?" Bo asked, instantly alert.

"There's a . . . a snake back here!"

Even at that distance, Bo and Scratch heard the faint, unmistakable buzzing that told them Luella had almost stumbled over a rattlesnake.

"Don't move!" Scratch told her urgently. "Is he coiled up?"

"Y-yes," Luella quavered.

"Stay here," Bo snapped at the other young women. From the looks of them, he didn't have to worry about them disobeying that order. They all seemed terrified, and they couldn't even see the snake.

As Bo and Scratch started quickly for the rocks, Bo said, "Stand just as still as you possibly can, Miss Luella. He's ready to strike, or he wouldn't be rattling like that, but he might not if you don't move."

They drew their revolvers as they split up and closed in on the rock from opposite directions. Bo was on the side where Luella was standing. Scratch came up behind the snake.

As Bo rounded the bigger rock, he saw the thick, mottled shape coiled up on itself. The snake's head was raised, its tongue was flickering in and out of its mouth, and the rattles on its tail were vibrating so fast they were just a blur. The varmint was ready to strike, all right, but somehow the clearly terrified Luella had managed to hold still enough not to provoke the rattler.

Quietly, Scratch said, "I don't have a shot, Bo. Too big a chance I'd hit Miss Luella."

"All right," Bo said. "Step on back. Miss Luella, you're doing fine. You just keep on being still—"

It didn't really matter anymore, though, because the snake had run out of patience. The wedge-shaped head flashed forward.

The Colt in Bo's hand boomed. The rattlesnake's head disintegrated in a bloody spray just before it was able to sink its fangs in Luella's leg. Even though she was safe now, the shot made her nerves snap. She screamed and leaped backward so violently, she lost her balance and sat down hard.

"Luella!" Cecilia cried as she ran toward the rocks, her fear momentarily forgotten. The other three young women trailed behind her.

"She's all right," Scratch called as he holstered his Remingtons and hurried to intercept the young women. "It's all over."

The now headless rattlesnake flopped around grotesquely. Bo caught it by the tail, pulled out his knife, and cut off the rattles. Then he dropped it back on the ground, turned to Luella, and reached down to give her a hand getting to her feet.

"I . . . I was never so scared in all my life," she said as she stared wide-eyed at the still thrashing snake.

"You had good reason to be scared," Bo told her. He held up the rattles. "They add one for each year they're alive. That old boy has been around for ten years. You'd have been mighty sick if he'd bitten you . . . assuming you pulled through."

"One thing it'd be good for you to remember," Scratch said as the others gathered around them, "and this goes for all you ladies . . . is if you see a cluster of rocks, or even just one good-sized one, in this part of the country, there's a good chance there's a rattler somewhere around it." He pointed down at Rose's feet. "You want to watch out for those varmints, too."

Rose looked down, saw the scorpion, which was a good two inches long, scuttling over the toe of her right shoe, and shrieked. She jumped, and the scorpion went flying off.

Scratch was ready when it landed. He brought his boot heel down on it and twisted back and forth, crunching the venomous little devil into oblivion.

"This is insane," Cecilia said. "Just how many ways are there to die out here in the West, anyway?"

"Too many to count," Bo said.

After what easily could have been a fatal encounter between Luella and the rattlesnake, nobody felt like doing any more practicing with the Winchester, not even Rose. Bo and Scratch hitched up the team, and soon they were rolling west again.

It was a subdued bunch of mail-order brides who rode toward Silverhill, Bo thought. Maybe they had begun to realize that surviving on the frontier was a serious business most of the time.

Over the past couple of days, a dozen riders had passed them, also heading west. Some had just ridden on by, casting curious glances at the five lovely young women in the wagon but not stopping to chat. Others had ridden alongside to pass the time of day briefly before urging their mounts on.

Several of the men had admitted that they were headed to Silverhill to check out the boom there and maybe stake a claim that would make them a fortune. Bo had a hunch that most, if not all, of the others were bound for the same destination. They were also bound for disappointment, more than likely, but that had never stopped any man who dreamed of finding a fabulous bonanza of his own.

They hadn't met anyone coming from the opposite direction, though, which was something of a surprise. That changed in the middle of the afternoon, when Scratch nodded toward something ahead of them and said, "Riders comin'."

Bo had spotted the figures on horseback just a second after his old friend did. The day was hot enough that faint distorted heat waves rose from the ground in the distance, so at first the men were nothing more than small dark blurs. As the space between them and the wagon closed, however, Bo was able to make out more details.

There were three riders, two wearing tall, steeple-crowned sombreros.

Scratch said quietly, "If we were south of the border, I'd say those hombres look like *Rurales*."

"I don't reckon we've strayed that far off course," Bo said.

"Shoot, we couldn't get that lost if we were ridin' in our sleep." Scratch paused. "Fella in the middle is a white man, judgin' by his hat."

"Yeah, I agree. A couple of vaqueros and one puncher who ride for a spread north of here?"

The terrain in this area was too arid for raising cattle—not enough graze—although some bullheaded men had attempted that in the past and probably would again. Off to the right, though, lay a low gray line that marked a long range of hills where conditions were better and a few ranches had been established.

"Could be," Scratch said. "They're headed the wrong direction to be fellas who figure on makin' a fortune minin' for silver."

"Yeah, there's nothing behind us but a bunch of empty land, all the way to El Paso."

"Well, there's one way to find out who they are and where they're headed."

"Yeah," Bo said. He reached for the rifle in the saddle scabbard, loosened it a little, and rode on.

Chapter 16

Bo's wariness grew stronger the closer he and Scratch came to the three riders. He said, "Drop back beside the wagon, and tell Rose that when I rein in to talk to those gents, she should stop the team, too."

"Got it," Scratch said. "You think they could be lookin' for trouble?"

"Don't know, but I don't want those girls crowding us from behind if they are."

Scratch turned his horse and rode back to join the young women. Bo continued moving steadily forward. He held the reins in his left hand. His right rested on his thigh, not far from the butt of the holstered Colt.

The two Mexicans were both bearded. One was burly and broad shouldered; the other smaller and wiry. Bo didn't like the looks of either of them. He had run into too many hard cases who resembled them.

Their gringo companion was a different story, though. Dressed in a fringed buckskin shirt and trousers, he was young, maybe not even out of his teens. He had tried to grow a beard, but all he had managed to raise was a little peach fuzz, which was so light in color, it was almost invisible. He had a friendly, open face and a shock of fair, curly hair under a pushed-back hat.

"Howdy," he called to Bo as he raised a hand in greeting when twenty feet separated them. "Mighty warm this afternoon, ain't it?"

"That it is," Bo said as he reined in. He wanted to look back and make sure Rose was bringing the wagon to a halt, but he figured it might not be wise to take his eyes off this mismatched trio. Anyway, he had complete confidence that Scratch would see to it.

The three men—or two men and a boy, you might as well say—came to a stop, as well. The blond youngster leaned a little to the right in his saddle, as if he was trying to look around Bo.

"What you got back there in the wagon, mister?" he asked.

"Just some friends of mine."

"The one on the seat, handlin' the team, looks like a gal," the youngster said. He grinned. "A sort of pretty gal, at that."

Bo didn't respond to the comment. Instead, he asked, "Where are you fellas headed?"

"Us? Why, we're headed to El Paso, I reckon. We're goin' the right direction, ain't we?"

"El Paso's back behind us a ways, all right," Bo said with a nod.

"Turnabout's fair play, or so they say. Where might you folks be goin'?"

"We're bound for Silverhill."

The blond boy laughed and said, "We just came from there, and you couldn't pay us to go back. Ain't that right, boys?"

The two Mexicans didn't say anything, just sat easily in their saddles and watched Bo with an intentness that made him think of a couple of hawks waiting for a mouse to venture out too far into the open.

"What's wrong with Silverhill? The mines playing out?"

That might actually be information worth knowing. If Silverhill was bound to become a ghost town in the next few months, the ladies might not want to stay there, after all.

The youngster laughed again and shook his head, though. "No, sir, as far as I could tell, those mines are still producin' a heap of silver. But all the good claims are taken already, and the only way poor but honest lads like me and Ernesto and Juan can make any dinero is to go down in those tunnels with a pick and shovel and dig for it to make some other fella rich. That didn't suit us."

"Don't care for hard work, eh?"

With an even bigger grin, the boy said, "Me and hard work ain't never been on what you'd call friendly terms!"

All three of the strangers, even the young one, wore guns that looked like they had been well used. Bo was waiting for them to slap leather and try to rob him and his companions. He was ready if they made such a move.

Going by instinct, he had already picked out the smaller Mexican as the fastest of the three, so he decided it would be best to kill him first. One of the others would probably get some lead in him, but he was confident he could put a second man on the ground before he went down himself.

And then Scratch would blow the remaining bandit out of the saddle with his Winchester. The young ladies would be safe.

Instead of things playing out that way, the big Mexican said in perfect English, "Let them be, Howie. We've got no business with these folks, and I want to get on to El Paso."

The youngster looked confused. He said, "Well, hell, Ernesto, I was just passin' the time of day with this fella."

"It's too hot for that," Ernesto growled. "Come on."

"Whatever you say, amigo." The boy Howie ticked a finger

against the brim of his hat and told Bo, "Good luck to you and your pards in Silverhill, mister."

The three of them pulled their horses to the side and rode around Bo. He moved his hand to the rifle, just in case they charged the wagon, although that seemed unlikely now that he was behind them.

The three riders swung to the south, giving the wagon a wide berth as they rode past it. Howie waved to the ladies and called out something, but Bo couldn't make out the words. Then the youngster put the spurs to his horse and dashed ahead. He was showing off for the pretty girls, Bo realized. He hoped Howie wouldn't run the horse too hard or too long in this heat. That wouldn't be good for the animal.

The men and the boy moved on into the distance. Bo kept an eye on them as he rode toward the wagon. The three of them didn't turn back. Their figures dwindled as they put more ground between themselves and the wagon.

"What in blazes was that all about?" Scratch asked as Bo came up to the vehicle.

"I'm not sure," Bo said. "When I first started talking to them, I thought for sure they were road agents."

Rose said, "You mean robbers?"

"That's right. The two Mexicans definitely had the owlhoot look about them. Not the kid, though. He didn't fit with them at all."

"He waved at us," Rose said. "He called out and said for us to enjoy our trip. He seemed rather nice."

"Maybe," Scratch said, "but you can tell a lot about a fella by the company he keeps."

From behind the seat, Cecilia said, "You're not being fair. Just because those men were Mexicans, that doesn't mean they were criminals."

"That's right," Bo said. "We've known plenty of honest,

hardworking Mexicans who are some of the finest people on the face of the earth. But we've run into plenty of bandits in our time, too, and those two boys have done some riding on the wrong side of the law, or my name's not Bo Creel."

Scratch rubbed his jaw and said, "Bo, you recollect what I told you back in El Paso about Jaime Mendoza?"

"Who's Jaime Mendoza?" Rose asked.

Bo didn't answer her question. Instead, he said to Scratch, "I remember, all right. Mendoza's supposed to be a pretty smart fella. That's the reason he's been able to dodge the *Rurales* for so long. You think maybe he spotted the wagon and sent those three to find out what's in it?"

"Like scouts, you mean?" Scratch nodded. "That's what I'm worried about, all right."

Cecilia asked the same question Rose had. "Who is Jaime Mendoza?"

"A bandit," Bo said. "He and his men used to operate on this side of the line in New Mexico and Arizona, but lately, they've been down south of the border. Rumor has it they're starting to venture in this direction again, though."

"Best get the wagon movin' again, Miss Rose," Scratch said. "Don't run the horses, but keep up a good pace."

Rose frowned under the wide-brimmed hat she wore. "You and Bo are kind of scaring me, Scratch," she said.

"No need to get scared," Bo said. "We're just being careful. Those fellas told me they were coming from Silverhill, that they left because they decided they didn't want to be miners and that's the only work they could get there. Maybe they were telling the truth."

He didn't really believe that, but it was possible, he supposed.

Rose slapped the reins against the backs of the horses. They leaned forward into their harness, and the wagon lurched into motion. Rose called out to the team and snapped the reins again. The horses began to move faster.

Bo and Scratch dropped behind the wagon for a moment.

Scratch said quietly, "If they come at us, there ain't no tellin' which direction they'll come from. They could'a circled around and could be anywhere by now."

"I know," Bo said. "Why don't you take the point, and I'll ride drag? We'll need to watch both sides, too."

"Too bad those Jensen boys ol' Cyrus mentioned didn't come along on this trip, too. We could use some flankers right about now."

Bo nodded, knowing his old friend was right. But they didn't have any help. Keeping those young women safe was up to him and Scratch, nobody else.

Scratch rode past the wagon, calling, "Keep 'em movin'!" to Rose as he did so. Bo trailed about twenty feet behind the vehicle. He had his head on a swivel, constantly moving to check all points of the compass.

One good thing about hot, dry country like this: a group of riders couldn't move across it at any great rate of speed without raising some telltale dust. If Jaime Mendoza's gang was after them, they'd know about it before the bandits got there.

Something ahead of them caught Bo's eye. It was a gray butte with a deeply seamed face, a short distance south of the trail. Such formations dotted the landscape, jutting up abruptly. A few others were faintly visible farther to the south.

Bo's attention lingered on the butte only for a second; then he turned his head to check the area north of the trail. Not seeing anything that alarmed him, he hipped around in the saddle to look behind them.

A brown haze that hadn't been there the last time he'd checked, less than thirty seconds earlier, hung in the air. As Bo stiffened and watched, the haze thickened and coalesced into a cloud of dust.

Had to be a dozen riders to kick up that much dust. Probably more. He didn't wait any longer. He heeled his horse ahead sharply and drew even with the wagon. Pale, nervous faces looked out at him from the opening in the back as he rode past.

He waved at Rose as he came up beside the driver's box and called to her, "Head for that butte!"

Chapter 17

Rose looked scared, but she slapped the reins against the horses' backs and called out to them. The horses lunged ahead harder, and the wagon picked up speed.

Bo tried to look in all directions at once. The bandits could be trying to lure them into a trap by seeming to pursue from behind. Fleeing toward the butte could be exactly what Jaime Mendoza wanted them to do.

However, they didn't have much choice. Letting the bandits catch them out in the open would be a disaster, probably a fatal one. At least this way they had a chance of finding a good place to hole up and make a stand.

The same thoughts must have crossed Scratch's mind. As Bo pulled up even with him, he called, "Mendoza could have men waitin' for us over there!"

"I'm going to check it out! Fall back with the wagon, in case the ladies need help!"

Scratch nodded and hauled his horse around. Bo galloped on toward the rough, massive chunk of sandstone that jutted up from the landscape a few hundred yards away.

As he drew closer, he spotted what he had been hoping to see. In times past, erosion had loosened chunks and slabs of sandstone on the butte's walls, and they had plummeted to the ground to litter the area around the formation's base.

If no bandits—human snakes—were lurking in those rocks, that would be a good place for Bo, Scratch, and the young women to seek shelter.

His eyes searched among the boulders as he approached. He didn't see anyone hiding there. He drew his Colt and rode into a large cluster of boulders, halfway expecting someone to open fire on him at any second.

Nothing of the sort happened. As far as Bo could tell, the area around the butte was deserted. Mendoza might well have set a trap there if he'd had time, once he found out who was traveling in the wagon, but the butte had been too close. The bandits' intended prey had reached it first.

Bo holstered his gun, rode back out into the open, and waved his hat over his head. Scratch would see that signal and hustle the wagon on toward the butte.

Bo dismounted, led his horse to what he hoped would be a safe spot deep in the rocks, and weighted down the reins with a chunk of sandstone the size of a man's head. He pulled the Winchester from its sheath and hurried back to a rock slab with a slanting top that commanded a view of the wagon's approach. Bo stretched out on the rock and snugged the rifle butt against his shoulder.

The bandits, riding like devils out of hell, had closed the gap between themselves and the wagon. They were only a couple of hundred yards behind it now.

But the wagon was within a hundred yards of the butte, and Bo didn't think the bandits could catch it before it reached safety.

Especially not if he slowed the varmints down some.

Bo raised the Winchester's barrel a little as he estimated distance and elevation. When he thought he had his figuring about right, he opened fire. Half a dozen shots blasted out in a steady roll of gun thunder, with Bo cranking the Winchester's lever between each round.

He could see the line of men on horseback at the bottom of the dust cloud now. Suddenly, that line bunched up in the middle, breaking up the gang's steady advance. Bo thought it likely at least one horse had gone down. That was what he was hoping for when he started shooting. He wanted to break the back of the attack, or at least blunt it.

He could hear the wagon rattling now, along with the pounding hoofbeats from the team. The ground was fairly level, but it had enough bumps to make the wagon bounce a little now and then. Bo hoped the ladies were hanging on in there and weren't getting jolted around too badly.

Better a few jolts, though, than falling into the hands of ruthless bandits.

The pursuers had slowed down, but not all of them had stopped. Bo levered the Winchester and sprayed more lead in their direction.

The wagon had almost reached the rocks. Rose leaned far back on the seat as she hauled on the reins to slow the horses.

There wasn't room behind the rocks for the wagon itself, so following Scratch's shouted directions, Rose turned the vehicle and brought it to a skidding, dust-spraying stop next to one of the boulders. As she leaped to the ground from the driver's box, the other four young women scrambled out the back, over the tailgate, and ran for cover.

Bo grimaced as he heard bullets ricocheting off the rocks. Some of the bandits had opened fire, too, although shooting from horseback that way, they weren't likely to hit anything unless it was by blind luck.

Unfortunately, blind luck could be just as deadly as the best aim in the world.

Bo slid down from the slab and ran to take Scratch's horse from him. While Bo led the mount closer to the butte, Scratch started unhitching the team.

"Beth!" Bo called, not worrying right now about being properly respectful and calling her Miss Beth. When she hurried over to him, he handed her the rifle and told her, "There are still five rounds in here. Get behind one of those rocks, brace the rifle on it, and fire toward those men out there while I help Scratch with the horses."

"But I might hit one of them!" she protested.

"That's what they're trying to do to us. They'll do worse if they get their hands on you."

Rose urged, "Give me Scratch's rifle! I can fight, too."

That wasn't a bad idea. Bo pulled his friend's Winchester from the saddle boot and passed it to Rose.

"Ought to have a full magazine," he said, "but try to make your shots count."

She nodded, a grim expression on her face, and then hurried over to the rock slab where Bo had been stretched out earlier. She climbed onto it and thrust the rifle out just like he had.

Bo put Scratch's horse next to his. A stray slug might penetrate back here and strike one of the animals, but this was the best he could do for them. He heard another spat and whine as a slug angled off a nearby rock.

Rose and Beth opened fire with the Winchesters.

Bo ran to help Scratch unhitch the team and lead the horses into the rocks. If the bandits were to kill several of the animals, they would be stuck here, with no choice but to sit and wait for whatever fate Jaime Mendoza's gang had in store for them.

It wouldn't be good for any of them, Bo knew.

They got the horses into the rocks without being hit. Scratch glanced at Cecilia, Luella, and Jean, who were sitting on the ground, huddled against a boulder. Quietly enough that they wouldn't hear him over the shooting, he said, "They can just sit out there and lay siege to us. There's too many of 'em for us to fight our way out."

"I know," Bo said, nodding. "And before nightfall, they'll ring this butte so we can't slip away in the dark, either."

"We got enough food, water, and ammunition to hold out for a while. But it's gonna run out sooner or later."

"I know, but we have one thing in our favor. We're not far from the main trail to Silverhill, which means somebody's going to come along sooner or later and hear the shooting."

"You reckon they'll help us?" Scratch asked.

"What would *we* do if we were riding down the trail and saw somebody pinned down by a bunch of bandits?"

Scratch smiled and said, "We'd be right in the big middle of the ruckus 'fore very much time went by. But ever'body ain't trouble-hungry fools like us."

"We'd better hope somebody is," Bo said.

Beth slid down from the rock where she had been shooting at the bandits and handed the rifle back to Bo.

"It's empty," she said. "I don't know if I hit any of them or not."

"I did," Rose said as she relinquished Scratch's rifle back to him. "I know I saw at least a couple of them go down."

Jean practically gasped as she said, "Rose, you shouldn't talk like that."

"I don't see why not. They're shooting at us, so I think I'm perfectly justified in calling them bastards. And in hoping that I . . . What do they call it in the dime novels? Hoping that I ventilated a couple of them?"

"That'll do," Scratch said. "I hope you did, too."

Another bullet whined through the rocks. Bo said to Rose and Beth, "You ladies sit down with your friends. Stay where you've got rocks on both sides of you. It's more likely that a ricochet won't hit you there."

Cecilia asked, "What are we going to do, Mr. Creel? We can't fight off all those men."

"No, we can't," Bo admitted. "We can't outrun them in that wagon, either."

Rose said, "Maybe we could leave the wagon and get away on horseback."

Bo shook his head. "Those draft horses wouldn't be any match for the mounts the bandits have," he said. "A lot of times their lives depend on a fast getaway, so they make sure they have the fastest horses they can find. No, the only thing we can do now is hold them off and wait for somebody to help us."

"Who's going to do that?" Cecilia asked.

"Somebody's bound to pass by on the trail."

"And if they have any sense, they'll keep right on going! No one's going to want to get mixed up in a battle with bandits."

Rose said, "I'd help if I was a man and saw something like that going on."

"So would I," Beth added.

Scratch had turned to keep an eye on the bandits, who appeared to have come to a halt for the time being about two hundred yards away. They were within range of the Winchesters, but not close enough for really accurate shooting. Both Bo and Scratch knew it would be smart to save their ammunition and make it last as long as possible, now that they were forted up in the rocks.

Something caught Scratch's eye, though, and he said, "Bo, you'd better take a look at this."

"What's going on?" Bo asked as he joined his friend.

"They've stopped shootin', and now a few of 'em are headed this way on horseback."

"A feint, maybe, to distract us while some of the others try to flank us?"

"I don't think so," Scratch said. "Unless my eyes are playin' tricks on me—and there's always a chance of that at our age—one of the varmints has a white flag tied on the barrel of his rifle. I think they're askin' for a parley."

Chapter 18

Bo didn't believe for a second that Scratch's eyes were playing tricks on him. Despite his age, Scratch still had eyes like a hawk. Bo's vision was almost that good.

Scratch was right. Bo saw the piece of white cloth flapping in the breeze as the riders came closer. The flag of truce was tied to the barrel of a Winchester, as Scratch had said, and the man holding it rested the rifle butt against his thigh as he rode, so the barrel stuck straight up into the air.

Bo and Scratch knelt behind adjacent rocks. Scratch said, "You reckon that's Mendoza his own self?"

"Might be," Bo said. "Or it might be his *segundo*."

"They get a little closer, we could blast 'em right outta their saddles."

"That's a flag of truce," Bo said.

"I know, I know. You think they'd honor somethin' like that if *we* rode up to *them*, wavin' it?"

"I'm not going to shoot a man down in cold blood, even a bandit."

"All right," Scratch said. "I was just makin' an observation."

And the suggestion was very tempting, Bo thought. If he was

certain that one of the men on horseback approaching them was Jaime Mendoza, he might give it some consideration.

Shooting some minor bandit hanger-on wasn't going to make any difference in their situation, though. And to be honest, killing Mendoza himself probably wouldn't do them any good in the short run. Some other cutthroat would just assume command of the gang.

"Hold on a minute," Scratch breathed. "What's that there on my left?"

"You mean the man riding on that end?"

"Yeah. He sure don't look like the other two."

As the riders slowly came closer, Bo saw that Scratch was right. The man holding the flag of truce was in the middle. He wore a high-crowned sombrero, and so did the man to his left.

The man to his right, though, sported a flat-crowned straw boater, which made him look like a Yankee. So did the tweed suit he wore and the round, rimless spectacles that perched on his nose and were attached to a ribbon tied to the button on his coat pocket. A brush of a brown mustache was underneath his nose. His face was pale, even at a distance. He didn't look like any Mexican bandido Bo had ever seen.

Bo thought for a moment and then said, "Remember when we were talking about Mendoza in El Paso?"

"Yeah. What about it?"

"One of the big newspapers back East sent a reporter down here to find Mendoza and ride with his gang."

"Son of a gun, you're right," Scratch said. "I thought it was a damn fool idea. Figured Mendoza probably killed the poor varmint as soon as he showed up."

Bo said, "I've got a hunch we're looking at that reporter fella right now."

"Yeah, he looks odd enough to be some newspaper scribbler," Scratch admitted. "I guess Mendoza didn't shoot him, after all."

The three riders had closed to within fifty feet of the rocks.

Bo called out to them, "That's far enough!"

He had thumbed fifteen fresh rounds through the Winchester's loading gate, so now he worked the lever to load one in the chamber. The distinctive clacking noise was loud enough for the men on horseback to hear it.

"Come any closer and you're liable to get your hair parted," Bo went on. "What do you want?"

"I think you know what we want, señor," one of the men responded in English. "That wagon of yours . . . and everything in it."

"I think you should shoot him," Cecilia said coldly.

Bo lifted a hand and motioned to her to stay quiet for the moment. He called back to the man with the white flag, "And I think *you* know that's not going to happen, mister."

"Oh, but it will, amigo. Sooner or later, one way or another."

The man was a Mexican, but unlike the two they had encountered earlier, he was clean shaven. His face was smooth and unlined, but Bo had a feeling he wasn't young. Well preserved was more like it. He wore a black sombrero and a black charro jacket over tight black trousers. An ivory-handled revolver rode in a black holster at his waist.

Bo had a hunch he was looking at the infamous Jaime Mendoza. Mendoza had a reputation for arrogance. He would want to handle this parley himself.

The third man was burly Ernesto, one of the scouts they'd met earlier. If Bo needed any further confirmation that those three had been part of the gang, Ernesto's presence was it.

The gringo in the funny clothes spoke up. "Sir, if I might prevail upon you for a private word?" he called.

"Who in blazes are you?" Scratch asked.

"Philip Armbruster, sir. One *l* in Philip. I'm a journalist for the *New York World*."

So that hunch was right, too. Bo said, "Mr. Armbruster, you've fallen in with bad company."

Armbruster glanced over at his companions and said, "A journalist's duty calls him to associate with every sort of person in the world, honestly and objectively, making no sorts of judgment, moral, legal, ethical, or otherwise, in advance, so that we may report only the plain, unvarnished truth."

Ernesto chuckled and said, "He does go on, doesn't he?"

"What is it you want to say, Armbruster?" Bo asked.

"If I come forward, you'll extend the protection of the flag of truce to me?"

"You don't look like the sort who'd try a double-cross," Bo said. "Come ahead."

Armbruster edged his mount forward, while Mendoza and Ernesto backed their horses away to give the reporter the privacy he had asked for. Armbruster rode all the way up to the edge of the rocks before Bo told him to stop. As far as Bo could see, Armbruster wasn't carrying a gun.

"All right, mister, say what you've got to say," Bo snapped.

"And don't try anything funny," Scratch added. "As best I recollect, I never shot a journalist before, but they say there's a first time for everything."

Armbruster swallowed and said, "I assure you, gentlemen, I intend no treachery." He started to dismount.

"Just stay in your saddle," Bo told him.

Armbruster settled back down on the leather and nodded. "Very well. What I came to tell you is that it might be wise for you to cooperate with Señor Mendoza. I believe if you do, he will spare your lives."

"What in the bloody hell makes you think that?" Scratch asked, obviously astounded at Armbruster's claim.

"Señor Mendoza would like to be General Mendoza and eventually President Mendoza."

Scratch groaned and said, "Not another bandit who's a would-be revolutionary."

"Well . . ." Armbruster glanced nervously over his shoulder

and then said in a voice that wouldn't carry to Mendoza and Ernesto, "Personally, I believe it's a rather far-fetched ambition, but nevertheless, he's sincere, and he's intelligent enough to know that it will further his cause to have support on the American side of the border. That's why he wrote to the editor of my paper and suggested that the *World* send someone down here to chronicle his activities. Since my arrival, he and his men have curbed their usual activities—"

"Robbing, raping, and killing," Bo said.

"Exactly. Well, they've still been robbing—raising funds for his political activities, Señor Mendoza calls it—but he's been trying to alleviate some of his bloodthirsty reputation. That's why I believe you and your companions will be safe if you co-operate."

Bo said, "You *do* know who we have with us, don't you?"

Armbruster's face took on a pink flush under the boater's brim.

"Several very attractive young women, according to the re-port delivered to Señor Mendoza by Ernesto, Juan, and Howie," he said. "Their youth, and the fact that you're heading for Silver-hill, led us to believe that they're, ah, working ladies—"

That was as far as he got before Cecilia said, "Oh!" She pushed up onto her knees and was about to get to her feet as she went on, "We are not—"

"Shut up!" Bo shouted at her, and the sheer shock of him speaking to her that way made her stare at him and fall silent. He motioned curtly for her to sit down again. Slowly, she did so.

Bo's brain worked rapidly. Cecilia had nearly complicated things and quite possibly made them worse. It was bad enough that Mendoza and the rest of the bandits believed the five young women to be soiled doves. If they found out that Cecilia and the others were mail-order brides and presumably inno-cent . . .

No matter how much Mendoza wanted to convince an

American newspaper reporter of the rightness of his cause, that might be too much temptation for his men to resist. The bandits would go on a spree of lust that would end very badly for their victims.

"Look, Armbruster, we're not carrying anything valuable," Bo went on. "Just supplies for the trip, that's all. No gold or money, and if Mendoza thinks he can get some sort of big ransom for these girls, he's wrong. They're not worth anything to anybody but my partner and me."

Bo hated playing the part of a whoremonger, but he had to convince Mendoza that losing a good number of his men just wouldn't be worth it.

"I hate to say it, sir," Armbruster replied, "but attractive young women are always, ah, currency of a sort below the border."

"Not these," Bo said, his voice hard and flat. "I'll put bullets in their brains myself before I let Mendoza have them."

Several of the ladies gasped in horror at that grim declaration. Cecilia seemed to be catching on, though. She looked like she might understand what he was trying to do.

She proved that by saying loud enough for Armbruster to hear, "You won't have to, Bo. We'll kill ourselves rather than let those beasts have us."

She motioned for the others to stay silent and not protest.

"I reckon that sums it up, Armbruster," Bo said. "We can't really stop Mendoza from getting in here among these rocks if he wants to bad enough, but if he tries, we'll kill six or eight or more of his men—and maybe him, too—and then he'll be left with nothing. If he wants to throw away those lives, that's up to him."

This stratagem had a slim chance of working, Bo thought . . . a very slim chance. But that was better than none at all.

Armbruster sighed and said, "I'll discuss the matter with Señor Mendoza, but I confess, I'm not optimistic about the outcome of that conversation. His men have gone quite a while without any sort of . . . diversion. They're going to be rather insistent about availing themselves of this opportunity."

"There's not going to be any opportunity," Bo said. "Try to get that through his head."

Armbruster nodded and turned his horse. He rode back to where Mendoza and Ernesto waited. Bo watched as they talked. Ernesto got mad and waved an arm in the air. Mendoza spoke sharply to him. Then Mendoza sent his horse prancing forward a few steps toward the rocks.

"You are making a bad mistake here by spitting in the face of my generosity, amigo," Mendoza called. "Once I return to my men and give them the order—"

Bo lifted the Winchester to his shoulder, peered over the sights at the bandit leader, and said, "What makes you think you're gonna be going anywhere and giving any orders?"

Chapter 19

Mendoza stiffened in the saddle.

"This is a flag of truce!" he said angrily. "By allowing me to ride up here unmolested, you have entered into a bargain with me, señor!"

Without taking his eyes off Mendoza, Bo turned his head just long enough to spit to the side. Then he peered over the Winchester's barrel.

"I don't reckon I'm obliged to keep any bargains made with a bandit," he said.

"You have no honor!"

"What I have is a forty-four–forty slug with your name on it, mister."

Mendoza stared at Bo for a couple of heartbeats longer. Then suddenly he whirled his horse, bent low in the saddle, and shouted, "Kill them!"

Bo fired and saw the sombrero leap from Mendoza's head as the bullet drilled the big hat. Still leaning forward, Mendoza galloped away from the butte. Armbruster trailed him, using one hand to hold the straw boater on his head as he rode frantically after the bandit leader.

Ernesto had yanked out a pistol and started blasting away at the rocks. Scratch's rifle cracked twice. Ernesto rocked back in the saddle, dropped his gun, and clapped his hand to his chest, where blood started to well out of the wounds and between his fingers. He managed to stay mounted and got his horse turned around so he could flee.

Bo put a rifle round between the big bandit's shoulder blades. Ernesto flung both arms in the air and toppled off his horse. The animal raced on with an empty saddle now.

"That was a pretty good idea you had," Scratch called over to Bo, "tryin' to make them think we'd never let 'em have those gals alive."

"Let's hope it doesn't come to that," Bo muttered under his breath.

"What'd you say?"

"Never mind. Here they come!"

The rest of the bandits surged forward, guns blazing. The Texans returned the fire as swiftly as they could, working the Winchesters' levers so fast, the shots began to sound like one continuous roar. Powder smoke hazed the air above the rocks. Ricocheting bullets buzzed like a swarm of angry bees.

Several men fell from their saddles. A couple of horses went down and caused chaos as the men behind them tried to leap their mounts over the fallen animals. Once again the solid line of attack broke up as men and horses began to mill around.

Then they were falling back, trying to retreat out of range. Bo and Scratch hurried them along with a few last, well-placed shots.

"They didn't keep it up as long as I expected," Scratch said as he lowered his rifle and began to reload.

"We hurt them too much," Bo said. "It'd be the smart thing for Mendoza to do if he lit a shuck."

Scratch shook his head and said, "He ain't gonna do that. His pride's wounded too bad."

"I know," Bo said. "And I reckon I'm to blame for that. I was just taking the only chance I thought we had."

From the little nest in the rocks where the young women were huddled, Cecilia said, "Are they going to attack again?"

"More than likely," Scratch told her.

"You should let us fight, too," Rose said. "We have guns, remember?"

Bo said, "And you remember we told you those little pistols aren't good for much of anything more than ten feet away?" He paused. "Unfortunately, it may come down to that before this is over. You all have the hammers resting on empty chambers?"

"Just like you taught us," Beth replied.

"Well, maybe you'd better go ahead and slip another bullet in there. Just in case."

The ladies looked at each other and then followed that grim suggestion.

Time dragged, and the heat trapped among the rocks at the butte's base didn't help matters any. Bo knew the young women were scared and miserable, but there wasn't anything he could do to help them right now.

"What are we going to do about food and water?" Cecilia asked. "All our supplies are in the wagon."

"The wagon's close enough that we can get to it if we need to," Bo said. "The way it's turned, it'll provide cover, too. Once it starts to get dark, and they can't see what we're doing, Scratch or I will get some food and water. I know you're thirsty, but you'll have to put up with it for a couple more hours."

"We'll be all right," Rose said. Bo could tell she was trying to sound more confident than she really felt. "You don't have to worry about us."

Scratch said, "That's what ol' Cyrus is payin' us to do. It's our job to get you safely to where you're goin'."

"Did you know we'd run into this much trouble along the way?" Cecilia asked.

"There was always a chance of it," Bo said. "Maybe someday the frontier will be cleared of hostiles and outlaws, but that's still a long way off."

"That's just what we need now," Rose said. "For some Apaches to come along."

"Hush!" Jean said. "Don't wish for such a thing."

"But maybe the Apaches would kill the bandits, or at least chase them off."

"And then we'd be left to deal with savages!"

Bo didn't think they had to worry about Apache renegades from below the border interfering in this standoff. If any Apaches *were* around, likely they would just keep their distance, wait until all the shooting was over, and then maybe jump the survivors, if they felt like it. It was almost impossible to predict what an Indian would do.

The sun lowered behind the butte and, thankfully, gave them some shade. The air was still hot, but at least the harsh sunlight wasn't glaring down on them anymore.

Cecilia said, "Once it gets dark, will they try to sneak up on us?"

"There's a good chance of it," Bo answered honestly.

"So that's why you told us to load our guns fully. You believe we're going to be fighting them at close range."

Luella said, "Should . . . should we save the last bullet for ourselves?"

Bo said, "That's up to you, but I'm still hoping it won't ever come to that—"

Gunfire crackled out on the flats.

Bo tightened his grip on his rifle and raised himself up slightly to peer toward the bandits. He expected to see them charging toward the butte again. Instead, although the shooting continued, no one rode toward them.

Scratch was watching, too, and he frowned as he asked, "What in blazes is goin' on out there? Did they start fightin' among themselves?"

"Could be, I suppose," Bo said. "Maybe some of them decided they don't want Mendoza running things anymore."

The sounds of battle went on for a minute or so, and then dust began to rise. A column formed and moved off to the northwest. Another pillar of dust followed.

Scratch peered into the distance and said, "I can't see any riders out there now, Bo. They must've pulled out."

"Or got chased out. There were two dust clouds."

"Yeah," Scratch said. "Looks like one bunch turned around and is headin' this way now."

"Keep an eye on them," Bo said as he stood up.

"What's happening?" Cecilia asked.

"That's what I intend to find out."

Bo went quickly to his horse, opened one of the pair of saddlebags, and took a pair of field glasses from it. He returned to the rock he had used for cover during the fight and raised the glasses to his eyes.

After a moment of adjusting the glasses and searching, he located the group of riders coming toward them. He counted ten men, and none of them looked like bandits. They were all gringos, and judging by their range garb, they were cowboys.

All the newcomers were young except for the man who rode in the lead. He was clearly older, with a short gray beard and jug-handle ears. When the group was fairly close, he motioned for the others to stop and urged his horse on so that he approached the butte by himself.

When he finally reined in, he called, "Hello, the rocks! Anybody left alive in there?"

"Alive and ready for trouble!" Bo shouted back. "Who are you?"

The man crossed both hands on his saddle horn and leaned forward. "Name's Rance Plummer," he replied. "Foreman of the SJ Ranch, about thirty miles north of here. Who might you be, and why was Jaime Mendoza tryin' to kill you? Not that that varmint would need much of a reason other than sheer meanness."

"I'm Bo Creel, and my partner's Scratch Morton. Mendoza figured on stealing our wagon, and we didn't much cotton to the idea."

Plummer nodded slowly. "Can't say as I blame you for that, but you must be carrying something mighty special in that wagon for Mendoza to throw his whole bunch against you like that."

Bo dodged the implied question for the time being by saying, "You got a good enough look at Mendoza to recognize him?"

"We heard the shooting and decided to take a look," Plummer replied with a shrug. "I have a good spyglass, and I've been around these parts long enough to remember when Mendoza was raiding before. He raised enough hell, folks ain't likely to forget him. We figured out he had somebody pinned down here, and decided to take a hand in the game."

That was exactly the sort of thing that Bo had hoped would happen.

"I guess Mendoza reckoned he'd already been stung enough today," Plummer went on. "They put up a little fight, then fogged it out of there. We got 'em running good, then turned back. I don't plan on leadin' my boys into an ambush."

"That's the crew from your ranch out there behind you?"

Plummer grinned and said, "Saltiest bunch of cowhands you'll find in the territory. But they're good lads."

"We're mighty lucky you came along when you did," Bo said.

Plummer cocked his head slightly to the side. "Wasn't entirely luck," he said. "Are you headed to Silverhill?"

Bo glanced at Scratch, who shrugged. Neither of them saw any reason not to tell the truth.

"That's right," Bo said.

"So are we. We aim to take in all the big doin's."

Chapter 20

Frowns creased the foreheads of both Bo and Scratch.

"What big doings?" Bo asked.

"You haven't heard? They're about to have themselves a big fandango in Silverhill."

This was the first Bo had heard about such a thing. Cyrus Keegan hadn't mentioned anything about a celebration. Of course, Keegan might not have known about it.

Not only that, but Bo also had a feeling that Rance Plummer wasn't revealing everything he knew about what was going to occur in Silverhill. Bo couldn't say why he had that hunch, but it rumbled around in the back of his brain, anyway.

"If you'll let us come on in without shootin' at us, I can tell you more about it," Plummer continued.

He and the other cowboys appeared to be trustworthy, Bo thought. Those punchers might be rough around the edges, probably were, but most Western men would never harm a decent woman and even watched how they talked around her.

"Come ahead," Bo called to the ranch foreman. He added, "Just you, though, at first."

Plummer chuckled. "Bein' careful, eh, Creel? Well, I suppose that's to be expected. You ain't from around these parts, so you don't really know who we are."

He rode a little closer and then dismounted. Bo and Scratch both covered him as he led his horse into the rocks.

Up close, Rance Plummer was a leathery old cowboy of the sort that Bo and Scratch knew well. They had met dozens, if not hundreds, just like him. Plummer slouched, thumbed his hat back on rumpled gray hair. He was nodding a greeting to them when he glanced to the side and suddenly straightened up.

Bo knew he had seen the five young women sitting on the ground between two boulders.

Plummer snatched his hat off and swallowed hard. "Ladies," he said. "I'm mighty pleased . . . I mean, it's an honor . . . I mean . . ."

Cecilia got to her feet and said, "Thank you for helping us, sir. Those bandits would have overrun us if you hadn't come along."

"Yes'm, I, uh, I reckon they would have. I'm sure glad we could give you folks a hand." He gave Bo a look of utter confusion.

Bo tried to clear that up by saying, "Scratch and I are escorting these young ladies to Silverhill. They're supposed to meet the fellas they're going to marry there."

Plummer's bushy eyebrows rose. "You mean they're the ones who—" He stopped short.

"The ones who what?" Scratch asked.

Plummer didn't answer the question. Instead, he held his hat in front of his chest and said, "It's a plumb pleasure to meet you ladies. I've heard a lot about you."

"You have?" Rose asked as she got up and stood next to Cecilia. The others climbed to their feet, as well, now that the trouble seemed to be over.

"What have you heard about us?" Cecilia asked sharply.

"Just that there were some mail-order brides comin' to Silverhill. Reckon you could say it's big news."

"I don't know why it would be," Rose said. "Surely, we're not the first."

"As a matter of fact, miss, you are," Plummer said. "Word's got around. You got to understand, the frontier's a hard, monotonous place most of the time. Any stranger livens things up, but when it's a handful of young, beautiful gals comin' to town . . . Well, folks take notice of that."

"I suppose," Cecilia said. "It still seems like a lot of unnecessary fuss to me."

Luella said, "Wait a minute. That celebration you mentioned . . . is it for *us?*"

Plummer cleared his throat, looked uncomfortable, and said, "I reckon that's part of it, ma'am."

Luella and Jean looked pleased to hear that news, and Rose and Beth seemed somewhat impressed, as well. Cecilia was just suspicious.

So was Bo. He felt like there was something Plummer wasn't telling them.

That feeling grew stronger when the ranch foreman went on, "Me and the boys are gonna be heroes around here when folks find out it was you ladies we saved from Mendoza's bunch. They'll be slappin' us on the back and buyin' us drinks in Forbes Dyson's saloon."

"Who's that?" Bo asked.

"Dyson? He owns the biggest saloon in Silverhill. He's the one who come up with the idea to—"

Once again Plummer didn't finish what he started to say, strengthening Bo's feeling that something else was going on. If Plummer didn't want to explain himself, though, there wasn't much they could do to force the man to talk, especially considering how Plummer and his companions had saved their bacon.

"It's fairly late in the afternoon," Bo said. "It might be best if we just made camp here tonight. We don't want to keep you men from going on with your plans—"

"No, sir," Plummer interrupted with a vehement shake of his head. "The boys and me ain't goin' nowhere. We won't intrude on your camp here, but we'll pitch our bedrolls close by, in case Mendoza decides to come back. And then, in the mornin', we'll ride with you. It'll take another couple days to get to Silverhill. Plenty of time for more trouble to crop up. Nobody'll bother you, though, if you've got a bunch of salty cowpokes like us ridin' with you."

That suggestion annoyed and relieved Bo at the same time. He and Scratch were responsible for the ladies' safety, and they never left a job unfinished.

On the other hand, accepting the help that Plummer was offering would insure that the young women reached Silverhill without any further mishaps, and in the end, getting them there safe and sound mattered more than anything else.

"I suppose that's all right," Bo said. "We're obliged to you for the help. I guess if you want to bring the rest of your men in—"

"No, sir," Plummer said. "Nope. I'm too old to do more'n admire these ladies for their beauty, like you fellas. But that bunch of young hellions ridin' with me, they'd start pawin' the ground and snortin' smoke out their noses if they spent too much time around the ladies. You know how boys like to show off and scuffle whenever there's a pretty girl around. Five of 'em would create a heap of commotion. No, we'll keep our distance."

That plan didn't bother Bo. In fact, he was grateful Plummer felt that way. Having the cowboys close enough to lend a hand if needed but not close enough to stir up a lot of turmoil was the perfect solution.

"All right, if you're sure," Bo told him.

Plummer nodded gravely.

Cecilia said, "Thank you again, Mr. Plummer."

"No, ma'am, it's us that ought to be thankin' you for all the excitement you're bringin' into our lives." Plummer put his hat on and continued, "I'll go explain to the fellas who you are and what we're gonna do."

"I hope they're not upset with your decision to escort us," Rose said.

"Oh, they ain't gonna be the least bit upset, ma'am. I can promise you that."

Plummer swung up into his saddle and rode out of the rocks, heading back to the group of cowboys waiting fifty yards away. Cecilia frowned after him as she watched him go.

"Is it just me," she said, "or did anyone else get the feeling something's going on that Mr. Plummer didn't tell us about?"

"It's not just you," Bo said.

The burst of raucous laughter that came from the cowboys after Plummer had spoken to them just made Bo's hunch stronger.

A few greasewood bushes grew among the boulders around the butte's base. Scratch was able to gather enough dry, broken branches to build a small fire, so they were able to enjoy hot food and coffee that evening.

Plummer and the cowboys from the SJ Ranch had a campfire, as well. Bo, Scratch, and the ladies could see them moving around by the light of the flames. Luella, Jean, and Rose were particularly interested in watching them.

"We really should have invited them to join us, you know," Luella said. "I mean, after all they did to help us."

"They practically saved our lives," Rose said.

Bo said, "I did tell Plummer he could bring them in if he wanted to. He's the one who decided that might not be a good idea, but I'll admit, I'm a mite relieved he felt that way. Those cowboys seem trustworthy enough, that's true, but it wouldn't hurt to get to know them a little better before we invite them to share our camp."

"Mr. Creel is right," Cecilia said. "This is the frontier. It's always better to be careful."

A little later, while Bo and Scratch were tending to the horses, Scratch said quietly, "We're still gonna stand guard tonight, even though those cowpokes are right close by, aren't we?"

"We are," Bo confirmed. "Like I told the ladies, they seem trustworthy, but I'm sure Plummer told them what he found over here. Or rather, *who* he found. Some of those cowboys might find the temptation to come courting too much."

Somewhat to Bo's surprise, though, nothing of the sort happened overnight, nor was there any sign of Jaime Mendoza and his remaining men returning.

The cowboys kept their distance, even in the morning, when Plummer rode back over to the butte while Bo and Scratch were hitching up the team and the young women were cleaning up after breakfast.

Plummer pinched the brim of his hat respectfully and said, "Mornin', ladies."

"Good morning, Mr. Plummer," Cecilia said.

To Bo and Scratch, the ranch foreman said, "I figured I'd send some of the boys ahead a ways to scout. The rest of us'll ride flank and drag. We want to make darned sure these ladies get to Silverhill all right."

Once again Bo had the feeling that something unsaid was behind Plummer's words. He considered refusing to budge until Plummer had come clean about what was really going on, but the best way to find out was probably just to go ahead and see what happened.

Whatever it was, he and Scratch would be prepared for trouble, because they always were.

This time, they would be heavily outnumbered if the cowboys tried any funny business, though, so Bo knew he wouldn't be relaxing anytime soon, probably not until they got the ladies safely to Silverhill.

Bo nodded to Plummer and said, "We're obliged to you for the help." Then, when the foreman had ridden back to join the other cowboys, he added to Scratch, "I want you to drive the wagon today."

"What's the matter with my driving?" Rose wanted to know. "I thought I'd been doing a fine job handling the team."

"You have been," Bo assured her. "I just want Scratch to be close to you ladies in case of any trouble."

"What trouble could there be?" Luella asked. "We're going to be surrounded by a bunch of handsome young cowboys, aren't we?"

"That's what's got me worried," Bo said.

Chapter 21

A couple of miles along the trail leading west toward Silver-hill, another low butte rose several hundred yards to the north. A ledge curved around it and served as a trail leading to the top. Sparse grass grew in clumps on the butte, and there were several rocky depressions that functioned as natural cisterns, catching the occasional rainfall that collected in shallow pools.

Because of the ledge and the availability of grass and water, from time to time travelers used the top of the butte as a campsite.

This morning, Jaime Mendoza and the men who had survived the battle waited on the butte, keeping an eye on the trail in the distance. Mendoza had ordered them to keep themselves and the horses farther back on the butte, so they wouldn't be as visible to anyone passing by.

After the arrival of the group of wild, fast-shooting gringo cowboys forced them to flee from their attempt to capture the wagon with the beautiful young women in it, most of Mendoza's men had expected they would circle around and head south, closer to the border, in case they needed to dash over it to escape the authorities.

Instead, Mendoza had led them here, and this was where they had been ever since.

Philip Armbruster pulled a handkerchief from his pocket and wiped sweat from his face. Even though the sun had been up for only a few hours, the day was already hot. No shade was available on top of the butte.

Mendoza wasn't budging, though. He was going to wait right here until his quarry had gone past.

Armbruster had heard considerable muttering among the men about everything that had happened. They had all been enthusiastic about taking those five attractive señoritas prisoner and putting them to good use before selling them below the border. It would have been a good deal all around for the group.

No one had expected the two old gringos with the women to put up such a deadly fight, however. Several members of the band had been killed, and they had lost horses, too, which was almost as important. Ernesto Reyes, who had been Mendoza's second-in-command, was dead.

Some of the men believed it would be wiser just to let the women go by and not risk any more losses. After all, they said, there were other women in the world, and these didn't possess anything all the others lacked.

But others in the group felt like they couldn't allow the gringos who had inflicted such damage on them to go unpunished. They still wanted the women, as well. Mendoza had kept all his followers on a tight leash in recent weeks, ever since Armbruster had shown up and sold the bandit leader on the idea of having stories about him and his "glorious cause" published in an American newspaper.

"The stories will probably be picked up by other papers, too," Armbruster had told Mendoza. "People all across the country will read about you."

Armbruster was fairly young, but he had been a journalist long enough to know how to appeal to a person's vanity. Most people would say whatever a skillful reporter wanted them to say and could even be manipulated into *doing* things that would make for a good story.

And, of course, any journalist worth his wages could always just make something up if he needed to. The gullible public would eat up any load of malarkey the newspapers fed to them. That had been proven over and over again.

The increasing heat didn't help matters when it came to the potential split brewing among the group. The men were on edge. But Mendoza didn't seem to care. He stood at the edge of the butte facing the trail, with a pair of field glasses in his hands, waiting for the wagon to come by.

Mendoza's voice had an impatient note in it when he turned his head long enough to call, "Howie! Come over here."

Howie Barton had been tossing a bowie knife so that it pierced the ground then retrieving it and throwing it again. When Mendoza summoned him, he picked up the knife and slipped it back into its sheath. He ambled toward the edge of the butte.

Curious, Armbruster followed the youthful-looking gringo.

"What can I do for you, boss?" Howie asked as he came up to Mendoza.

Looking intently at him, Mendoza said, "You are certain those men with the wagon said they were going to Silverhill?"

This wasn't the first time Mendoza had asked that question.

"That's right. I wouldn't have made a mistake about that. They said they were takin' those gals to Silverhill." Howie grinned. "I figured right then and there that they must be doves the hombres plan on puttin' to work. Why else would anybody haul a wagonload of gals to a boomtown?"

"Perhaps," Mendoza said, nodding slowly. "But why have

they not passed by? That is the only trail through this part of the territory that leads to Silverhill."

"Couldn't say, boss," Howie responded with a shrug of his shoulders. "Maybe they got a late start this mornin', or maybe they're just not in a hurry."

While talking to Howie, Mendoza wasn't paying as close attention to the trail as he had been a few minutes earlier. Armbruster caught sight of something moving in the distance, though, and pointed to the east as he said, "Señor Mendoza, is that them?"

Mendoza turned sharply and peered through the field glasses as the broad brim of his sombrero shaded his eyes. After a moment he said, "That is the wagon, but those damned gringo vaqueros are still with it!"

No one in Mendoza's bunch knew why the American cowboys had happened to come along when they did and ruin everything. All they knew was that they had been forced to flee, or risk being wiped out by staying and fighting.

Mendoza and the other men had hoped that the cowboys would have pressing business elsewhere and would have to leave the wagon to continue the journey to Silverhill alone.

Armbruster had believed all along that this was too much to hope for . . . although, as had happened numerous times since he had joined Mendoza's force, he wasn't exactly sure of what he himself hoped for.

He considered himself an honorable man, and what Mendoza and his cohorts had in mind for the women was hardly honorable. In fact, it was just the opposite.

But Armbruster also valued his own skin, and he knew that if he protested too much, Mendoza or one of the other bandits might lose patience and shoot him. He would be just one more luckless gringo who vanished into the vast, empty stretches of the border country.

So he had kept his mouth shut about the situation so far,

other than telling those two old gringos what Mendoza had told him to say when they approached the butte under the white flag. It would have been nice if Mendoza had just forgotten about the women, but it seemed certain now that that wasn't going to be the case.

Mendoza turned abruptly and thrust the field glasses into Armbruster's hands.

"Look," the bandit chief ordered. "Look at the wagon."

Armbruster lifted the glasses to his eyes and peered through them. He had never been good at such things, but after a minute of the view he saw through the glasses jumping around all over the landscape, he located the wagon and the men riding around it. He focused on the vehicle itself.

One of the older men was on the seat, handling the reins. Next to him sat a young woman with hair dark as midnight under the broad-brimmed hat she wore and a lovely faintly olive-skinned face. She was beautiful enough that Armbruster's heart suddenly gave a funny little thump in his chest.

"You see her?" Mendoza asked. "The woman sitting next to the *viejo* driving the wagon?"

"I see her," Armbruster said.

"That woman is going to be my wife," Jaime Mendoza declared.

Rose didn't like giving up her seat on the driver's box, but she had agreed—grudgingly—to let the other young women take turns riding up there with Scratch. Luella was on the seat at the moment, sitting close enough to the silver-haired Texan that he felt it when she shivered suddenly.

"Something wrong?" he asked.

"You know that old saying about how people feel a cold chill go through them when somebody walks over the ground that will be their grave?"

"Yep, I've heard folks say that many a time."

"So have I, but I never really believed there was anything to it." Luella paused. "Until now. But now I'm not so sure, because I just felt the oddest sensation. I don't know how else to explain it. Almost like . . . something evil was watching me. Something that intends a terrible fate for me."

"Don't you worry about that," Scratch told her, trying to sound reassuring. "Bo and me are gonna see to it that nothin' bad happens to any of you ladies. And now we've got Plummer and those cowboys helpin', too, so I reckon you and the other gals are just as safe as if you were in your folks' parlors back in Four Corners, Iowa."

Scratch hoped she believed that. He wished he felt as absolutely certain of it as he sounded. . . .

Despite Luella's premonition, if one wanted to call it that, which Scratch told Bo about later, nothing happened that day except that the wagon rolled on and put more miles behind it on the way to Silverhill.

Bo hadn't been over this particular trail before. The last time he and Scratch were in this part of New Mexico Territory, the trail hadn't been there, because Silverhill itself hadn't existed.

So he didn't know exactly how close they were to the boomtown or how much longer it would take to get there. He hoped they might arrive the next day, but he supposed they would have to wait and see.

While riding out ahead of the wagon, he experienced a similar feeling to what Luella had reported, like someone was watching them. Bo's eyes scanned the surrounding landscape constantly, all the way out to the horizons, searching for any signs of lurking danger.

But if it was out there, it was staying well hidden.

The cowboys camped a short distance from the wagon that night, as they had the previous night. Rance Plummer came over and shared a cup of coffee with Bo and Scratch.

"Those boys of yours are behavin' themselves," Scratch commented.

"Of course they are," the foreman said, sounding a little offended. "I only hire good hombres, and I trust my judgment in pickin' 'em. Oh, sure, they're cowboys through and through, which means they like to head to town and do some hell-raisin' on payday, but I run off anybody who gets too rowdy . . . and that includes disrespectin' decent women. You don't have to worry about them."

"At least as long as we don't put too much temptation in their path, right?" Bo said.

Plummer chuckled and nodded. "Well, a little discretion sure won't hurt nothin'," he agreed.

Bo sipped his coffee and said, "You know this part of the country better than we do. Do you think we'll reach Silverhill tomorrow?"

Plummer considered the question and nodded. "Ought to pull into town late tomorrow afternoon, if nothin' happens to delay us."

"I'm lookin' forward to it," Scratch said. "It'll be nice to get the ladies there and have the job over with."

"What are you boys gonna do after that?" Plummer asked. "Do you have to take that wagon back to El Paso?"

Bo shook his head. "The man we rented it from told us to turn it over to the office of his freight company in Silverhill. They'll probably load some sort of cargo in it and send it back. But Scratch and I won't have to worry about it."

"There ain't a telegraph line into the settlement yet, is there?" Scratch asked.

"Nope," Plummer said. "It'll come in if and when the railroad runs that spur line down there, I reckon. Got mail service twice a week on the stagecoach, though."

Bo said, "We'll write to Cyrus Keegan in Fort Worth and let

him know the ladies arrived safely. He runs the matrimonial agency that set this trip up."

"Until we hear back from him, though," Scratch said, "we won't know if he has any more work for us." He grinned. "I reckon that gives us a mighty good excuse to hang around Silverhill for that fandango you talked about, Rance."

"It'll be a good one," Plummer said.

Again, Bo was curious what the ranch foreman *wasn't* telling them, but he supposed they would find out soon enough, if they reached Silverhill the next day.

The night passed peacefully, and the wagon, still accompanied by the SJ crew, got an early start the next morning. Scratch handled the team and kept the horses moving at a steady pace as the miles unrolled behind them.

Small mountain ranges began to appear during the day. These peaks were more substantial than the buttes rising to the east but nowhere near as tall as the Sangre de Cristos to the north and the majestic Rockies beyond them. The ranges ran roughly north and south, with wide, flat valleys between them. Bo knew the silver mines that were the reason for Silverhill's existence were located in the mountains, with the town being in a nearby valley.

The trail curved to the southwest, into the bootheel-shaped region that extended down between Mexico and Arizona. The route followed easy passes between the scattered mountain ranges.

When Cecilia was riding on the wagon seat next to Scratch, she commented, "This is beautiful country, in a stark sort of way."

"Yes, ma'am. A hard land, but a mighty good one if you know how to get by in it. And a land where a man can make his fortune if he's tough and smart enough."

"It's nothing like the agricultural region we come from."

Rose, riding inside the wagon, just behind the seat, said, "There's nothing but fields to look at around there. I like this better."

The rougher terrain meant that the wagon couldn't travel quite as fast. Late that afternoon, the two cowboys Plummer had sent ahead to serve as scouts hurried back to join the foreman, who was riding out ahead of the wagon with Bo. They were moving at a pretty good clip, which made Bo stiffen in the saddle.

Out here on the frontier, especially in the hotter regions like this, if anybody got in a hurry, it usually meant trouble.

But not in this case. The young punchers reined in and grinned. One of them said, "Silverhill's just on the other side of that gap up there. Not more'n two miles away."

"I knew we were gettin' close," Plummer said, "but it's been a while since I was in these parts."

Bo was relieved to hear the news. After the run-in with Mendoza's bandits, he had expected more trouble before they reached the boomtown, but now they were practically in spitting distance and nothing else had happened.

Better be careful, he warned himself. He didn't want to jinx things by getting too overconfident.

He half turned in the saddle and waved Scratch and the wagon on; then he and Plummer rode ahead, urging their mounts to a trot, which carried them through the pass. They stopped at the far end, at the top of a fairly gentle slope, where the trail led down into the valley.

At the end of that trail lay Silverhill.

And the settlement was booming, all right.

Chapter 22

The valley was about two miles wide, with Silverhill sitting in the middle, where a small creek bordered by scrubby trees and bushes meandered along. The mountains on the far side were slightly smaller and more rounded than the more rugged range to the east, where Bo, Scratch, and their companions were moving through the pass.

Smoke rose from the smelter located at the base of those western mountains. Even from here, Bo could see the wide, rutted trail formed by the wheels of ore wagons as they made hundreds, maybe even thousands, of trips back and forth from the smelter to the settlement.

The trail they had followed from El Paso turned into Silverhill's broad, dusty main street. Two smaller streets ran parallel with it, one on each side. Half a dozen cross streets intersected the three longer streets. All these were laid out in a neat grid, although the adobe houses around the edges of the settlement were arranged in a more haphazard pattern, as the outlying residents had built wherever struck their fancy.

Businesses lined the main street. Many of these were made of adobe, too, but Bo saw frame buildings, as well, some of them false fronted and even a few with actual second stories. Lumber would be expensive in a mostly treeless region like this, although some timber grew on the mountain slopes. Most of the lumber used in the town's construction would have been hauled in by wagons from forests far to the north.

In a boomtown such as Silverhill, though, a successful business could make a lot of money in a short period of time, so some entrepreneurs likely considered the expense of a nice building to be a worthwhile investment.

As they sat there looking down at the valley, Bo wondered idly which of the buildings was the big saloon owned by Forbes Dyson, the man Rance Plummer had mentioned.

The wagon came up behind Bo and Plummer. Scratch hauled back on the reins and brought the team to a stop. Rose had reclaimed her place on the seat beside him. The other four young women clustered right behind them, looking over their shoulders.

"That's Silverhill?" Rose asked excitedly. "That's where we're going?"

Bo turned his horse toward the wagon and smiled as he said, "That's it, all right. Looks like a pretty nice settlement."

"It's not very big, is it?" Cecilia said.

"Bigger than some," Scratch told her. "Bigger than a lot of settlements out here, actually. And the houses look pretty nice, most of 'em, anyway. I don't reckon you ladies will want for much once you've settled down with your new husbands."

"I see a church steeple," Beth said. "And is that a building with some sort of bell tower attached to it, there on the north side of town?"

"That'll be a Catholic mission," Bo told her. "From the looks of it, it's pretty old. Been there awhile. More than likely, it was founded on the banks of that creek long before the town was here, back in the days when Spain and then Mexico owned this part of the country. The Church scattered missions all over, trying to civilize the Indians who lived here."

Scratch said, "If there's a school, then you got all you need for a settlement to take root. Leastways as long as the silver holds out. If the town grows enough, it might last even if the silver veins peter out."

Bo didn't dispute his old friend's statement, but he doubted if Silverhill would continue to exist for very long if the mines ever closed down. This area just didn't have anything else that appealed to settlers. Not even the Indians had ever been able to make much out of it.

After a short delay while all the men withdrew a good distance and the ladies changed into nicer outfits, as Bo had promised them they could do before entering the town, Bo and Plummer led the way down the slope toward the settlement. Scratch followed with the wagon, while the rest of the cowboys, who'd had to bunch up as they came through the pass, brought up the rear.

Bo thought this would be a good place for an ambush, but when nothing of the sort happened, he told himself that he was just worrying too much, wary of trouble erupting at the last minute, when the journey was almost over.

As they came closer, he saw how busy the town was. The several blocks of the main street that made up the principal business district were clogged with horses, mules, wagons, buckboards, buggies, and even a few fancy carriages with brightly polished trim, which probably belonged to some of the mining magnates.

The boardwalks on both sides of the street were likewise thronged with people. Bo heard a buzzing sound before they ever reached the settlement's outskirts, and realized it was the hum of loud conversation and laughter. Silverhill sounded a little like a beehive and reminded him of one, too, the way everybody swarmed around.

"What's everybody so worked up about?" Rose asked from

the wagon seat. "I never saw quite so much excitement in Four Corners, even on the Fourth of July!"

"The town's always like this, ma'am," Plummer said as he hipped around in the saddle to answer the question. "Leastways it has been every time I've been here. I'd say that folks are maybe worked up a mite more than usual today, because they know that you ladies are supposed to be arrivin' any day now. Fact is, somebody may have spotted us comin' through the pass and started spreadin' the word that you're almost there."

From behind the driver's seat, Cecilia said, "Surely, the arrival of five women shouldn't cause such a stir."

Beth added, "Yeah, it's not like we're two-headed monsters or something like that!"

Plummer chuckled. "No, ma'am, far from it. But you see, young women are in short supply in these parts. Especially ladies as pretty as the five of you, who not only ain't married, but you also ain't . . . well, a different sort than you . . . I mean—"

Tartly, Cecilia said, "We can imagine what sort of young women are usually to be found in mining boomtowns, Mr. Plummer. But there are only five of us. I fail to see how we could actually make a significant difference in the town."

"Except for the men we marry, of course," Luella put in. "They'll be happy."

"Very happy," Jean said.

Plummer nodded and said, "I expect so. Maybe folks think that this'll be the start of somethin', though. That more ladies like you will be comin' out here and makin' the town a better place."

Bo said, "You mean you think Cyrus Keegan will be getting some repeat business?"

"Could be," Plummer said as he lifted a hand and rubbed his beard-stubbled chin. "I reckon it depends on how ever'thing works out over the next few days."

By the time Bo and Plummer reached the eastern end of Main Street, the citizens of Silverhill definitely were aware of who was riding in the wagon right behind them. A crowd of whooping, cheering men surged toward them. Whistles and catcalls filled the air. The grinning bearded faces of miners, freighters, and bullwhackers beamed up at them. Men waved their hats in the air in sheer exuberance. The racket was enough to wake the dead.

Then it grew even louder and more jarring with the abrupt addition of the discordant strains of a brass band launching into a raucous melody. Bo looked along the street and saw the roughly clad musicians gathered on the boardwalk in front of a large building right in the center of town. It was one of the structures with an actual second floor, fronted with a balcony, and nailed to the railing of that balcony was an elaborately painted sign that ran almost the entire block.

DYSON'S SILVER KING PALACE – THEATER AND SALOON – FINEST WHISKEY AND COLDEST BEER IN THE TERRITORY!

Well, that settled the question of which building belonged to Forbes Dyson, Bo thought.

The men in the street clustered around the wagon and pressed in so close, it was difficult for Scratch to guide the team along without anyone getting trampled. At the same time, the men on the side where Rose was sitting reached up toward her. They didn't look like they wanted to pull her down from the wagon, but they definitely wanted to touch her, as if to make sure she was real. Seeing so many grimy hands groping in her direction made Rose's eyes widen with fear.

"Miss Rose, you better get inside the wagon!" Scratch told her as he sawed at the reins and struggled to keep the suddenly skittish team under control.

Rose stood up and swung a leg over the seat to clamber into

the back. That flash of stockinged calf was enough to set off even more howling and whistling and grabbing at the empty air where she had just been.

"Bo!" Scratch called. "Can you clear a path?"

Bo thought a few gunshots blasted into the air might make the crowd scatter, but that might also finish the job of spooking the horses. Not wanting a runaway, Bo left his Colt holstered and pulled his mount back and forth, causing men to jump out of the way if they didn't want to get knocked down and maybe trampled.

Rance Plummer did likewise and added a bellowed order to get out of the way.

"Rattle your hocks, you rannies!" he roared at the men in the street. "Clear out! Clear out, there!"

Meanwhile, the brass band continued its off-key blaring. The musicians seemed to be trying to make up for with enthusiasm whatever they lacked in talent.

Bo saw that something was stretched from the front of the Silver King to a building across the street and tied in place with ropes. Someone pulled another rope, loosening all the fastenings, and a banner emblazoned with red, white, and blue bunting unfurled and hung flapping about fifteen feet above the street. In bright red paint on the banner were the words WELCOME TO SILVERHILL!

From behind the seat, Cecilia raised her voice to be heard over the hubbub and said to Scratch, "My goodness, they certainly go all out to welcome visitors here, don't they?"

"I reckon they don't make such a fuss over ever'body, ma'am," Scratch said over his shoulder. "They've done all this for you ladies!"

Bo had never expected such a commotion to greet their arrival. He wasn't sure where they should go or what they should do.

Plummer must have seen the look on Bo's face, because he

leaned over in his saddle and shouted over the racket, "All this was Forbes Dyson's idea! He sort of runs things around here, so maybe you should talk to him first!"

At least that was a place to start, Bo decided. He nodded and guided his horse carefully through the crowd toward the big, impressive-looking saloon.

If Dyson was the one who had come up with the idea for this celebratory welcome, he ought to be out in front to greet the newcomers. Bo searched the boardwalk on both sides of the brass band and spotted a man in an expensive suit standing there with his thumbs hooked in the pockets of a fancy vest. A long black cheroot was clenched between the man's teeth and stuck out from his lips at a jaunty angle. He was sleekly handsome, with a mustache and silver-streaked dark hair.

Bo's instincts told him he was looking at Forbes Dyson.

He managed to reach one of the hitch rails in front of the saloon, but there were too many men pressed in around his horse for him to dismount. Plummer forced his way alongside, and Scratch brought the team to a stop a few feet away.

The man Bo guessed was Forbes Dyson stepped forward, took the cigar out of his mouth, and held up both hands, as if calling for quiet.

That was what he got, as the band stopped playing in midnote and the men in the crowd fell silent with surprising quickness. The few who continued whooping and hollering shut up in a hurry when they were on the receiving end of hard stares from several men who stepped up to the boardwalk railing on either side of Dyson.

Bo's eyes narrowed slightly as he looked at those men. Lean and rangy, they had a wolfish quality about them. The grips of the revolvers on their hips looked well used. Bo had seen enough hired-gun wolves in his life to recognize the breed when he laid eyes on it.

As the owner of a saloon in a boomtown, though, Dyson

probably needed such men just to keep the peace in his place, and Bo couldn't find fault with that.

As Dyson stood there with his hands still raised, the attention of the men in the street turned to him from the wagon. He seemed to enjoy having all eyes on him and allowed the moment to stretch out before finally raising his voice and saying, "Ladies, welcome to Silverhill! I take it you *are* the beautiful prospective brides sent to us by the Keegan Matrimonial Agency?"

Bo took it upon himself to answer.

"My friend and I work for Cyrus Keegan," he said. "These ladies are here to meet the men they've agreed to marry. If those men would step up . . ."

Whoops and howls erupted from the crowd again. Frowning, Bo glanced over at Rance Plummer and saw that the ranch foreman was grinning slyly. In that moment, Bo wished he had made a stronger effort to get Plummer to spill everything he knew about what was waiting for them in Silverhill . . . because in his gut, Bo knew something was wrong in this boomtown.

Dyson replaced the cigar in his mouth, puffed on it a couple of times, and blew out a cloud of smoke. Then he motioned for the crowd to be quiet again. When they were, he said, "That's going to be a little difficult, my friend."

Bo said tightly, "I don't see what's so hard about the men who plan to marry these women stepping up and identifying themselves."

"Well, the problem is, you see . . ." Dyson chuckled and waved the hand holding the cigar to indicate the entire large crowd of men in the street. "All these fine fellows are the prospective bridegrooms!"

Chapter 23

For a moment, Bo couldn't understand what the man was getting at. He stared at Forbes Dyson in confusion.

Scratch was equally puzzled, and he couldn't stop himself from exclaiming, "What the hell?"

Cecilia leaned forward, put a hand on Scratch's shoulder, and said, "What in the world is he talking about?"

Bo wanted an answer to that question, too. He said, "I reckon you'd better explain yourself, mister."

"Of course," Dyson said smoothly. "It's quite simple, really. Even though the ladies corresponded with five gentlemen from here in Silverhill and accepted their proposals of wedlock, it doesn't necessarily follow that those are actually the five men who will marry them."

"It most certainly does!" Cecilia said. "Where is Jasper Hobson? If he's here, I demand to see him."

Dyson chuckled. He put the cigar back in his mouth, clenched his teeth on it, and said around it as he beckoned to someone in the crowd, "Jasper, come on up here."

Scratch said to Cecilia, "This is the fella you're supposed to marry?"

"That's right." She didn't sound excited now at the prospect of meeting her intended bridegroom.

Apprehensive was more like it, Bo thought.

That apprehension was warranted. The crowd parted to let a man through. He stepped up onto the boardwalk, taking the hand that one of the hard-faced gunmen stuck out to him to help.

Jasper Hobson was short, bowlegged, and sported a ragged gray beard. His clothes were patched where they weren't threadbare. He wore a battered old hat with a pushed-up brim. One of his whiskery cheeks bulged with a chaw of tobacco.

"I thought you were marryin' a fella who owns a successful minin' claim," Scratch said to Cecilia.

"I am. I mean, I thought I was, too. But that man looks like . . . like . . ."

"An old desert rat who ain't got two dimes to rub together," Scratch said, finishing for her. "As red as his nose is, though, I reckon he got a snootful of whiskey somehow."

Jasper Hobson fumbled his hat off, revealing a fringe of lank gray hair around a mostly bald head, and slurred, "It's . . . it's mighty fine t' meet you, Miss . . . Miss Ceci . . . Cecilia. You're a—" He had to stop to hiccup, then continued, "You're a whole heap prettier'n I expected!"

"This can't be true," Cecilia said as her eyes widened in horror. "This can't possibly be Jasper Hobson. The man who wrote those letters to me was charming and urbane!"

From the way Forbes Dyson hooked his thumbs in his vest pockets again and practically preened, Bo suddenly had a pretty good idea who had written the letters to Cecilia and signed Jasper Hobson's name. He had a glimmering of what was going on here, although he didn't know the details yet.

"Mr. Dyson, I think you've got some explaining to do," Bo said. "The other men these ladies were expecting to meet, are they all like this Hobson hombre?"

"Well, not exactly," Dyson said. "Two of them are prospectors like Jasper, one is the blacksmith's assistant, and the other fellow clerks in Higginbotham's Store. I can bring them all up here if you'd like. You see, we had a lottery—"

"A lottery!" Cecilia cried. "You mean you gambled to see who was going to marry us?"

Dyson waved a hand and said, "Not at all, not at all. You misunderstand me. It was never intended that these men would marry you. Oh, they'll have their chance, like everyone else, but just because we used their names, they won't be given any unfair advantage."

"*You* wrote those letters, didn't you?" Bo asked.

Dyson looked very satisfied with himself again.

"I thought I did a commendable job of varying the style and vocabulary and attitudes in each one, so that the ladies would believe they were corresponding with five different men. I thought that with them being friends and coming from the same town, they might well pass the letters around among each other, so I put some real effort into it."

"Into tricking us, you mean!" Rose said. She glared at Dyson. "I ought to—"

"Ladies, ladies." Dyson held up both hands again, obviously a favorite gesture of his. "For any offense I've given, I sincerely apologize. You have to understand the situation here in Silverhill, though." He swept a hand toward the crowd. "These men need wives!"

Cheers and whistles erupted again.

Dyson allowed the commotion to go on for a minute or so, then motioned for quiet and went on. "But in the interests of fairness, it seemed that everyone should have a chance at wedded bliss! So we came up with the idea of bringing you ladies to Silverhill and staging a . . . tournament, let's call it . . . to determine who will have the privilege of marrying you."

Cecilia stared at him and said coldly, "That's the most insane thing I've ever heard."

"Not at all. Think of, say, the Trojan War. All the blood spilled, all the men who died, simply to determine who was going to be the husband of *one* woman. Helen of Troy, the face that launched a thousand ships, as the saying goes. But here, no real battles will be fought. No one will die. We'll just hold a series of contests, and the winners will claim the hands of you ladies in marriage."

"But what if we don't *want* to marry whoever wins?" Jean practically wailed.

"Don't worry," Dyson told her. "We'll come to an arrangement that's satisfactory to all the parties involved."

Bo shook his head and said, "Mister, this is loco. It's not what these ladies agreed to before they ever came out here. It's not right, and you're not going to do it."

Angry shouts burst out from the men crowded around the wagon and the horses. Bo's first impulse was to move his hand closer to the butt of his gun, but he knew that if he did that, the displeasure the men were expressing now might turn into a riot. A crowd could become a mob in the blink of an eye.

"Hear me out," Dyson said, raising his voice over the tumultuous racket. "While it's true there was a certain amount of . . . not being completely accurate—"

"Just call it lyin' and be done with it," Scratch snapped.

Dyson fixed him with a cold stare and said, "Not many men have ever called me a liar and gotten away with it, friend. But I'm going to overlook it since this is an unusual situation."

He turned back to Bo and continued, "Every sentiment expressed in those letters was genuine. I just helped these men put what they felt into words. Every man here"—again, he waved at the crowd—"wants a chance to show one of these ladies that he can be the sort of husband she came out here seeking. They were willing to put their hard-earned money on the line to earn that chance."

"You're saying they all went in together to pay Cyrus Keegan's fee and cover the expenses of the ladies coming out here?" Bo asked.

"That's exactly what I'm saying. Everyone chipped in, and as I mentioned before, we held a lottery to see whose names would be used on the letters, just to make everything fair and square. I volunteered to draft those letters. You see . . ." Dyson smiled ingratiatingly at the young women in the wagon. "You ladies should be honored that an entire community came together to bring you out here."

Cecilia said, "I don't consider having a bunch of men gambling for me to be that much of an honor."

"Neither do I," Jean said with a sniff. "It's very undignified."

"I don't know," Luella said. "It's kind of . . . romantic . . . isn't it? I mean, in olden times, knights in shining armor used to have tournaments to try to win the favor of fair maidens."

Rose said, "You read too many books. But, on the other hand, now that I think about it, it *is* kind of impressive that these fellows would go to so much trouble just to get us out here."

"And he did say it would be like a tournament," Beth added.

"Exactly!" Dyson said with a big grin. "I'm glad to see that you ladies understand and are getting into the spirit of the thing."

"Nobody said anything about getting into the spirit of the thing," Bo snapped. "Our job is to look out for the safety of these ladies—"

Dyson spread his arms wide and said, "What could possibly happen to them? They're surrounded by several hundred devoted guardians, men who would lay down their lives to protect them."

Bo frowned over at Rance Plummer and asked, "You knew about this, didn't you?"

Plummer shrugged. "The boys heard about the fandango and raised such a fuss about wantin' to come here for it, old man Jecks, who owns the SJ, finally agreed. They drew lots to see who'd stay and look after the spread, and the rest of 'em got to come here to Silverhill."

"We're lookin' to win us some wives," one of the cowboys said.

"Not if we've got anything to say about it!" responded a bearded hombre in the rough garb of a pick-and-shovel man. "The miners are gonna win them gals!"

A burly man in grimy buckskins, with a beard nearly down to his waist, yelled, "No miner could ever stand up to a bull-whacker in a fair contest!"

Angry shouts rose from all through the crowd. The rivalry between the factions might have turned into an out-and-out street brawl if Forbes Dyson hadn't shouted, "You men settle down! Do you want these fine ladies to think that you're all savage animals?"

That quieted the commotion. The hotly voiced challenges died away.

In the silence that fell, Cecilia said flatly, "We're not going along with this. As Mr. Creel said, it's not what we agreed to, and you can't hold us to the bargain."

"Nobody's going to force you to do anything, Miss . . . ?"

Cecilia hesitated before answering, "Spaulding. Cecilia Spaulding."

"All these men are asking for is a chance, Miss Spaulding. Let them show you how excited they are that you're here. Let them demonstrate that they're willing to risk not only money but also life and limb in order to win you over. This is the biggest thing to ever hit this part of the country! We're going to have a shooting competition, a horse race, a poker tournament, a test of strength, and even bare-knuckles boxing bouts to determine the winners. Wait and see. There's never been anything like this in New Mexico Territory!" Dyson laughed. "I'm not sure there's ever been anything like it in the entire country!"

He was probably right about that, Bo thought. No matter what Luella had said about those tournaments with knights in olden times, nobody had ever come up with an idea quite this crazy before. The more Bo mulled it over, the more confident he was about that.

"What do you say, ladies?" Dyson went on with a wheedling note in his voice. "If you agree, you're going to be responsible for making several hundred men very happy. Not many women can do that simply by saying yes."

Another cheer went up from the crowd.

Bo turned in the saddle to look at the women peering out through the opening at the front of the wagon. He shook his head and said, "You don't have to do this. We'll turn right around and go back to El Paso, and you can get a train back to Iowa."

"Go back without husbands?" Luella said. "That would be humiliating!"

"Yeah, it kind of would," Rose agreed. "I don't like being tricked like that . . . but I guess their motives weren't all bad."

Beth nodded and added, "And it really is a little romantic, like Luella said."

"I think it was a craven, cowardly thing to do," Cecilia snapped.

With a weary sigh, Jean said, "But we just got here, and despite what Mr. Creel said, we can't just turn around and go home right away. We'll have to wait until the morning to leave, at the very least . . . if we *do* leave."

"That's right!" Dyson said. "We have rooms for you in the Territorial House, the finest hotel in Silverhill. At least spend the night and think about it. Then, if you really don't want to stay, no one is going to force you to do so." He nodded and went on smugly, "But I believe that once you consider how all these men feel about you, you're going to want to stay and give them a fair chance to win you over."

Dyson was a persuasive varmint, Bo had to give him that. He was appealing to the ladies' sense of fair play, and it appeared as if this tactic might succeed, judging from the expressions on the faces of Beth, Rose, and Luella. Cecilia and Jean still looked opposed to the idea, but they seemed to be wavering, at least on the point of it being too late in the day to start back now.

"I suppose we're going to have to spend the night," Cecilia said. "What do you think, Mr. Creel? Mr. Morton?"

"This team could really use a few days of rest after the haul over here from El Paso," Scratch said.

"But we can get a new team," Bo said, "and start back first thing in the morning."

Shouts of "No!" rang out from the crowd.

Cecilia took a deep breath and nodded. "We can decide that in the morning," she said. "For now, like it or not—and I *don't* like it, Mr. Dyson—you can go ahead and have someone show us to the hotel."

Dyson bent low in a bow and swept an arm dramatically in front of him.

"I'll do that myself, Miss Spaulding," he said. "It'll be my honor!"

Chapter 24

The crowd moved back like snow melting in the hot sun as Forbes Dyson's gun wolves stepped down from the boardwalk and moved among them.

Dyson followed, a king surrounded by royal guards, and gestured for Bo, Scratch, and the ladies to follow him.

"Just swing that wagon around, friend," he told Scratch. "My men will see that you have room."

Bo and Scratch exchanged a grim glance; then Scratch lifted the reins and got the team moving again. He circled across the broad street as Dyson led the way toward another of Silverhill's actual two-story buildings, this one an adobe structure in the Spanish style, with a red tile roof.

Rance Plummer said, "I reckon we'll be seein' you around town, Creel. Hope you don't hold it against me that I didn't tell you exactly what you'd be runnin' into when you got here."

"Those cowboys of yours might have mutinied if you'd said or done anything to make the ladies turn back before we got here."

Plummer chuckled and nodded, saying, "Yeah, they sure

might have. They've plumb got their hearts set on winnin' those contests and gettin' 'em some good-lookin' young brides. Of course, the odds are against 'em, and the gals might not agree to come back to the ranch, anyway."

"Scratch and I aren't letting anyone take those ladies off somewhere against their will."

"If anybody tried to do that, I'd be right there beside you, backin' your play."

"Against your own men?"

"If they pulled somethin' as low-down rotten as that, damn right I would."

Bo believed the man. He nodded and said, "I'm glad to hear that, Plummer. I'd better catch up with the wagon now."

Plummer lifted a hand in farewell and followed his men, who were drifting on horseback toward the other hitch rails in front of the Silver King. If Bo knew cowboys—and he did—they were bent on lubricating their tonsils in the saloon.

Now that the ladies had agreed to spend the night in Silverhill, at least, the crowd was breaking up to an extent. Some of the men still followed the wagon toward the hotel, obviously intent on getting the best look possible at the five young women, but others wandered away. Bo was able to weave his way through the remainder and caught up with the wagon as Scratch brought it to a halt in front of the Territorial House.

Dyson's men took up positions on the hotel's gallery and stood there looking around, as if making sure no one came too close. Dyson himself waited beside the team while Scratch climbed down from the box and went to the back of the wagon to lower the tailgate. Bo dismounted, looped his horse's reins around a hitch rail, and joined his old friend in helping the ladies get out of the wagon.

When they were all on the ground, Dyson held out a hand to usher them into the hotel.

"Right this way, ladies," he invited them with a suave smile.

With varying degrees of reluctance, they walked into the hotel ahead of Dyson.

The saloon owner looked back at Bo and Scratch and said, "You can leave your horses and the team where they are. My men will take care of them. We have a good livery stable here in town."

Bo nodded. He didn't want to come right out and thank the man, not after Dyson had come up with that wild scheme to get the ladies here.

He and Scratch walked into the hotel behind Dyson. The Territorial House's lobby was shady and cool behind thick adobe walls. Heavy, comfortable-looking chairs were scattered around, some with potted plants beside them. Brightly colored woven Navajo rugs decorated the polished hardwood floor. The registration desk was straight ahead, with the entrance to a dining room off to the left.

The young women were gathered in front of the desk, where a clerk with spectacles was stationed. He greeted them with a smile as slick as the pomade on his hair and said, "Welcome to Silverhill, ladies. Speaking for the staff of the Territorial House, let me say what an honor it is to have you staying here with us."

"Just sign them in and give them their keys, Peavey," Dyson said. "I'm sure the ladies are tired and would like to rest and freshen up."

"That's certainly true," Jean said. She took off her hat and fanned herself with it. "I swear, I believe I've accumulated at least a pound of dust on my person in the past week. Would it be possible to have a bath?"

"All of us," Luella put in quickly. "We'd all like to have a bath."

"But not at the same time, in the same tub," Rose said.

The clerk cleared his throat and said, "We, ah, have only two tubs available, but I'll have them sent up to two of the rooms right away, and I'll let the maids know to start heating water immediately. Which of you ladies would like to go first?"

Cecilia said, "Jean and Luella spoke up about it first. Have the tubs taken to their rooms."

For a second Rose looked like she wanted to argue about that, but then she shrugged her shoulders in acceptance of Cecilia's decision.

The clerk assigned the ladies to rooms on the second floor. A couple of Navajo men who worked in the hotel brought their bags in and carried them upstairs. The clerk called a middle-aged Navajo maid in a starched apron and told her to show the guests to their rooms.

As they started up the stairs, Dyson told them, "I'll call for you ladies in a couple of hours, and then you'll have dinner with me at Harbinson's Restaurant. It's the finest food Silver-hill has to offer."

Cecilia turned and frowned down at him. "I don't recall any of us accepting a dinner invitation from you, Mr. Dyson," she said.

He smiled and spread his hands. "You have to eat, don't you? Please, join me. I can explain everything that's going to happen over the next few days, so you'll have all the information you need to decide if you want to take part. I'm certainly hoping you will."

Cecilia looked at the others.

Beth said, "He's right. We have to eat."

"You say this restaurant is a good one?" Rose asked.

"The best in town," Dyson assured her.

Cecilia said, "That might not be saying much, considering that this is a mining boomtown. Still, I suppose we can give it a try."

"I'm very glad to hear that," Dyson said. "I'll be back in a couple of hours."

"Mr. Creel and Mr. Morton will accompany us," Cecilia said sharply.

Dyson didn't look quite as pleased about that, but he nodded. "Of course." He glanced at Bo and Scratch and added, "They'll be more than welcome."

Somehow, Bo couldn't quite bring himself to believe that.

The hotel clerk didn't look nearly as pleased to deal with a couple of dusty old saddle bums, but he gave them rooms on the second floor, as well.

"I hope you, ah, gentlemen won't be wanting baths anytime soon," he sniffed.

"As long as there's a wash basin in the room, we'll make do," Bo said. He held up the key the man had slid across the desk to him. "How close are these rooms to the ones where you put the ladies?"

"They're at the other end of the hall."

"Do you have anything closer?"

"You're lucky I had anything available at all," the clerk said. "We've been holding the rooms for the young ladies, of course, but as I'm sure you noticed when you came into town, Silverhill is a bit crowded these days."

When they reached the second floor, he looked up and down the hallway, with its carpet runner and doors on both sides. After locating the rooms that the ladies occupied, he pointed past them to a window at that end of the corridor. An armchair sat under it.

"Tonight we'll drag that chair down here and take turns sitting up in it."

"To keep watch over the girls, you mean?" Scratch asked.

"That's right."

Scratch fingered his chin and said, "You know, we only signed on to get 'em here safe and sound, and they're here, each in one piece. Some fellas would consider that their job was over at this point."

"With everything that we've found out since we came into town, do you *feel* like our job is over?" Bo asked.

"Well . . . no, not really," Scratch admitted. "I've kinda got in the habit of lookin' after those gals, and it seems to me like they might still need some lookin' after."

"I feel the same way." Bo paused, then added, "Besides, we're not exactly those 'some fellas' you were talking about."

"We dang sure ain't!" Scratch said. "We're a couple of ornery ol' sidewinders."

"And proud of it," Bo said.

A short time later, Bo had just finished washing some of the trail dust off his face with a rag dipped in water he'd poured from a pitcher into a basin on the side table in his room, when somebody rapped on the door.

Out of cautious habit, he rested his hand on the butt of his gun as he went over to the door, called, "Who is it?" and took a quick step to the side in case somebody opened up with a rifle or shotgun through the panel.

"Brought your belongings up, mister," a man's voice said. "The stable sent 'em over."

Bo didn't recognize the voice, but what the man said sounded reasonable. He kept his hand on his gun and used his other hand to open the door.

One of the Navajo porters trudged into the room, carrying Bo's saddle in his left hand and the Winchester in his right. Bo's saddlebags were slung over his shoulder. He dropped the saddle in a corner and handed the rifle to Bo.

"Obliged to you," Bo said. "Just put the saddlebags on the table."

The man did so, then said, "So you're one of the fellas who brought those brides into town."

"That's right."

"Big doin's. The biggest. Don't reckon Silverhill has ever seen the like."

"The town hasn't been here that long. It makes sense nothing like this would have happened before." Curious, Bo added, "The mission was here first, wasn't it?"

The man nodded and said, "Yeah. The Spanish built it more than a hundred years ago. They figured on taming my people."

Bo recalled stories he had heard about violent Indian uprisings against the priests and the Spanish soldiers and said, "That didn't work out so well for them, did it?"

"No. It took the Americans and their army to do that. I'm not complaining, though. At least I've got a decent job."

Despite those words, the man's voice held a slightly bitter note. The Navajo were a proud people who had not accepted "civilizing" easily.

Bo handed the man a silver dollar and said, "I appreciate your help. One more question?"

"Sure, mister."

"What do you think about Forbes Dyson and this fandango he's putting on?"

The porter shrugged and said, "Dyson's a big man in these parts. Got big plans. A man would be wise not to cross him, especially if Bouma's around."

Bo frowned and said, "Boomer?"

"No, *Bouma*," the Navajo replied with a shake of his head. "That's his name. Jack Bouma. He's the boss of that crew of gunmen Dyson has working for him."

"Dangerous man with a gun, eh?"

"Mister, you don't want to find out. But I'll say this. There's a cemetery up by the old mission, and business is as brisk there as anywhere else in town."

Chapter 25

After they had washed up, Bo and Scratch waited in the hotel lobby for the ladies to come down. While they were there, Forbes Dyson strode in as confidently as if he owned the place, accompanied by a lantern-jawed man in a red shirt, a black leather vest, and a black hat with a tightly curled brim. Bo recalled seeing him among the group of gunmen who had been with Dyson earlier.

Dyson wore a black hat, too, with a flat crown and a silver band. He nodded curtly to Bo and Scratch and said, "The ladies haven't come down yet?"

"No," Bo said. "When you came in just now and had the door open, I noticed that there's a crowd gathering outside again."

"You can't blame those men for wanting to catch a glimpse of such beauty. The ladies are probably the loveliest women who have ever set foot in Silverhill."

"I wouldn't doubt it," Bo agreed. He looked over at Dyson's companion, who was regarding him with a cool, enigmatic stare. "Who's this?"

"An associate of mine," Dyson said. "Jack Bouma."

"Howdy," Scratch said with a nod.

Bouma had a toothpick between his lips. He shifted it from one side of his mouth to the other but didn't say anything in response to Scratch's greeting.

"Talkative sort, ain't he?" Scratch asked.

"Jack speaks up when he needs to," Dyson said.

Bo had a pretty good idea what the saloon owner meant by that. Bouma did his talking with a gun.

"He's coming to dinner with us?" Bo asked.

"Not exactly. But he'll be around."

Bouma nodded slowly to confirm that. He was Dyson's bodyguard, Bo realized, in addition to bossing the crew of gun wolves.

Before the conversation, such as it was, could continue, Dyson glanced toward the staircase, and a smile appeared on his face. Bo turned his head to look in the same direction and saw Jean and Luella descending the stairs. Both wore stylish gowns now, and Bo had to admit they were sights to take a man's breath away.

Scratch grabbed his hat off his head and grinned at them. Bo removed his hat, too, as did Forbes Dyson. Jack Bouma grunted almost inaudibly and strolled over to one of the armchairs, where he sat down, cocked his right ankle on his left knee, and proceeded to worry at his teeth with that sliver of wood.

Bouma was too cold-blooded to even greet the ladies politely, Bo thought.

Neither man actually broke into a run, but it was still a close race to see who reached the foot of the stairs first, Scratch or Dyson. The saloon owner edged out the silver-haired Texan and bent low in another bow.

"Ladies," he said, "you both look stunning."

Bo couldn't argue with that. He had followed Scratch and

Dyson over to the staircase, although he hadn't got in such a hurry about it.

"Miss Jean," Scratch said. "Miss Luella. The two of you look mighty nice."

Jean said, "It helped getting all that trail dust off, didn't it?"

"It sure did," Scratch agreed. "Not that you didn't look fine before, I mean, trail dust and all."

"We know what you mean, Mr. Morton," Jean assured him.

"I told you, you can just call me Scratch."

"Even though you're old enough to be our grandfather?" Luella teased him.

"I'm still young where it counts." Scratch patted his chest with his free hand. "In here."

Dyson said, "What about the other ladies?"

"They should be down soon," Jean said. "It takes a while to heat up enough water between each bath."

"We should sit down and get comfortable while we wait for them," Dyson suggested. He held out a hand. "Right this way, ladies."

He guided them over to a corner of the lobby, where three armchairs were arranged in a semicircle. Dyson waited until Jean and Luella had sat down and then took the third chair himself. Bo noted that Dyson had made sure there was no place for him and Scratch to sit. A glance over at Scratch told Bo that his old friend had noticed the same thing.

Scratch shrugged and ambled over to a chair elsewhere in the lobby. He was easygoing enough that it was difficult to rile him. He sat down and kept an eye on the stairs, while Bo walked up to the hotel's front windows and looked out at the men gathering in the street.

Many of them had probably been in the crowd that had greeted the ladies earlier, he thought. He saw some cowboys he recognized from Rance Plummer's SJ crew. A lot of laughing and backslapping was going on as they waited to get another look at the five young women who had the settlement in such an excited state.

Scratch called his name quietly, and when Bo turned around, he saw that his friend was on his feet again, hat off and held in front of him. Bo followed Scratch's gaze up the stairs and saw Cecilia, Rose, and Beth descending, each of them looking fresh and beautiful as a daisy.

As had happened when Jean and Luella came down, all the men in the hotel lobby stopped what they were doing and stared in admiration at the ladies.

Forbes Dyson said, "Excuse me," to the pair he was with and stood up to make his way toward the staircase.

Bo and Scratch beat him there this time, however. With his hat in his left hand, Bo reached up with his right hand to Cecilia and said, "Allow me, Miss Cecilia."

Her hand was cool and smooth as she took his.

"Thank you, Mr. Creel," she said.

Scratch put his hat back on and held out both arms to the side as he said, "Ladies?"

Smiling, Rose and Beth linked arms with him, Rose on his right, Beth on his left. Bo wasn't sure he had ever seen Scratch grin quite so big. They all started across the lobby toward the others. The men who were in their path took their hats off and got out of the way, opening a passage, as if a royal procession were going through.

Forbes Dyson wasn't pleased that the Texans had claimed escort duty for the other three young women. Bo could tell that by the resentment that smoldered briefly in Dyson's dark eyes before he covered it up and smiled.

"I have a table reserved for us at Harbinson's," he said. "Shall we go?"

"By all means," Cecilia murmured.

Dyson took Luella's arm. Jean took Bo's other arm, opposite Cecilia. Dyson and Luella led the way toward the door.

Jack Bouma stepped out first, though, with his right hand hovering near the butt of his Colt. Bo figured that was almost always the case. Men who lived by the gun had to be ready to draw all the time.

Bouma's presence made the men outside draw back slightly to give him room. That made it easier for Dyson and Luella and the rest of the group to follow him. They angled across the street toward a building with brightly lit windows.

Harbinson's was no trail-town hash house, Bo saw as they entered the restaurant. He had seen fancier places in Denver and San Francisco and New Orleans, but for a mining boomtown in New Mexico Territory, it was pretty doggone impressive, with hardwood floors, paintings on the walls, crystal chandeliers, and white silk tablecloths instead of the blue- or red-checked coverings that most cafés used.

There was no counter with stools in front of it and a menu chalked on a board behind it, either. Instead, a man in a red jacket and brocaded vest over a white shirt greeted them and showed them to a large round table in the back of the room.

To get there, they had to go past other tables, where men in expensive suits sat dining. These well-fed hombres sported beards or muttonchop whiskers. They had glasses of wine next to their fine china plates, and fat cigars smoldered in ashtrays.

Bo knew wealthy mine owners and businessmen when he saw them. Forbes Dyson might be right at home here, but a couple of footloose Texans like Bo Creel and Scratch Morton were definitely out of place.

The good thing was that Bo and Scratch never let anything like that bother them. They had their freedom, which, to their way of thinking, put them ahead of those rich galoots.

When they reached the table, Dyson held Luella's chair for her, then did the same for Cecilia and Beth, while Bo and Scratch helped Rose and Jean get seated. Somehow, Dyson managed to arrange things so that he wound up sitting with his back to the wall, between Luella and Cecilia. Bo and Scratch had to sit next to each other, with their backs to the door. Jack Bouma was nowhere to be seen.

"I'm glad we ain't plannin' on playin' cards," Scratch said under his breath. "I'd be leery of drawin' aces and eights."

"What was that?" Beth said. She was seated to Scratch's right.

"Oh, nothin'," he said.

Bo was glad Scratch didn't explain how that combination of cards was known as the dead man's hand, Bill Hickok having been holding it when Jack McCall shot him in the head up in Deadwood a few years earlier. The Texans had had their own brush with trouble in Deadwood after that.

"I made arrangements to have a bottle of the finest wine sent over from the Silver King," Dyson announced. "It should be here soon. Harbinson has some decent wine, but this bottle is from my private stock. It comes all the way from Paris."

"That's quite impressive, Mr. Dyson," Jean said.

"Well, just because we're tucked into an out-of-the-way corner of New Mexico Territory, that's no reason we can't still enjoy all of life's pleasures."

Dyson managed not to smirk when he said that, but Bo thought he probably had a hard time of it.

Dyson went on, "Fine wine, the best cigars from Cuba . . . the prettiest ladies from Four Corners, Iowa . . . We're blessed to have such things in Silverhill."

"Being the prettiest girls in Four Corners might not be saying that much," Rose said. "It's not a very big place."

"I think it's saying a great deal." Dyson smiled. "Ah, here's the wine!"

The same red-jacketed waiter who had brought them to the table arrived with the wine. He opened the bottle and filled several crystal glasses. When everyone had a glass, Dyson raised his and said, "To the ladies, who, by gracing us with their mere presence, have lifted Silverhill to a whole new plane of existence!"

"You're embarrassing us with your flattery, Mr. Dyson," Cecilia said.

"On the contrary," Dyson insisted. "It's not flattery if it's true, and no truer words have ever been spoken than those that praise the beauty of you ladies."

Scratch whispered to Bo, "He sure does love to hear himself talk, don't he?"

Bo couldn't argue with that.

He had never cared for wine, and private stock from Paris or not, this particular vintage didn't impress him. It just tasted like vinegar to him, as all wine did. But he drank it politely, and he had to admit that Harbinson's put on a good feed. The steaks the restaurant served were perfect, tender and juicy, and the fixings that came with them were tasty, as well.

As they were eating, Bo was aware of the other diners in the room watching them. Those men had a stake in how successful Silverhill was. This so-called "mail-order bride tournament" idea Dyson had come up with, loco though it might be, had brought a lot of people into town, and those people had already spent quite a bit of money, Bo figured. Over the next few days, they would spend even more.

Of course, all the hoopla was a distraction, as well. Bo wondered if the men who worked in the mines were keeping up with their jobs, or were they sneaking off to town to take part in the festivities?

The mine owners would probably be glad when the whole thing was over.

When they had finished eating, the waiter brought snifters of brandy. Dyson leaned back in his chair, swirled the brandy around in his snifter, and said, "I suppose we should talk about everything that's going to happen over the next few days."

"We haven't determined that anything actually *is* going to

happen," Cecilia pointed out. "At this point, all my friends and I have agreed to do is listen."

"Of course. As I said earlier, we plan to have a poker tournament, which will start tomorrow morning and last as long as it takes to determine a winner, a shooting competition, a strength competition, a boxing tournament, and a horse race. Five events, five beautiful prizes."

"We're not prizes," Cecilia snapped. "We're human beings."

Dyson nodded and said, "Of course. I phrased that badly. But I hope you understand just how excited the men here in town are, as well as all those who have come in from other parts of the territory. Many of them have already signed up to compete, some in more than one contest."

"Are they paying entry fees to sign up?" Bo asked.

"As a matter of fact, they are. But if you think I'm doing this simply to make money, you couldn't be more wrong, Creel. I want to help Silverhill grow into a real town, a town that will last, and you know as well as I do that the first step is to have more fine, upstanding female citizens, such as these ladies. Women always bring civilization with them wherever they go."

Bo knew enough history to realize that Dyson was right about that. Men were more likely to keep tighter reins on their barbarian natures when decent women were around. But he still didn't like the idea that these five young ladies were considered prizes to be won, and there was no getting around *that*, either.

"How is this going to work, exactly?" Rose asked. "When a man wins one of these contests, does he get to pick and choose a bride from those of us who are left?" She rolled her eyes and added, "I wouldn't want to be picked last."

"Rose!" Cecilia said. "That's terrible."

Rose shrugged and said, "I just want to know what the plan is."

"Actually," Dyson said, "we'll wait until all five winners have been determined, and then they'll sit down with the five of you to work things out. No one will be forced to enter into any arrangements that aren't agreeable to them, I assure you."

Beth said, "This whole idea of being mail-order brides *is* sort of a business arrangement, Cecilia."

"I suppose," Cecilia agreed grudgingly.

"But there's nothing wrong with a little romance going along with it," Luella added.

Scratch said, "Pardon me for buttin' in here, but you said some fellas have signed up for more than one contest, Dyson. What happens if an hombre *wins* more than one?" Scratch chuckled. "You don't intend to allow a fella to have more than one wife, do you, like the Mormons?"

"I will *not* go along with that," Cecilia said.

"If that happens, we'll work something else out," Dyson said. "Maybe give the fellow a cash prize and allow whoever finished second to sit in on the meeting with the ladies. But we'll deal with that when and if it actually takes place."

"You've put some thought into this," Bo said.

"And with good reason. This is the biggest thing to happen so far in Silverhill's relatively brief existence. And it may be the biggest thing that will *ever* happen in Silverhill." Forbes Dyson leaned back in his chair, with a look of extreme self-satisfaction on his face. "I assure you ladies, no one in this part of the country will ever forget what's going to happen in Silverhill over the next few days!"

Chapter 26

The Silver King was the biggest and busiest saloon in Silverhill and, therefore, likely the best, Philip Armbruster reasoned as he paused in front of the batwing doors. From the looks of the place, the best source of information he was likely to find, too.

He took a deep breath, inhaling the fumes of tobacco smoke, whiskey, and beer that mingled with the less pleasant aromas of cheap perfume, unwashed flesh, vomit, and human waste.

All the smells blended into a potent mix, which floated out of the entrance onto the boardwalk before the night breezes dispersed it. That distinctive miasma was the same from the Bowery in New York to the Barbary Coast in San Francisco and probably in other towns around the world.

It was the smell of a saloon.

After that moment's hesitation, Armbruster gripped the tops of the batwing doors and pushed them aside. He walked into the Silver King, knowing that in his suit, hat, and spectacles, he might be a bit out of place among the cowboys, miners, and freighters who had crowded into the place. But there were enough townsmen in the saloon that he didn't stand out too much, he realized as he looked around.

If the smells were something of an assault to the senses, so was the racket. A piano player pounded the ivories in a corner, but the talking and laughter were so loud, Armbruster couldn't hear the music well enough to tell if the man had any talent or not. Quite likely, it was limited at best. If he *was* any good, he was a diamond in the rough.

The sound of cards being slapped down on green felt, the rattle of dice, and the whir of a spinning roulette wheel formed a counterpoint to the music, as if they were all instruments in this orchestra of vice and depravity.

The Silver King had long hardwood bars on both sides of the room, each manned by a pair of bartenders, who hurried back and forth, pouring drinks and sliding mugs of beer to their thirsty customers.

The games of chance were in an area to Armbruster's left, surrounded by a wooden railing and elevated a couple of steps from the level in the rest of the saloon.

Bordering that area, in an L shape, was the part of the saloon filled with tables, where men drank and laughed and fondled the feather-covered rear ends of serving girls, who wore scandalously low-cut outfits short enough to reveal stocking-clad thighs and calves. The sight of all that female flesh on display was enough to make Armbruster swallow hard.

Beyond the tables, in the rear of the room, was another raised area, where the piano was located. It was big enough to serve as a stage whenever entertainers came in and put on a show. It was a dance floor, too, and several roughly dressed men were taking advantage of the chance to stomp around awkwardly with saloon girls in their arms while the slick-haired maestro in the corner provided the music.

Armbruster shoved those thoughts aside. He was here for a reason, and he didn't want to let Jaime Mendoza down.

Disappointing Mendoza was a good way to get killed.

The bar to Armbruster's left was full, but he spied a few open spaces at the bar to his right and headed in that direction, being careful not to bump into anyone as he weaved through the tables. These Westerners were touchy about such things—"proddy," they called it—and he didn't want to offend anyone and draw attention to himself.

Mostly, he didn't want to wind up in any kind of fight where he might easily be hurt or even killed.

He eased into one of the open spaces and rested his hands on the bar's front edge. Neither of the red-jacketed bartenders seemed to notice him. He waited a few moments for one of them to come over and ask what he wanted. When that didn't happen, he raised his right hand and cleared his throat.

Still no response. They probably hadn't heard him over the hubbub in the room. He cleared his throat again and then said, "Excuse me." When that didn't do any good, he raised his voice. "Excuse me!"

The man at his right elbow chuckled and said, "That ain't gonna do you any good, son. Looky here. This is the way you do it." The man's callused hand slapped down sharply on the hardwood. He gave a piercing whistle and then bellowed, "Hey, drink juggler! Get your ass down here."

The closest bartender walked over with a scowl on his face.

"What do you want, Seamus?" he demanded. "You've still got beer."

"Yeah, but my friend here don't." The man slapped Armbruster on the back hard enough to make him bend forward toward the bar for a second. "What'll you have, son?"

"B-beer will do just fine, thank you," Armbruster said as he tried to catch his breath.

"You heard the man," Seamus snapped.

The bartender nodded, grabbed a mug off a shelf, and started filling it from a tap. When the foaming amber liquid began to overflow, he set the mug on the bar in front of Armbruster.

"Four bits," the bartender said.

Armbruster was reaching for his pocket when Seamus tossed a coin onto the hardwood.

"Ain't seen you around here before, so the first one's on me. My way of sayin', 'Welcome to Silverhill.' You *are* new in these parts, ain't you?"

"Yes. I just got here this evening," Armbruster replied. "I appreciate the gesture."

"Glad to do it. Drink up, son."

Armbruster lifted the mug, which left a ring of foam and liquid on the bar, and took a cautious swallow. He wasn't really all that fond of beer, but this one tasted surprisingly good, he discovered, and it was bracingly cold, as well.

"Pretty good, ain't it?" Seamus asked. "Dyson don't skimp on the booze."

"Is that the bartender's name?" Armbruster asked. "Dyson?"

"Oh, hell no. I don't know that varmint's name. Forbes Dyson is the fella who owns this here saloon. Big man in Silverhill."

Armbruster nodded and said, "I see." He drank some more of the beer, then set it down and stuck out his hand. "I should introduce myself. I'm Philip Armbruster. One *l* in Philip."

Seamus seemed to him the garrulous sort, a likely source of information.

The man's big paw fairly swallowed up Armbruster's hand. He said, "Seamus Donnigan is my name. Sounds Irish as the day is long, I know, but I was born in this country, in Chicago. Worked on the railroad for a while, then came out here to try my hand at mining."

Donnigan looked like a miner. He was half a head taller than Armbruster and had shoulders that an ax handle might not be able to span. Rust-colored bristles covered his slab of a jaw, and a thatch of hair the same shade stuck out from under the battered derby jammed down on his head. He wore a flannel shirt, canvas trousers with suspenders, and laced-up work boots.

"What's your line of work, Phil?" Donnigan went on.

Armbruster didn't see any point in concocting an elaborate

lie. That would just give him something to keep up with. He said, "I'm a newspaperman."

Donnigan's shaggy red eyebrows rose. "You don't say! Sil-verhill's got a newspaper. The *Enterprise*. You gonna try to get a job there?"

This was the first Armbruster had heard about a newspaper in Silverhill, but since it existed, he might as well play along with Donnigan's assumption.

"That's my plan," he said. He ventured a smile. "I don't think I'm exactly cut out for the same sort of work that you do."

Donnigan threw his head back and guffawed. "No, I reckon not," he said. "No offense. I never had much truck with readin' myself, newspapers or books or anything else, but if that's what you're suited for, that's what you ought to do. I reckon a whole heap of the world's unhappiness comes from fellas forcin' them-selves to do things they really don't want to do, just 'cause they think for some reason that they ought to."

"That's very profound, Mr. Donnigan. Do you mind if I quote you?"

"Don't quite know what that means, but sure, go ahead."

Armbruster drank more beer, then got on with the task that had brought him into the settlement tonight: finding out what Jaime Mendoza wanted to know.

"Why in the world is the town so crowded? Is it always like this, simply because of the mines?"

Donnigan laughed again and said, "Silverhill's a boomtown, all right, but what's goin' on right now is something special. It's the brides!"

"The brides?" Armbruster frowned and shook his head. "I don't know what you mean."

"The mail-order brides. Five of 'em Dyson brought in, and all beautiful enough to take a man's breath away and make him feel like he's been punched in the gut."

Five beautiful women, Armbruster thought. Donnigan had to be talking about the women from the wagon, the ones who had been accompanied by those two old men who'd put up a far better fight than Mendoza had ever expected.

Armbruster, like Mendoza and the other members of the gang, had assumed those women were prostitutes. Now, according to what Donnigan was saying, it seemed that they were something else.

"Two blondes, two with very dark hair, and one with lighter brown hair?" Armbruster asked as he tried to recall what the women had looked like, based on the glimpses he had gotten of them through Mendoza's field glasses.

"Yeah, that's right. You've seen 'em, huh? Ain't they just about the prettiest fillies you ever laid eyes on?"

Armbruster didn't answer those questions. Instead, he asked another of his own.

"If they're mail-order brides, who are the prospective grooms? Who are they going to marry?"

Another laugh boomed out from Donnigan, and once again he slapped Armbruster on the back hard enough to stagger him.

"That's just it! Nobody knows yet, 'cause it ain't been decided. There's gonna be contests to decide who gets hitched with 'em. I signed up for the strongman contest and the bare-knuckles boxin' tournament." Donnigan's massive right fist smacked into the palm of his left hand with a sound like a gunshot. "I figure I've got a good chance to win one or both of 'em!"

Armbruster took another drink while he struggled to grasp what Donnigan had just told him. He had never heard of such an arrangement before.

"The ladies, they've agreed to this?"

"Well, I reckon it took 'em a mite by surprise when they got here and found out what Dyson's plannin', but they'll go along with it. I mean, they came out here to get married, right? And if they marry up with the fellas who win these contests, they're bound to get pretty good husbands. It makes sense to me that they'd go along with it."

Looking at the matter from that perspective, Armbruster

supposed his newfound acquaintance was right. Simply by becoming mail-order brides, the women had agreed to marry men
they had never met.

Armbruster was enough of a cynic to believe it was usually a
mistake to depend on logic where females were concerned,
though.

"When is all this going to happen?" he asked.

"The poker tournament starts tomorrow mornin'," Donnigan
said. "And the strongman contest will be held tomorrow afternoon, while the poker games are still goin' on. The shootin' contest and the horse race will be the next afternoon, and then the
boxin' tournament that morning and evenin', as long as it takes
to declare a winner." His rugged face split in a grin. "Which
means however long it takes for me to knock out all the other
contestants!"

"Well, I wish you luck," Armbruster said. He had found out
almost all he needed to know. He drank the last of the beer in
the mug and then asked, "Do you happen to know where the
ladies are staying while all this other business is going on?"

"Dyson's puttin' 'em up in the Territorial House, across the
street. It's the best hotel in Silverhill, or so they say. I wouldn't
know firsthand, 'cause I've never had reason to set foot in the
place myself."

Armbruster nodded. He said, "I've enjoyed our conversation, Mr. Donnigan—"

"Seamus," the miner said. "Call me Seamus."

"I've enjoyed it, but I have to be going now. Before I do,
though . . ." Armbruster slapped his hand on the hardwood
and yelled, "Barkeep!"

The man came over again and asked, "Another round?"

"Just for my friend here," Armbruster said as he slid a coin
across the bar. "This one's on me, Seamus. I always repay any
favors done for me."

"You're an honorable man, Phil. I hope I run into you again.

Come watch the strongman competition tomorrow. If you get a job with the newspaper, you can write about it!"

Armbruster just smiled and nodded. He didn't know what he would be doing in the future. That was up to Jaime Mendoza. The bandit chief was expecting him back tonight, at the camp up in the hills where Mendoza and the others waited.

First, though, Armbruster had to make another stop in Silverhill.

Chapter 27

By the time Bo, Scratch, the five young women, and Forbes Dyson left Harbinson's Restaurant, Cecilia had agreed to take a wait-and-see attitude toward the activities of the next couple of days as Dyson had outlined them. Since the other ladies seemed to regard her as their natural leader, they were willing to go along with that.

Actually, Rose, Beth, and Luella were more than just willing to go along, Bo thought as he walked with the others back toward the Territorial House. They had been won over completely by Dyson's smooth talk and the romanticism of the idea. To them, it really was like noble knights jousting over fair ladies . . . although as far as Bo could tell, most of the hombres crowding into Silverhill were about as far from being knights as a man could get.

Jean was more reserved in her support for the idea, and Cecilia was downright skeptical. Bo didn't know if Dyson could win her over or not, but clearly, the saloon owner intended to try.

One thing he *hadn't* sensed was that Dyson had any interest in any of the ladies himself. As far as Bo could tell, Dyson was doing this simply out of a desire to help Silverhill grow, as he claimed.

That didn't mean Bo had lost all his suspicions of the fellow, though. He still planned to keep a mighty close eye on Dyson, just in case he was up to something more than was apparent.

The crowds in the street had thinned out a little during the evening, but a lot of people were still moving around. Dyson led the way toward the hotel, with the ladies behind him and the two Texans bringing up the rear. Because of that, when a cowboy lurched drunkenly toward the young women, it was Dyson who got in his way.

Dyson put a hand on the cowboy's chest and said around the cigar clenched between his teeth, "Better back off there, friend. You don't want to go crowding the young ladies."

"I don't intend to crowd nobody, mister," the cowboy responded. "I just want to get a better look at them gals. I paid good money to enter the shootin' contest, and I think I got a right to see just what I'm tryin' to win." His voice rose angrily. "And you'd best get your hand off'a me. I don't cotton to bein' touched like that."

Jack Bouma appeared as if out of nowhere, making Bo realize that he'd probably been lurking somewhere close by all evening. Dyson gave the cowboy a shove that made him stumble back a couple of steps. Bouma moved in smoothly to get between Dyson and the cowhand.

"You've had too much to drink," Bouma said in a low, hard voice. "Better move on now, amigo, while you've still got the chance."

The cowboy pointed past Bouma at Dyson and yelled, "He pushed me!"

Bouma began, "You'll get worse than a push if you don't—"

The drunken cowboy cursed and clawed at the holstered gun on his hip.

When the confrontation began, Bo had nodded for Scratch to stay where he was and then had moved around the ladies to get a better look at what was happening. He might have taken a hand himself, but then Bouma had shown up.

So Bo was in perfect position to see the speed of Bouma's draw as the gunman's hand flickered down and then up again, filled with a revolver. The cowboy's gun was less than halfway out of leather when flame spurted from the muzzle of Bouma's weapon and the crash of the shot filled the street.

The cowboy let go of his gun and it fell back into its holster as the slug from Bouma's gun slammed into his chest. The impact knocked the cowboy back another couple of feet. He gasped, and his eyes opened wide. He brought up a trembling hand and patted clumsily at the blood-welling hole in his chest as he swayed back and forth.

Then his eyes rolled up in their sockets, his knees buckled, and he collapsed.

It had all happened so fast, the ladies were all standing there, staring in shock.

Bouma stepped over to the fallen cowboy, apparently satisfied himself that the staring eyes were indeed lifeless, and took a cartridge from one of the loops on his shell belt to replace the one he had fired.

Dyson turned hastily toward the young women and held up his hands as he said, "Ladies, I'm so sorry you had to witness that. I wish that young fool had listened to reason."

"He . . . he killed him," Rose said.

With a solemn shake of his head, Dyson said, "The man gave Jack no choice. It's accepted practice out here that when a man tries to draw on you, you have a right to defend yourself." Dyson glanced over at Bo. "Isn't that right, Creel?"

"Generally speaking," Bo agreed. "That hombre was drunk, though, and from the looks of it, not that slick on the draw to start with. Why didn't you just buffalo him, Bouma?"

The gunman's mouth twisted in a sneer. "Don't try tellin' me how to handle my affairs, old-timer. It's none of your business."

Dyson said, "Take it easy, Jack. No one's blaming you for this. We both gave that young fool a chance to back off."

"He was never going to back off," Bo said. "Not with all the whiskey he had in him and pretty girls around to try to impress."

"That was still his choice to make," Bouma drawled with a smirk on his lean face.

"Yeah, I reckon it was," Bo said grimly.

The shooting had caused a large area to clear suddenly around the group in the street. People began to come forward now, though, as they peered curiously at the dead cowboy.

"Where are the authorities?" Cecilia asked. "Isn't there any law in this town?"

"We have a marshal," Dyson said, "but his main duty is locking up drunks who try to cause trouble. It's a shame he didn't get this one behind bars before things went as far as they did. A killing like this, where it's a clear-cut case of self-defense and there are plenty of witnesses . . ." Dyson shrugged. "Well, there's really no need for any authorities to get involved."

"And you expect us to marry and settle down in a lawless place like this?" Cecilia said.

"It's not lawless," Dyson responded with a faint note of impatience in his voice now. "It's just a different sort of code from what you ladies are used to."

Jean said, "Shouldn't someone at least get that poor young man's body off the street?"

"Undertaker's on his way now," Bouma said, nodding toward a wagon creeping through the crowd toward them. A man in a black suit and top hat sat on the driver's box, handling the team.

"We should get on to the hotel, ladies," Dyson said. "My deepest apologies for this tragic delay."

Cecilia sniffed and the others still looked a bit shaken, but they all followed him toward the Territorial House.

Bo and Scratch trailed behind them.

Scratch glanced over his shoulder and said quietly, "Bouma's already gone. Slipped back into the shadows like a snake, I reckon." The silver-haired Texan paused, then added, "He's fast, Bo. Faster than me and maybe faster than you."

"Let's hope we don't have to find out," Bo said.

Philip Armbruster was trying to persuade the clerk in the hotel to tell him which rooms the young ladies were in—a five-dollar gold piece hadn't done the trick, but a ten-dollar eagle might—when the gunshot roared out in the street.

Quite a few people were in the hotel lobby. They hurried to the windows to look out and try to see what was going on.

Armbruster was among them, but at first he could see only a crowd surrounding an open space in the middle of the street. Then, through a gap, he caught a glimpse of a man sprawled in the dirt and several people standing near him, including the five young women.

Armbruster's heart lurched inside his chest. If anything happened to that woman Mendoza had set his sights on, there was no telling what he might do in his rage.

He might even try to burn Silverhill to the ground, but he didn't have enough men left to pull off such a raid successfully. Chances were, all he'd accomplish would be to get all of them killed.

Thankfully, as far as Armbruster could tell from his vantage point, all five of the ladies appeared to be all right. After a few minutes, the well-dressed man with them ushered them on toward the hotel.

Armbruster stiffened as he spotted the two older men following the ladies. He recognized them from the several times he had seen them before. He had no idea what their names were, but they were the hard-fighting old-timers who had put up such a battle against Jaime Mendoza's band of thieves. And they had gotten a good look at him, too, during that parley, Armbruster reminded himself. A little shudder went through him as he recalled how that had ended with bullets flying around his head. He didn't want them seeing him and probably recognizing him, so as the group reached the hotel porch, he drew back and faded into the crowd, keeping his head down.

A lot of people called excited questions as the group entered with the well-dressed man in the lead. Remembering what Seamus Donnigan had said in the Silver King, Armbruster wondered if this man was Forbes Dyson, owner of the saloon and organizer of the bizarre competition for the hands in marriage of the five young ladies. It seemed likely he was.

Armbruster used his elbow to nudge the man standing next to him and asked quietly, "Is that Forbes Dyson?"

"Who else would it be, squiring around those beauties like that?" the man replied. He hooked his thumbs in his lapels and went on, "Folks are going to be calling him the King of Silverhill before this is all over."

Perhaps, Armbruster thought. Given the name of Dyson's saloon, that might be exactly what the man had in mind. But Jaime Mendoza might have something to say about that.

Dyson lifted his hands, which quieted the crowd in the hotel lobby immediately. He said, "Friends, I'm sorry you had to witness that unfortunate display out in the street just now. You all know it's my fondest wish to see Silverhill growing into a large, thriving, and, above all, peaceful community."

"You've got a funny way of showing it," snapped one of the men in the crowd, "having a gunfighting killer like Jack Bouma working for you."

A lot of eyes swung to the well-dressed middle-aged man

who had spoken, including Dyson's. Armbruster saw the way Dyson's smooth-shaven jaw tightened. He caught the flare of anger in the saloon man's eyes.

But Dyson controlled those reactions quickly and said, "I'm still a businessman, Lester, and Silverhill is still a boomtown. I have to have someone protecting my interests. You hire men to guard your mine, don't you?"

"Of course I do," the man replied. "But it's different—"

"I don't think so. Jack was just looking out for me, keeping me and these ladies from being hurt. You wouldn't want anything to happen to our lovely visitors, would you?"

"No, of course not," the man called Lester blustered. "But still, a young cowboy being shot down in the street like that—"

"Will more than likely prevent any other young cowboys— or any of your miners—from getting too liquored up and causing trouble tonight. Sometimes the harsh lessons are the most effective."

Lester looked like he wanted to continue the argument, but several of the other men spoke up, saying things like, "That's right, Mr. Dyson," and "It's not your fault, Forbes."

Lester scowled, shook his head, and turned away to push through the crowd and out of the hotel. Dyson steered the ladies toward the staircase again.

The two rugged old-timers followed.

Armbruster managed to stay on the fringes of the crowd, inconspicuous, until they had all gone upstairs. A part of him wanted to follow them and see which rooms they went into, but he couldn't risk being spotted, and besides, he told himself, it didn't really matter. The Territorial House was one of the biggest buildings in Silverhill, but not so big that five women couldn't be found in it, when the time came.

He slipped out of the hotel and headed for the hitch rail where he had left his horse when he rode into town earlier this evening. Mendoza was probably growing impatient by now, and Armbruster wanted to pass on everything he had found out.

Mendoza would have to go about making his plans differently now. He had lost enough men that he couldn't just come barging into a place and take what he wanted anymore. That diminished force was why he hadn't ambushed the travelers while they were still out on the trail, before they ever reached Silverhill. It had been just too risky.

But over the past few days, Armbruster had seen how obsessed Mendoza was with that young, dark-haired beauty, and there was plenty of loot in Silverhill for the other men in the gang to get their hands on, as well, in all the confusion of this so-called bride competition.

They might even be able to grab the other four young women, as they had tried and failed to do earlier.

Big doings in Silverhill these days, all right, Armbruster thought as he swung up into the saddle . . . but the people who had flocked here didn't know just how big those events were going to be.

Chapter 28

The Territorial House had a small, unpretentious dining room attached to the lobby, and that was where Bo and Scratch escorted the five young women for breakfast the next morning.

The ladies all looked lovely, of course, but to Bo they didn't appear all that well rested.

"How did you sleep?" he asked the group as they sat down at a round table already set with cups of coffee and plates of ham, eggs, and biscuits.

"I was rather restless," Cecilia replied. "I suppose seeing a young man shot down right in front of my eyes has that effect on me."

"That *did* make it harder to sleep," Jean said. "I don't believe he meant any harm. He was just excited about . . . about, well, seeing us there. In the flesh, so to speak."

"He should have backed off," Rose said. "Even if he hadn't been drunk, I don't think he would have stood a chance against Bouma. That man is *fast*."

Luella said, "Like one of your dime-novel gunfighters?"

"That's right. I'm not sure even Smoke Jensen could have matched his speed."

Scratch said, "I don't know about that, Miss Rose. Our trail's never crossed that of ol' Smoke—the real fella, I mean, not the dime-novel character—but we've heard enough about him from hombres who've seen him in action to figure he's just about the fastest there is."

"I wouldn't mind seeing that someday," Rose said. "Smoke Jensen in action, I mean."

Cecilia shook her head and said, "Not me. I've already witnessed enough violence during this journey to last me the rest of my life."

Bo hoped that would be the case and Cecilia would never encounter any more trouble. Out here on the frontier, though, that was a lot to hope for.

They dug into the food, which was good. Rose and Beth had the best appetites among the ladies, with Jean being the pickiest eater in the bunch.

As they were finishing their meal and lingering over the cups of coffee, Forbes Dyson walked into the dining room, carrying his hat in one hand. He didn't have one of his usual cigars burning at the moment.

He came to the table and greeted them by saying, "Good morning, ladies."

Bo thought Dyson had a slightly dissipated look about him. This was probably a pretty early hour for a saloonkeeper to be up and around.

"Good morning, Mr. Dyson," Cecilia said.

"You slept well, I trust? Not too disturbed by the unfortunate events of yesterday evening?"

"We're fine," Cecilia said coolly.

The others just nodded in agreement, even Jean. Bo was somewhat touched that they had been more open and honest with him and Scratch about how the shooting had affected them than they were being now with Forbes Dyson.

"I thought you might like to come over to the Silver King

with me and meet some of the men who'll be playing in the poker tournament," Dyson said.

Scratch said, "This is sort of early for most of the poker players I've known. Unless they'd been up all night in a big game, that is."

"Most of them are normally night owls, all right," Dyson agreed. "That just goes to show how excited they are about this opportunity." He smiled and gestured with the hat he held in his right hand. "What do you say, ladies? I'm sure the competitors would appreciate the visit."

Jean said hesitantly, "I don't believe I've ever set foot in a . . . an actual saloon."

"The Silver King is a classy establishment, not the sort of squalid dive you read about in popular entertainment," Dyson assured her.

"We're finished with breakfast," Cecilia said, "so I suppose we can go." She drank the last of her coffee and set the empty cup back on its saucer.

The others finished their coffee, as well, and stood up. Dyson ushered them out of the dining room and through the lobby. Bo and Scratch trailed behind, spreading out slightly so they could cover both flanks in case of any trouble. Bo didn't really expect any, but it was better to be prepared.

Silverhill wasn't roaring like it had been the night before, but quite a few riders and wagons were moving along the street, and the boardwalks were busy, as well. This morning, though, it looked more like a normal boomtown.

Despite that, the ladies drew a crowd as they crossed the street toward the Silver King with Dyson, Bo, and Scratch. Most of the men in town were interested in getting a good look at them.

No one approached too closely, though, maybe remembering what had happened the night before to that eager young cowboy who'd had too much to drink. Bo hadn't seen Jack

Bouma so far this morning, but that didn't mean the gunfighter wasn't around. Bo was sure he would show up if anything threatened Forbes Dyson or his plans.

Bo and Scratch hadn't been inside the Silver King before, so as they entered the saloon, they took a good look around. From the outside, it appeared to be an impressive place, and the interior confirmed that impression. The Texans had been in fancier saloons, but this one was mighty nice, especially considering its location.

The gleaming hardwood bars, one on each side of the room, were mostly empty at this time of day. One bartender was on duty at each, and they were busy pouring cups of coffee for the handful of customers.

Some of the coffee in those cups got a sweetening jolt of Who-Hit-John from various bottles of whiskey, Bo noted. That was one way to start the day.

To the left, in a raised section behind carved wooden railings, were half a dozen baize-covered poker tables. The roulette wheel and the faro and keno layouts, also in that section, were deserted at the moment, but men sat at four of the six poker tables, and cards were already being shuffled and dealt.

"We'll open up the other two tables as it becomes necessary, to accommodate the contestants," Forbes Dyson explained as he led the ladies up three steps into the gambling area.

The dealers stopped in the middle of what they were doing as they caught sight of the five young women. All eyes turned to them. Several of the players got to their feet politely, and that caused the others to stand, as well.

"Gentlemen, I'd like to present the finest ladies ever to grace Silverhill with their presence," Dyson said. "Miss Cecilia Spaulding, Miss Jean Parker, Miss Luella Tolman, Miss Beth Macy, and Miss Rose Winston."

A stocky man in a cream-colored suit plucked a wide-brimmed hat of the same shade from his head and gave them a courtly bow. He had a rugged, deeply tanned face under gray-ing red hair. When he spoke, his voice held a soft Virginia drawl.

"Ladies, it's an absolute honor and privilege to meet you," he stated. "Having you here definitely raises the stakes in this game."

"Don't be crude, O'Keefe," Forbes Dyson said.

"Crudity is the farthest thing from my mind, I assure you. I meant only that a mere smile from one of these ladies would be a great prize indeed."

Still down on the saloon's main level, Bo leaned toward Scratch and said quietly, "That fella's got a silver tongue, just like you."

"Yeah, but he ain't near as handsome," Scratch said.

The other players were a mixture of well-dressed hombres who had the look of professional gamblers, businessmen from here in Silverhill, and miners and cowboys, who must have scrimped and saved their wages for quite a while to be able to afford to buy into this game. All of them were fascinated by the young women, and when Dyson told them to go back to their games, some of them seemed to have a hard time focusing their attention on their cards.

Instinct soon took over, though, and they concentrated on the hands they had been dealt.

"If you ladies would like to watch, I'm sure these men wouldn't mind having an audience," Dyson said.

"I don't think we need to be distracting them," Cecilia said. "We can go back to the hotel."

"Why not allow me to show you around the town instead?" Dyson suggested. "After all, once you're married, Silverhill is going to be your home."

Rose said, "Yes, let's do that. All right, Cecilia?"

Cecilia nodded and said, "I suppose that will be fine," but she didn't sound or look too enthusiastic about the idea.

Dyson led the way out of the saloon as he had led the way in.

Bo got the idea that the saloonkeeper really enjoyed being at the head of this parade of beautiful young women. All eyes were turned their way, and that appealed to Dyson's vanity.

As they headed up the boardwalk, he pointed out the various businesses. After a while they came to a large barn with attached corrals, and an adobe office building beside the barn. A sign on the building read ANIMAS FREIGHT COMPANY.

Smiling, Dyson said, "Now, right here is probably the most important business in Silverhill . . . and I'm including my own saloon in that. George McCallum's freight wagons carry all the silver that comes from the smelters up to the railroad at Lordsburg. Other freight lines bring in supplies from there and from El Paso, but it's the silver shipments that give the town its life."

Several men sat in chairs on the porch of the freight company's office. They had shotguns and rifles across their laps, but they stood up and held the weapons at their side as the ladies approached. Their faces were solemn as they took off their hats and nodded politely.

A portly man with a mostly bald egg-shaped head and pince-nez spectacles came out of the office and said, "Good morning, Mr. Dyson. I take it these are the lovely young women I've heard so much about?"

"They certainly are, Mr. McCallum," Dyson replied. He introduced each of the ladies in turn.

"It is a pleasure to meet you, ladies, and an honor, as well," the freight company owner said.

"Are you involved in this . . . competition . . . Mr. McCallum?" Cecilia asked.

McCallum laughed and shook his head. "If you mean, am I taking part, then good heavens, no, my dear. I already have a wife, a dear lady to whom I have been happily married for nearly thirty years." He raised a finger. "Ah, but if I was thirty-*five* years younger, I might well risk competing for a chance at wedded bliss with one of you ladies."

"If you were thirty-five years younger, that might be all right," Rose said with her typical bluntness.

McCallum cocked his head to the side for a second, as if puzzled, then laughed again. "Your honesty is very charming, my dear," he told her. "I wish all of you the best, and I hope the contests turn out to your satisfaction."

Dyson asked, "Are you going to be watching any of them, George?"

McCallum shook his head and said, "No, I'm afraid not. This is a pretty busy time for us right now, you know."

"Well, we'd best be on our way and continue our tour of the town," Dyson said to the ladies.

As they started to turn away, Cecilia said over her shoulder, "It was nice to meet you, Mr. McCallum."

"Likewise, my dear, likewise," he called after her.

As they were crossing the street, Rose dropped back a little and said to Bo and Scratch, "Who are those men with rifles and shotguns, sitting out in front of the freight office?"

"Guards," Bo said.

Scratch added, "I reckon McCallum must have some silver in there he's gettin' ready to ship to Lordsburg."

"You may have noticed that there's no bank here," Bo said. "In cases like that, where a bank hasn't been formed yet in a community, the freight company office usually has a safe, or at least a room with a good sturdy door and walls, where valuable cargo can be locked up."

"Those men looked really serious . . . and dangerous."

Bo smiled and said, "They're not a threat to anybody . . . unless you're trying to rob the place."

It was past mid-morning before Dyson finished the impromptu tour of Silverhill, including the old Spanish mission, which had some beautiful stained-glass windows, golden candleholders, and paintings and tapestries, which had been faded by time but were still quite impressive.

As the group walked back toward the Territorial House, the crowd that had been following them earlier had thinned out to only a few curious onlookers. The novelty of having the ladies in town had worn off a little, Bo mused . . . but it would come roaring back once the contests that involved more than playing cards got under way. He expected those other competitions would have plenty of spectators.

He and Scratch were still alert. Officially, the job they had agreed to do for Cyrus Keegan was over, but they still felt a considerable amount of responsibility to look out for the young women, who had become their friends.

Because of that wary attitude, Bo spotted the group of riders reining to a stop in front of the hotel. They were covered in dust, as if they had been on the trail for quite a while, and the horses looked tired, like they had been pushed long and hard. The six men swung down from their saddles and looped the reins around the hitch rail, then stepped up onto the porch.

As they did, one of them glanced along the street and stopped short at the sight of the young women. He straightened, a determined expression coming over his face.

It was a face that Bo recognized, despite the trail dust and beard stubble. So did Scratch, judging by the way he muttered, "Oh, shoot," under his breath.

Hugh Craddock took a step off the porch and said to tthe ladies in a loud, clear voice, "There you are, Miss Spaulding. I knew I'd catch up to you. I'm not just about to let the woman I'm going to marry get away from me!"

Chapter 29

The five men with Craddock were cowboys from his ranch. Bo vaguely remembered most of them from the encounters in Fort Worth.

They spread out in a line behind Craddock, clearly ready to back any play that he might make.

Forbes Dyson had come to a stop, too. He regarded Craddock with a cold stare as he moved smoothly to get between Craddock and the five young women.

"Excuse me, sir," he said. "Do you know these ladies?"

"Of course I do," Craddock snapped impatiently. He stepped to the side to look around Dyson and went on, "You remember me, don't you, Miss Spaulding?"

"Unfortunately, I do," Cecilia said.

"Now, that's no way to talk about the fella you're going to marry!"

"The only one who's ever said anything about the two of us getting married is you," Cecilia told him. "I have no intention of taking you as my husband, Mr. Craddock."

"That's right. You need to go back and marry that poor

woman you brought out West and then abandoned," Rose added.

Craddock pointed a finger and said, "Now, that was Keegan's fault for letting that old maid fool him. Once I saw her in person, there was no way anybody could've blamed me for not wanting to go through with the arrangement."

Dyson moved again to block Craddock's path.

"I don't know exactly what you're talking about, friend," he said, "but you definitely have the wrong idea where Miss Spaulding is concerned. You can't marry her, because she's come here to Silverhill to marry someone else."

Craddock sneered and demanded, "Who? Sure as hell not you, fancy pants!"

Dyson's jaw tightened. At the same time, Bo saw a lean figure appear on the hotel porch.

He wasn't surprised that Jack Bouma had put in an appearance just as the confrontation between Dyson and Craddock started to heat up.

The gunman was behind Craddock and the cowboys he had brought with him from Texas. Bo could tell they had no idea the sort of threat that lurked at their backs.

Cecilia must have seen Bouma, too, and she knew the danger he represented. She stepped forward quickly, planted herself beside Dyson, and said, "Mr. Craddock, I'm willing to talk with you, but I make no other promises. Right now, though, you must let us pass. I'll send word to you when we can meet. Where will you be staying?"

Before Craddock could answer, Dyson said, "You don't have to do that, Miss Spaulding. You don't owe this man anything, whoever he is—"

"If this is where you're staying, then I am, too," Craddock broke in. "I'm not going to let you slip away from me again."

"You can't stay here," Dyson said. "The hotel is full."

"Reckon I'll find that out for myself," Craddock snapped.

Bo stepped forward and said, "Dyson's telling you the truth, Craddock. In case you hadn't noticed, the whole town's pretty much full."

Craddock stared at him in surprise and said, "You're still here?" His gaze flicked toward Scratch and back. "And that other old pelican, as well? I figured the two of you would have started back to Fort Worth by now."

"We're stayin' around here for a spell," Scratch drawled. He had both thumbs hooked in his gunbelt, so his hands weren't far from the Remingtons.

Craddock looked around, obviously puzzled by the crowd and the festive atmosphere, and said, "What in blazes is going on in this town, anyway?"

"You can ask anyone about that," Dyson said. "I'm sure there are plenty of people in Silverhill who would be glad to tell you. Now step aside."

For a moment, the two men stared at each other with hate in their eyes. It had to be a purely instinctive thing, Bo thought, since Dyson and Craddock had just met.

Up on the porch, Jack Bouma was like a string pulled taut, ready to snap. And if he did, guns would blaze. Bo was poised to grab Cecilia, who was closest to him, and drag her to the ground, hopefully out of the line of fire. He knew Scratch would do what he could to protect the other young women.

Then Hugh Craddock said, "All right, but this isn't over." He looked at Cecilia. "I'll send word to you here at the hotel once we've found a place to stay."

"You're wasting your time," Dyson said, but Cecilia nodded her agreement with Craddock's statement.

Bouma stepped aside as Dyson ushered the ladies onto the porch and into the hotel. For the first time, Craddock noticed the gunman, who lounged against a post with a smirk on his face. Craddock frowned, and Bo thought maybe the rancher recognized the sort of man Bouma was and realized what had almost happened just now.

Quietly, Bo said to Scratch, "You go on inside and make sure the ladies are settled in their rooms. I'm going to talk to Craddock."

"Best be careful," Scratch said. "That hombre's half loco when it comes to Miss Cecilia."

"Maybe more than half," Bo said.

He walked over to Craddock, who said, "I didn't expect to see you again, Creel, but maybe it's a good thing you're here. You can explain to me what the hell is going on in this town. I know there's some sort of mining boom, but this seems like something else."

"You remember the ladies were coming out here to meet the men they thought they were going to marry?"

"Of course I remember."

"Well, that's not the way it turned out," Bo said. "The whole thing was . . . well, kind of a trick, I guess you could say."

"They don't have husbands waiting for them, after all?"

"They have a whole *town* full of potential husbands," Bo said.

He went on to explain about the competitions that would decide who won the right to ask for the hands of the young women.

"A lot of the businessmen in town chipped in to pay Cyrus Keegan's fee, and some of the men who signed up for the contests contributed, too."

Craddock stared at him as if he couldn't believe what Bo had just said.

"That's the craziest thing I've ever heard," he said. "You mean to say that Miss Spaulding and the other ladies are going along with it?"

"They haven't promised to abide by the results of the competition," Bo said, "but they're at least willing to talk about it.

To tell you the truth, I think some of them sort of like the idea. It seems romantic to them."

"It seems insane to me," Craddock said.

His men had been listening to the conversation as they stood in the street, beside the horses. One of them grinned and said, "Hey, boss, sounds to me like you ought to enter some of those contests. You're a damn good shot. You've won a few turkey shoots back home."

"And we've got some fast horses, if they get a chance to rest up a mite," another puncher said. "Might stand a chance in that horse race."

"Shut up," Craddock barked at them. "I'm not entering some stupid contest to get a woman to marry me, when she ought to have the good sense to do it just because I want her to."

Now, *that* was a loco idea for any man to have in his head, Bo thought, and if Craddock genuinely believed in what he was saying—and he certainly seemed to—then Bo didn't really see the sense in talking to him anymore.

There was something else Craddock needed to know, though, so Bo said, "Did you see that fella who was standing on the porch when you turned around toward the hotel?"

"Fella with the red shirt and black vest?"

"That's him," Bo said. Bouma had faded from sight again, but he was probably still around somewhere close by. "His name's Jack Bouma. He's a gunfighter, and he works for Forbes Dyson. Last night he killed a man who got in Dyson's way."

"Is that supposed to scare me?" Craddock asked.

"Whether you're scared or not is none of my business. I'm just telling you what happened, that's all."

"I'm not worried about some shootist. I can take care of myself."

Craddock sounded confident. A couple of his men looked a little concerned, though. They were tough, swaggering cowboys, but they probably weren't fast-draw artists.

"Dyson's got a lot tied up in this fandango he's putting on,"

Bo said. "He's not going to let anything get in the way of it being successful. You might do well to remember that, Craddock."

With that, he turned away and stepped up onto the porch to go on in the hotel. He hadn't had any obligation to warn Hugh Craddock, but he had gone out of his way to do so, anyway.

Now whatever happened was on Craddock's head, just the way it should be.

Bo met Forbes Dyson on the stairs in the hotel. The saloon owner was on his way back down from the second floor.

Dyson stopped and said, "Did you get that lunatic to understand that he can't just waltz in here and claim Miss Spaulding as his bride?"

"He tried to do the same thing back in Fort Worth," Bo said. "He's used to being able to just take whatever he wants."

Dyson grunted contemptuously and said, "Well, he can't do that in Silverhill."

That was probably because Dyson already filled that position in Silverhill, Bo thought. He didn't like being challenged for it, either.

"He's liable to cause trouble," Bo warned.

Dyson shook his head and said, "I'm not worried about trouble. I can handle it."

"You mean Jack Bouma can handle it."

Dyson gave him a flat, angry look. "Bouma works for me. He takes my orders and is an extension of my will. Understand?"

"Sure," Bo said easily.

"Anyway, don't underestimate my personal capabilities, Creel. I've run into plenty of men who thought they could force me into doing what they wanted. But I'm still here, one of the biggest men in this town . . . hell, in the whole territory . . . and they're not."

Bo changed the subject by nodding toward the second-floor landing and asking, "Did the ladies get into their rooms all right?"

"They did. Your friend Morton checked every one of the rooms first and made sure no one was lurking in any of them."

Bo nodded. He was glad to hear that Scratch was being careful. He didn't expect any less from his old trail partner.

Dyson went past him and on down the stairs. Bo finished the climb to the second floor and found Scratch sitting in the armchair, which they had put back under the window at the end of the hall. The silver-haired Texan had his right ankle cocked on his left knee, but he put his leg down and stood up as Bo approached.

"Were you able to talk any sense into Craddock's head?"

"What do you think?"

Scratch chuckled and said, "I'd bet a hatful of pesos you didn't. I ain't sure you could drive any sense through that hombre's skull with a sledgehammer."

"I warned him about Jack Bouma," Bo said. "I figured he deserved to know what he was getting himself and his men into if he's determined to be stubborn about this."

"How'd those cowboys take it?"

"Some of them weren't too happy about it, but I got the feeling they'd stick with Craddock, anyway, and do whatever he wants."

"You got to admire a man who rides for the brand, even if it ain't always the smartest thing to do."

Bo leaned his head toward the nearest door to a room where one of the ladies was staying and asked, "Everybody get settled in all right for a while?"

"I'd say so. I ain't heard a peep from any of 'em since they went in their rooms. Miss Cecilia said they'd rest for a spell before they went to dinner." Scratch grinned. "And then this afternoon is the strongman competition. You ready for that?"

Bo frowned and said, "What do you mean? *I'm* not competing in that or any of the other competitions. At my age, the last thing in the world I need is a young wife!"

"I meant just in case there's any trouble."

"With Hugh Craddock in town," Bo said with a sigh and a slow nod, "that could be what's waiting for us, all right."

Chapter 30

Philip Armbruster felt like a complete and utter fool as he rode down Silverhill's main street on a mule with such a rough gait and bony back that every step the animal took jolted the reporter unmercifully.

It was bad enough that he was riding this ugly beast, but in addition, he had traded his tweed suit for the rough homespun of a Mexican peasant's pajama-like garb. The wide, ragged brim of a straw sombrero shaded his face, which had mud rubbed on it to darken it.

No one who looked very closely at him was going to take him for a Mexican, but the odds of anyone paying that much attention to such a pathetic specimen were small, claimed Jaime Mendoza.

To make discovery even less likely, Armbruster's spectacles were hidden inside his shirt rather than perched on his nose. Not wearing them made his vision a bit blurry, but he could see well enough to get around without them.

Now that they knew the two old men who had been with the young women before were also here in Silverhill, Mendoza deemed it too dangerous for Armbruster to walk around in his normal clothes. They had gotten too good a look at him during the confrontation. The old-timers might spot him, recognize him, and realize that if Armbruster was in Silverhill, Mendoza might be, too.

"You have done well, Señor Armbruster," Mendoza had said the night before, after Armbruster delivered his report. "The news you bring about this . . . this competition . . . is surprising, but I see no reason not to believe what you say."

"It's the truth," Armbruster had replied as they sat beside the campfire. "I've never really heard anything like it, either."

The men had been listening to Armbruster tell Mendoza what he had discovered. One of them grinned and called out, "Maybe you can win the señorita who has stolen your heart, Jaime!"

Mendoza smiled and nodded at that gibe, but a second later, his gun slid swiftly and smoothly from its holster and rose to point at the man's face. Mendoza's expression turned suddenly hard as stone.

"Jaime Mendoza does not *compete* for what he wants," the bandit chief said in a low, dangerous voice as he eared back the revolver's hammer. "He *takes* it."

Wide-eyed with fear, the joker stammered out, "Of . . . of course, Jaime. I meant no offense . . . *Es verdad*, Jaime, I meant nothing!"

"A man who means nothing should keep his mouth shut." Mendoza kept the pistol pointed at the man's face for a moment longer, then lowered the hammer and pouched the iron. "You would do well to remember that."

"*Sí*, Jaime, I will remember—"

Mendoza had swung back toward Armbruster, clearly dismissing the other man. He said, "Did you see many Mexicans in Silverhill?"

"Some," Armbruster replied. "The town seems to be mostly Americans, but there were a good number of your people, too."

"Then no one will notice a few more riding into town, one by one, eh?" Mendoza looked around at his men and got the expected mutters and nods of agreement.

So that was the plan. The bandits would filter into town individually, at different times and from different directions, so it was unlikely that anyone would pay attention to them.

None of them owned a fancy saddle except Mendoza, and he had a spare that was plain and strictly functional. He would use that one and ride in on one of the extra mounts instead of his fine black stallion. If he left off his ornately decorated charro jacket, the rest of his garb was nondescript enough.

Armbruster was actually the one who had had to make the most changes to his appearance. That morning, they had stopped at a small homestead a dozen miles from the settlement and had "borrowed" the clothes and sombrero from the farmer who struggled to scratch a living out of the place.

Mendoza had thrown the man a few pesos to compensate him for his trouble. He could have just as easily gunned him down, and the peasant had known that and had been appropriately, gushingly, grateful to have his life spared.

He had thrown the mule into the deal, as well. Whether the animal or any of his clothing would ever be returned was doubtful, but at least he'd still been breathing as the bandits rode away.

Now the reporter was in Silverhill, and as he drew back on the reins and brought the mule to a stop in front of a hardware store where there was a vacant space at the hitch rack, he thought once again that perhaps it would be better for him to find some hole and hide until whatever was going to happen here . . . was over.

He had known when his editor sent him here to this godforsaken border country that the assignment would be dangerous. But if he was successful . . . if he wrote a series of dispatches about life with a band of Mexican bandits and it appeared in newspapers all over the country . . . his reputation as a journalist would soar.

He could probably even turn those stories into a popular book, and fame and fortune would follow. Those rewards were worth the risk, Armbruster had decided.

His confidence had been shaken when he rode into the bandit camp after a meeting had been arranged through a go-between in El Paso. Seeing the wild, careless killers who made up Jaime Mendoza's band had made Armbruster's belly go hollow. Mendoza had seemed to be the worst of them all, and Armbruster had been convinced he would never get out of there alive.

Instead, Mendoza had taken to him right away, perhaps sensing that Armbruster was also an ambitious man, just like him, and by now he almost seemed to regard the reporter as a member of the gang.

Mendoza certainly hadn't hesitated to send him on that scouting mission into Silverhill the previous evening. He had trusted Armbruster to come back and report accurately . . . and that was what Armbruster had done.

But it was probably a good thing the railroad hadn't reached Silverhill yet. If there had been a train pulling out last night, Armbruster knew there was a good chance he would have been on it, putting all this insanity of pretending to be a Mexican bandido behind him.

Hoping for the best, he swung down from the saddle and tied the mule at the hitch rack, then joined the crowd drifting toward the Silver King Palace.

At one of the poker tables in the raised gambling area inside the saloon, Kenton O'Keefe looked at the cards he'd been dealt, and with the experience of years spent playing in big games, he knew immediately what he needed to do.

When the dealer came back to him, he discarded two cards, a five and a seven. The two new cards didn't help, though. He'd had a pair of tens and a jack, and he didn't catch anything that would improve them. A pair of tens wasn't worth risking much on, but if the bets weren't too big, he might stay in a time or two, just to assess the chances of bluffing with them.

But when one of the other players pushed in a gold eagle and another raised that bet ten more, O'Keefe dropped out. No sense in throwing money away.

And money was why he was here, after all. He had no interest whatsoever in "winning" a bride, although he had to admit that all five young women were very lovely. If he *had* been looking to get married, any of them might have tempted him.

The life of a drifting gambler was nothing to subject a young woman to, however, and O'Keefe had been following the cards for too long to ever give them up. He would die at a poker table, or in some lonely hotel room, and he accepted that fate.

Until then, he loved the competition, and he enjoyed taking money from less skilled players. The last man standing in this tournament got the right to ask one of those young women to marry him, but before it reached that point, Kenton O'Keefe would take his winnings and move on.

One of the other players raked in the pot and said, "I don't know about you fellas, but I could use a break to stretch my legs and move around a mite."

Mutters of agreement came from the other men. O'Keefe nodded and reached down to the floor beside him to pick up his hat. He flicked some dust off it with a finger and put it on as he got to his feet.

"Back here in half an hour?" he asked.

"Sounds good to me," a man said.

O'Keefe crooked a finger at one of Forbes Dyson's men who stood nearby. The bouncer ambled over with a shotgun tucked under his arm.

"We're taking a short break," O'Keefe told him.

The man nodded, understanding that he would stand guard

over the table, with its piles of coins and greenbacks in front of each chair. No one would bother the money with the burly shotgun wielder watching it.

And if the guard himself happened to be tempted, the thought of what would happen to him if Dyson ever found out would keep him from acting on the impulse. For this big competition to work, Dyson had to run clean, honest contests.

Kenton O'Keefe went down the steps from the gambling area and walked over to the bar. The bartender knew his preferences by now and brought him a shot of rye whiskey and a beer.

After downing the rye, O'Keefe picked up the mug of beer and half turned to look across the big room. As he did, Forbes Dyson came through the batwings and strode toward the stairs. The gunman Jack Bouma was with him, trailing behind Dyson with an easy, almost lazy stride. Arrogance radiated from him like a mirage rising from the desert sands in the heat.

Like most gamblers—like most *successful* gamblers—O'Keefe knew when to play a hunch. He indulged the one he felt now. When Dyson and Bouma had disappeared up the stairs, he swallowed more of the beer but left the mug half full as he ambled toward the stairs and headed up after them.

When he reached the landing, he looked along the hall toward the door of what he knew to be Forbes Dyson's office. It was just swinging closed. Since Dyson and Bouma weren't in sight, O'Keefe assumed both of them had gone into the office.

His steps quiet on the carpet runner, he walked along the hall until he reached the door. He leaned closer to it so his keen ears could make out most of what was being said inside.

"Biggest crowd for the boxing match," Forbes Dyson was saying.

Bouma responded, "And that's when . . . make our move."

The gunfighter's voice had faded out in the middle of that sentence because clinking sounds interfered with O'Keefe hearing it. The gambler knew by those sounds that someone in the office, probably Dyson, was pouring drinks.

"It'll be up to you to make sure all the men are in place," Dyson went on.

"I know the job, Forbes," Bouma said with a note of irritation in his voice.

Out in the hallway, O'Keefe heard that and thought that the gunman sounded more like someone who was partners with Dyson, not necessarily an employee.

That might well be the case. Whatever they were up to, they could have gone into the scheme together, with Dyson providing the money and an air of respectability while Bouma furnished the necessary gun skills and the men to carry out some violent chore.

O'Keefe was pondering that when he heard a footstep near the door. He drew back, turned, and moved swiftly and soundlessly along the hall. He turned again when the doorknob rattled, so that when Jack Bouma stepped out into the hallway, sauntering toward the office with a smile on his face.

Bouma stopped short and frowned.

"You want something, O'Keefe?"

"I thought I'd see if Mr. Dyson could change some large bills for me," O'Keefe replied easily. As it always did in situations such as this, his brain worked quickly.

Dyson appeared in the doorway behind Bouma in time to hear what O'Keefe said. He asked, "How much did you have in mind, O'Keefe?"

"A couple of hundred," the gambler replied, shrugging.

Dyson nodded and waved him on. "Come on in. Jack, I'll see you later."

"Yeah," Bouma said. He cast a narrow glance from the corners of his eyes at O'Keefe as the two men passed in the hallway. The gambler saw the look but appeared to take no notice of it.

He already knew that Bouma didn't like him. But Bouma

didn't like much of anybody, so O'Keefe didn't take it personally.

Once he was in the office, O'Keefe took his wallet from an inside coat pocket and extracted two hundred-dollar bills from it. He dropped them on Dyson's desk while the saloon owner unlocked a cashbox and took out ten double eagles.

"Usually people want to trade in the coins for currency," Dyson commented, "not the other way around. It's easier to carry that way."

"I have always liked the heft of a handful of double eagles better than a piece of folding money," O'Keefe said. "Reckon I'm old fashioned."

"How's the game going downstairs?" Dyson took a cigar from his vest pocket and put it in his mouth. He didn't offer one to his visitor. "Are you out already?"

"No. My table is just taking a break," O'Keefe replied with a shake of his head.

"I have to say, Kenton, I'm a little surprised you signed up to play in this tournament. I realize we don't know each other all that well, but I wouldn't have figured you for a man who wants to win a wife."

"Never claimed that I do." The answer was framed in the gambler's soft Virginia drawl.

Dyson regarded him with renewed interest for a moment, then chuckled. "You plan to drop out and take your winnings before the tournament's actually over, is that it?"

"That's allowed, isn't it? Or does a man have to go broke to get out of this game?" O'Keefe's tone hardened slightly. "If those are the rules, they should have been made clear beforehand."

"No, no," Dyson said quickly, waving the hand that had just taken the cigar out of his mouth. "There's nothing stopping you from leaving whenever it suits you. Most of the other players won't care. That'll just be one less man they have to beat in order to claim the hand of one of the young ladies."

Weighing in his hand the coins Dyson had given him, O'Keefe asked, "Do you really expect those women to go along with your plans?"

"They've agreed to at least consider it. And let's face it . . . if they do back out in the end, that will hardly be my fault, will it? And by that time, a lot of money will have poured into Silverhill already. The town will be on more solid footing. The mines are operating at full blast right now. The biggest shipment so far will be rolling out on some of George McCallum's wagons in a day or two. But that may not last. What will Silverhill do then? The town will stand a much better chance of surviving if it has something else going for it."

"You sound like a civic booster from back East, Forbes. You plan on turning Silverhill into the mail-order bride capital of New Mexico Territory?"

Dyson laughed heartily and shook his head. "I wouldn't go that far. But if there's a healthy profit in it, who knows?"

O'Keefe thanked Dyson for changing the bills, then left the office. Trading the greenbacks for double eagles had been mostly a ruse, an excuse for him to be found in the corridor when Bouma stepped out of the office, but the brief conversation with Dyson—as well as the one he had overheard between Dyson and Bouma—had made the gambler more convinced than ever that Dyson had some sort of plan to enjoy a big payday while all this hoopla over the mail-order brides was going on.

And if that actually was the case, there was no reason in the world why Kenton O'Keefe shouldn't cut himself in on it.

Chapter 31

Bo and Scratch stood on the porch in front of the Territorial House. Next to the them were the five young women. Rose, Beth, and Luella all pressed up against the railing and rested their hands on it as they looked out with eager anticipation at what was going on in the street. Cecilia and Jean were a bit more subdued but still definitely interested.

Five wagons had been lined up side by side, and then the teams that pulled them into position had been unhitched and led away.

Today, instead of horses, men would pull these wagons.

The five contestants had sturdy ropes wrapped around their chests and attached to the wagons. The singletrees had been lifted and tied so they would be out of the way.

The contestants shook their arms and rolled their shoulders to make sure their muscles were loose. They kicked and scuffed at the dirt, looking for just the right spots to plant their feet when the signal came to start pulling.

Fifty feet ahead of them, a line had been drawn in the dirt and marked by a flag on a stick at each end. Each man had to pull his wagon that far by the sheer strength of his body in order to qualify for the next round of the competition. People crowded into the street beyond that finish line, as well as along the boardwalks, to cheer on the contestants.

Scratch pointed toward the burly redheaded man at the far end of the line and said, "That fella right there looks to me like the favorite. You can tell by his clothes he's a miner. Probably spent thousands of hours swingin' a pick or usin' a sledgehammer to bust rock."

"That builds up a man's arms and shoulders," Bo said, "but it's leg strength that's going to win this competition. Look at that hombre in the middle."

"His legs are the shortest in the bunch."

"Yeah, but they're as big around as a tree." Bo nodded. "That's the one my money would be on, if I were a betting man."

"But you ain't, except for a card game now and then."

Bo shrugged. "He's still the one I think will win."

"We'll just see," Scratch said confidently.

Cecilia looked over at them and said, "You almost sound like you're comparing the qualities of livestock."

"Well, a human bein' is an animal, too, Miss Cecilia."

"Yes, I'm all too aware of that," she said.

Bo nudged Scratch and said, "Here comes Dyson. I reckon he's going to get things started."

Wearing his expensive black hat to shield his face against the glare of the afternoon sun, Forbes Dyson strode to the middle of the street in front of the gathered contestants and raised his hands for quiet. Gradually, the crowd settled down and became attentive.

"Ladies and gentlemen," Dyson began, "especially five young ladies in particular, the reason we're here today . . ."

He stopped long enough to take off his hat and sweep it in front of him as he bowed to the young women on the hotel porch. Then he straightened, put the hat back on, and continued with his spiel.

"We're gathered here today to witness not only a competition but also a demonstration of strength unlike any that has ever been seen before in Silverhill. These men"—he flung out a hand toward the contestants—"these gallant sons of Hercules, will move those wagons, normally pulled by teams of horses or mules or oxen, by the sheer power of their own bodies. Here are the men who will attempt this prodigious feat!"

Dyson pointed at the burly redheaded miner.

"Seamus Donnigan!"

Donnigan waved as cheers and whistles came from the crowd. He clasped both hands together and shook them over his head like a prizefighter.

"Albert Powell! Big Dog McCreary! Fred Winchell! Joe Hammond!"

With each name that Dyson called out, one of the men grinned and waved to acknowledge the crowd's acclaim. The short, thick-legged man Bo had pointed out as his pick to win was Big Dog McCreary. His ruddy face, which had a distinct bulldog-like cast to it, had to be the reason for the nickname.

McCreary turned, grinned at the five young women lined up along the porch railing, and waved a hamlike hand at them. Rose and Beth laughed and returned the wave.

Once all the applause and cheering had died down again, Dyson called, "Gentlemen, take your places! Are you ready?"

He paused until he received eager nods from all five men.

"Then the contest begins *now!*"

Another wave of thunderous cheering rolled along the street as the competitors leaned forward and surged against the ropes that bound them to the wagons.

For a moment, as the men strained, it appeared that the wagons weren't going to move. Then, with a creaking of wheels and axles, the heavy vehicles lurched forward a few inches. The contestants threw their strength into the effort again.

The wagons began to roll. They didn't travel fast, but they moved steadily. As the competitors grunted and strained, the wagons slowly built up speed. Powerful legs churned against the dirt of the street as the men fought to keep the vehicles moving.

Big Dog McCreary reached the finish line first, as Bo expected he might, but this wasn't a contest of speed. Seamus Donnigan was close behind McCreary; then one by one the other men crossed the line, as well.

As the last man reached the goal, Forbes Dyson waved his arms to signal that this round was over.

"All right, everyone is moving on," Dyson announced. "The competitors will rest while we prepare the wagons for the next round."

The men shrugged out of the rope harnesses. A couple of them leaned over and placed their hands against their thighs to steady themselves as they dragged in great lungfuls of air.

A dozen burly men hurried out to turn the wagons around, and then they carried sandbags, stumbling a little under the weight, and placed them in the backs of the vehicles. When four sandbags had been loaded into each wagon, Dyson called the competitors out into the street again.

"They can't possibly move those wagons with that extra weight in them," Luella said. "They were barely able to budge them the first time."

"I bet they can. Some of them, anyway," Rose said. "You wait and see."

Bo was curious about what was going to happen, but as the contestants got ready to begin the second round, he also looked around the crowd, searching for any signs of potential trouble.

He was especially on the lookout for Hugh Craddock, and after a few minutes, Bo spotted the rancher. Craddock was on the opposite boardwalk with his men, but he didn't give any indication that he was planning to disrupt the contest.

Instead, he just stared across at Cecilia with an intent expression on his face. She must have noticed the same thing, because when she suddenly cleared her throat, Bo glanced over at her and saw that her features had taken on a pink hue.

She was blushing.

"I wish that man would stop staring at me that way," she murmured.

"Want me to go talk to him?" Bo asked quietly.

Cecilia shook her head. "As long as he's not doing anything else, I suppose he has a right to look," she said. "After all, there's no harm in that, is there?"

The crowd jostled the mild-mannered Mexican peasant back and forth. Philip Armbruster felt himself getting more annoyed every time someone casually jolted his shoulder and made no apology, and in fact didn't seem even to notice what they had done.

He didn't allow himself to display that irritation, though. He didn't know exactly what Jaime Mendoza was planning to do, but the bandit chief had made it clear that Armbruster shouldn't allow his masquerade to be discovered. Mendoza didn't want it known that he or any of his men were in town until it was time for them to make their move . . . whatever that was going to be.

In the meantime, Armbruster watched the strongman competition with interest. The big miner he had talked to in the Silver King the previous night, Seamus Donnigan, was one of the contestants, and he seemed to be doing well. He had finished second in the first round, not that the order of finish really meant anything, according to what Armbruster had overheard in the crowd. The weight of the wagons would continue to be increased until only one man could pull his vehicle over the finish line. That man would be the winner and would be allowed to sit down with the ladies and try to convince one of them to marry him.

Because of his friendly conversation with Donnigan, Armbruster supposed he might as well root for the miner to emerge triumphant in the competition.

The second round got under way, and as the crowd cheered them on, the contestants struggled mightily to pull the loaded wagons. Donnigan and the man called Big Dog McCreary got their wagons moving at the same time. The other three men took longer, but eventually, their wagons rolled slowly toward the finish line, too.

Before they got there, one man suddenly stopped, dropped to his knees, and shook his head. His face was so red, it appeared that he might pop at any moment. He fell forward and caught himself on his hands, then stayed there on all fours as he tried to recover.

Jeers from the crowd poured down on the man, which was hardly fair, thought Armbruster. It wasn't like any of those people could have done any better.

The other two contestants continued on and dragged their wagons across the finish line before collapsing, as well. Donnigan and McCreary leaned against their wagons, breathing hard as big drops of sweat rolled down their faces.

"What an incredible effort!" Forbes Dyson proclaimed as he came forward into the street and raised his voice. "Give all the competitors a big hand, ladies and gentlemen!"

Armbruster didn't applaud. He thought it would look odd for a peon like he was supposed to be to do such a thing. Instead, he stood there and kept his head tilted forward a little so the sombrero's brim obscured his face to a certain extent.

Someone bumped into him again, and as he tightened his jaw against the angry retort he wanted to make, the person leaned close to his ear and said, "Be ready, amigo. Soon you will witness daring that will thrill your readers when you write about it."

Armbruster glanced over and saw Jaime Mendoza standing there. He asked in a half whisper, "What are you going to do?"

"When the final round takes place and all eyes are on the

street, a distraction will take place. And then I will swoop in, claim my beloved, and leave this place behind us. As I said, be ready, or you will be left behind. There will be no time to waste. Where is your mule?"

Armbruster leaned his head toward the mouth of a nearby alley. "Tied up back there. I can get to him quickly. But how is a mule going to keep up with your horses?"

"Some mules are fast. Do your best, amigo. But if today marks our parting, remember your new friends fondly, eh? And write our story well."

"Of course," Armbruster said with a nod.

Unknown to Mendoza, the bandit had just given him a way out of the dilemma in which he found himself, Armbruster thought. When Mendoza and the others fled from Silverhill, he simply wouldn't go with them. Mendoza would believe that he hadn't been able to get away.

It meant giving up the opportunity to experience more of the bandido life, but Armbruster believed he already had plenty of material for his stories—and the book he would make from them.

"Good luck," he added to Mendoza.

"Luck?" Mendoza repeated. "I need no luck! I am—"

He stopped short, evidently realizing it wouldn't be a good idea to proclaim himself a notorious bandit in the middle of this crowd. With a cocky grin, Mendoza moved on instead, vanishing quickly into the press of people watching as the next round of the competition got under way.

More sandbags were loaded into the wagons. The straining was monumental this time as the contestants fought to move them.

Big Dog McCreary got his wagon rolling first, followed a moment later by Seamus Donnigan. A third competitor followed Donnigan toward the finish line, but the fourth man finally slumped back against his vehicle and waved his hands weakly to signify that he was giving up before even getting started in this round.

Over on the hotel porch, Scratch grinned and said, "Looks like it's gonna come down to those two fellas we picked to root for, Bo."

"I'm not actually rooting for any of them," Bo said. "I just pointed out the one I thought stood the best chance of winning."

Rose turned her head toward the Texans and said, "Well, I'm rooting for that big redheaded man. He's more handsome than the other two."

"I'm not much of a judge of that, I reckon," Bo said.

"Well, you won't wind up having to marry one of them."

Cecilia said sharply, "None of us *have* to marry any of the men who win the competitions. We don't *have* to get married at all."

"Speak for yourself," Beth said. "I came to Silverhill to get a husband!"

Cecilia might have argued, but at that moment the third man gave up short of the finish line, too, just as Seamus Donnigan crossed it. Big Dog McCreary was already past the line.

"Now it's down to just the two of 'em, like I thought it was gonna be," Scratch said. "Looks like we got the final round comin' up!"

Chapter 32

Donnigan and McCreary were given a little extra time to rest after more sandbags had been piled into the backs of the wagons. Then Forbes Dyson called the competitors back to their marks.

"This has been an epic battle, ladies and gentlemen," he told the crowd, "and it will continue as long as necessary until we have crowned a winner! If both men reach the finish line, more sandbags will be added to the load!"

A groan came from Seamus Donnigan.

"Are you tryin' to kill us, Mr. Dyson?" he asked, but the big grin on his face seemed to indicate that he didn't mean the question seriously.

"Not at all, not at all, Donnigan," the saloon owner replied. "We just have to make certain that the winner is truly worthy of the hand of one of these fine ladies!"

He waved toward the five young women at the railing of the hotel porch. That brought more cheers from the crowd.

"Let's get on with it," McCreary rumbled. "I'm ready to send this bumpkin packing."

"Bumpkin, is it?" Donnigan demanded. He was still grinning, but the fires of competition burned brightly in his eyes. "Get ready to eat my dust, you stumpy little varmint!"

They pulled on the rope harnesses and leaned against them, ready to start pulling.

Over on the hotel porch, Scratch said, "I don't think they'll be able to budge those wagons. The fellas put too many sandbags in 'em. I ain't sure a team of mules could pull 'em!"

"I hope those poor men don't give themselves apoplexy," Jean said.

"They can do it," Rose said, and Beth and Luella nodded agreement.

Frowning, Cecilia muttered, "This is getting a little barbaric."

Scratch heard her and said, "Wait until the bare-knuckles boxin' matches tomorrow evenin'."

"I may not be able to watch those," Cecilia responded with a shake of her head.

In the street, Forbes Dyson shouted, "Go!"

Donnigan and McCreary surged forward against the ropes. Their legs drove hard. They leaned so far ahead, their bodies formed a sharp angle with the ground. The thick ropes were drawn so taut, they fairly hummed.

The wagons remained motionless.

Lips drew far back from teeth as the two men grimaced from pain and effort. Donnigan clenched his fists and slowly swung his arms back and forth in an attempt to build up more force. McCreary just grunted and strained. Donnigan's face was as red as his hair, and McCreary was equally flushed.

Donnigan's wagon suddenly moved about an inch.

He stumbled and tried to right himself in time to keep the wheels turning, but the wagon had already settled down again and didn't move. A great bellow came from Donnigan as he strove to budge it a second time.

McCreary's wagon inched forward. Donnigan's began to move again, as well. Bit by bit, the wagons crawled toward the finish line.

That fifty feet had to feel more like fifty miles to the two contestants, Bo thought as he watched them with pity in his eyes. He wondered if their hearts might give out before they reached their goal.

Donnigan's wagon drew ahead slightly. Bo wasn't sure, but despair appeared to flicker in McCreary's eyes for a second. There wouldn't be another round. If any more weight was loaded onto the wagons, the men would have no chance of moving them.

Forbes Dyson must have known the same thing. He cupped his hands around his mouth and yelled over the shouting and whistling and stomping of feet, "First man to the line wins! First man to the line wins!"

McCreary pulled even with Donnigan. The muscles in his thick legs bulged out so much from the effort that it seemed like his trousers might split at the seams.

At the same time, Donnigan's massive chest rose and fell like a bellows. McCreary was probably slightly stronger, but would Donnigan's superior wind bring him the victory?

The roar of the crowd was so deafening that it seemed to make the very ground tremble underneath Silverhill. Step by step, inch by inch, Donnigan and McCreary approached the finish line. With the goal only five feet away, Donnigan moved ahead of McCreary again.

Bo saw the excitement on Donnigan's face and thought for a second that overconfidence might take hold and cause the rugged miner to ease up and then fail, but Donnigan continued pulling until his feet blurred the redrawn line in the dirt.

Only inches behind, McCreary saw that he had lost and fell to his knees with a huge groan. Just on the other side of the line, Donnigan flung his arms up and shouted in triumph.

No one heard the shot, but everyone in the crowd saw the result as Donnigan suddenly jerked back and blood welled from the hole that had appeared in his chest. He pawed at the wound for a second, and then, still attached to the wagon by the ropes, he pitched to the ground.

McCreary saw him fall. Eyes widening in shock, the man tried to struggle to his feet, but before he could make it, a piece of his skull leaped in the air as a bullet struck him in the head. He toppled sideways and was dead by the time his massive body hit the ground.

The shots might have gone unnoticed at first, but the two brutal deaths did not. Screams ripped from the throats of several soiled doves who had taken the afternoon off from their normal work to watch the strongman contest. Men shouted curses and questions at the top of their lungs.

Chaos erupted along the boardwalks and in the street as people scrambled to get to cover in case the deadly gunfire continued.

The possibility that whoever had shot Donnigan and Mc-Creary had done so as a distraction immediately occurred to Bo. His hand dropped to the Colt on his hip, but he didn't pull the iron just yet. With two men cut down by a mysterious gunman in front of practically the whole town, if he started waving around a revolver, he'd just add to the panic.

And some hombre might decide *he* was to blame for the killings and open fire on him.

"Spread out so we can keep a better eye on the girls," he told Scratch. "Let's get them back inside."

That order might be easier given than carried out. The porch was packed with hotel guests and townspeople, and they suddenly surged around the Texans and the five young women, like quicksand enveloping them and trying to pull them down in its deadly embrace.

Scratch tried to shoulder through to the other end of the area where the ladies had been lined up at the railing. He hadn't

made much progress when he spotted several men in sombreros who, instead of scrambling to get inside the hotel for
protection against the hidden killer, seemed to be trying to
reach the young women.

Bo noticed the same thing and called to his old friend, "Look
out for those Mexicans!"

One of the men darted through a sudden gap in the crowd
and grabbed Luella's arm. She screamed as he jerked her toward
him. His other arm whipped around her waist and closed
tightly.

Scratch palmed out the Remingtons, but in this mob of innocent bystanders, he couldn't even think about shooting, nor could
he get a shot at Luella's captor without endangering her, too.

But as more Mexicans sprang in front of him to block his
path, he didn't hesitate to lash out at them. The long barrel of a
Remington smashed one man's jaw and sent him staggering
back. The other gun thudded against a man's skull and made
his knees buckle. He went down under the trampling feet of
the mob.

Bo took a different route. Leaving his gun in its holster for
the moment, he swung up onto the railing that ran along the
front of the porch. That top rail was only about three inches
wide, but Bo was able to stay balanced on it and slide along for
several feet before he saw the opening he was looking for.

He dived off the railing, flew through the air, and crashed
into the man who was trying to wrestle Luella out of the
crowd.

With so many people around, the impact was like a game of
ninepins. Bo and the would-be kidnapper fell, and so did the
people with whom they collided. A tangled sprawl formed at
the end of the porch.

The good thing was that the man's grip on Luella had been
jolted loose. She pulled away.

The whole business knocked the air out of Bo's lungs. He

knew he was way too old for such daredevil stunts, but there hadn't seemed to be any other way to reach Luella in time.

He was still lying on top of the man he had knocked down, trying to catch his breath, when the man writhed and Bo caught a glimpse of a knife blade flashing toward his face. Bo jerked his head aside. The knife missed his face but raked along the top of his left shoulder, cutting through his coat and shirt and leaving a fiery line drawn across his flesh.

Bo's left arm and hand still worked just fine despite the minor wound. He grabbed the wrist of the man's knife hand to hold the blade away from him and hammered a punch with his right into the Mexican's snarling face. Bo hit him again, fast and hard, and the man went limp.

A scream made Bo jerk his head up. Another man in a sombrero had hold of Luella and was trying to drag her away. She was putting up a fight, though.

More shots blasted, enough that it seemed like a small war was breaking out on Silverhill's main street.

"Stop fighting!" Philip Armbruster cried. "I'm not going to hurt you!"

The dark-haired young woman struggling in his grasp twisted her head around so that her face was only inches from his. As he peered into her wide, frightened eyes, he asked himself again what in the world he was doing.

Armbruster had acted totally on impulse. He had seen one of Mendoza's men trying to drag the young woman away, only to be knocked down by one of the old men who had proven to be such thorns in the bandit chief's side. Armbruster wouldn't have believed that an old-timer was capable of such athletic derring-do, but clearly, even the old men were tough out here on the frontier.

When the woman had pulled free of the bandido's grasp, however, she had stumbled right into the reporter's arms. He'd grabbed her without thinking and started trying to drag her off the porch. If he succeeded in capturing her, Mendoza would be pleased. Maybe Armbruster wouldn't abandon this assignment, after all . . .

But then she writhed around, and he gazed into her eyes, eyes such a dark blue that they were like the night sky or a bottomless lake, and in that moment, Philip Armbruster was lost. All he could do was stare helplessly at her.

Now he understood why Jaime Mendoza had become so obsessed with this woman.

Only a split second passed, even though it seemed much longer to Armbruster's addled senses. Then the woman's hard little fist came up and cracked sharply into his nose.

He exclaimed in pain as he drew back from the punch. Blood spurted hotly from his nose. He had never been a fighter. He was a physical coward, and he knew it, which was one reason why he had decided to make his living with the words that flowed from his brain.

He tried to keep hold of her, but she hit him again, slugging him in the chest. Armbruster's grip loosened even more. She put her hands on his chest and pushed him away. She whirled to flee.

That took her right into the arms of Jaime Mendoza, who scooped her up and carried her, kicking and screaming, off the porch and into the chaos of the street.

Chapter 33

With all the incredible racket going on, Bo was never sure what made him notice one particular scream, but just as he fought his way back to his feet, he heard it and swung around.

Another Mexican had hold of Luella, had lifted her off the ground so that her feet kicked wildly as he reached the street with her.

A glance over his shoulder told him that Scratch was trying to struggle through the fear-crazed mob toward him, but his old friend wasn't going to reach him in time to help. Another few seconds and Luella and her captor would vanish into the chaos.

Bo thought about trying to vault over the railing, but he knew he wasn't up to that. He ducked under it instead and dropped to the street.

He grabbed people by the shoulders and thrust them aside as he went after Luella and the Mexican. Panic-stricken hands fumbled at him, but he shrugged them off. Through the bobbing heads around him, he tried to keep an eye on Luella and the man who had hold of her, but it was growing more difficult to do so.

Bo didn't think there had been any more shots, but it didn't really matter. This mob couldn't be any more crazed than it already was. All the spectators had been worked up into a frenzy over the strongman competition, and then sudden, unexpected death had pushed them over the edge into temporary madness.

At least Luella was putting up a fight, Bo saw. She kicked and hit at her captor, and her struggles made him stumble a little, slowing him down. Bo drove through a narrow gap in the crowd, widening it with his shoulders, and then he was right behind them.

He tackled the man around the waist, driving him off his feet. Still caught in his grasp, Luella went hard to the ground, too. As they landed, Bo rammed his elbow into the small of the would-be kidnapper's back, hoping to paralyze him momentarily. The man cried out in pain.

Feet thudded against Bo's ribs and tromped on his back. The people who did that weren't trying to hurt him. They just wanted to get away before somebody shot them. Bo knew that, but he felt like he was caught in a stampede, anyway.

He looked around for Luella and saw that she had rolled away. She tried to get up, but people kept running into her and knocking her down again. Bo crawled to her and hovered protectively over her.

"Grab on to me!" he told her. "I'll get you out of here!"

Her arms went around his neck. He got his feet underneath him somehow and heaved upright, bringing her with him. As they both stood, someone screamed close by. A gun roared. A man running past Bo and Luella cried out as a bullet struck him in the back of the shoulder.

Bo turned, thrusting Luella behind him as he continued trying to protect her with his own body. The gunshot had opened a narrow path as terrified people scrambled out of the line of fire. Bo saw that the Mexican he had just tackled was back up on one knee, gun in hand, ready to fire a second shot.

No matter how fast you were, beating an already drawn gun

was nearly impossible. Bo wasn't sure if even Rose's hero Smoke Jensen could do that.

But right now, he had to try. His hand flashed to the holster on his right hip.

It was empty. In all the fighting and jumping around, the Colt had fallen out of the holster.

In the fraction of a second that passed, Bo saw the face of the man who was about to kill him, and recognized Jaime Mendoza. Judging by the grin on the bandit chief's face, he recognized Bo, as well, and was glad for the chance to drill one of the men who had thwarted his will earlier. His finger tightened on the trigger.

Before the gun went off, the barrel of one of Scratch's Remingtons crashed down on Mendoza's head. The bandit slumped forward just as he pulled the trigger. The gun in his hand roared, but the bullet went into the dirt right in front of him.

Mendoza followed, collapsing in the street from the blow, which had knocked him cold.

Bo nodded his appreciation to Scratch. With two such old friends, that fleeting moment was enough to acknowledge what had happened.

"Are you all right?" Bo asked Luella.

She seemed to be having trouble catching her breath, but she managed to nod and say, "Yes, I . . . I think so."

Bo looked at the hotel porch, the last place he had seen the other four young women. None of them were in sight now.

"Scratch, the other ladies—"

"I saw all of 'em make it inside the hotel," Scratch replied as he kept the Remington trained on the senseless Jaime Mendoza. "Miss Cecilia sort'a took charge, the way she usually does. She mother-henned 'em out of harm's way, looked like."

That was a relief, thought Bo, but he wanted to see the other young women for himself. He wasn't sure how many more of Mendoza's men were still lurking around. With their leader unconscious and captured, though, they might decide to cut their losses and get out of Silverhill as quickly as they could.

The chaos in the street was beginning to ease as the crowd thinned. Bo looked around, but although he saw some Mexicans running here and there, he didn't spot any that he recognized as Mendoza's men. Mostly, they were farmers and their families who had come into Silverhill for the excitement.

Bo wanted to search for his gun, but right now it was more important to check on the other ladies. A Colt could be replaced.

He put a hand on Luella's shoulder and told her, "Go on in the hotel and join the others. I'll be there in just a minute. Scratch and I need to figure out what to do with that fella he buffaloed."

"Are *you* all right, Mr. Creel?" Luella asked.

Bo smiled. "I reckon I'll be a mite stiff and sore in the morning from being knocked around," he said, "and I've got a cut on my shoulder, too, but nothing that I won't get over. It won't slow me down any, either."

"Thank you. You saved my life, you and Mr. Morton."

"That's our job."

"Not really. Not now. Or have you adopted us from now on?"

Bo patted her shoulder and said, "I doubt that. You go on and find the others. Make sure they're all right."

Luella nodded and headed for the hotel. Bo walked over to Scratch, and they both peered down at the still unconscious Jaime Mendoza.

"What are we going to do with this varmint?" Bo asked.

"I was thinkin' a bullet in the head might be just what he needs."

"It's tempting," Bo admitted, "but that would be cold-blooded murder."

"More like shootin' a snake 'fore it has the chance to bite somebody again," Scratch muttered. "But I suppose you're right.

We been accused of a lot of things and been guilty of some of 'em, but we ain't murderers."

Bo looked up as Jack Bouma strode through the stragglers from the mob. The gunman's Colt was holstered, but his hand rested on the butt, ready to draw.

"Who's this?" he asked curtly.

"Jaime Mendoza," Bo said.

Bouma cocked an eyebrow. "The bandit boss who's been raiding from below the border? He's got a sizable price on his head."

"One and the same. Is there somewhere he can be locked up, Bouma?"

"Why don't you just kill him and cut off his head? You can send it back to El Paso to claim the reward."

"I'm not interested in the reward. I just want him locked up so he can't cause any more trouble."

A new voice said, "I absolutely agree, Creel."

They all turned as Forbes Dyson came up to them. Dyson hooked his thumbs in his vest and looked down at the unconscious man.

"Did I hear you say that's Jaime Mendoza?" he asked.

"That's right," Bo said. "He and his men tried to steal the ladies while we were out on the trail, on our way here. Rance Plummer and the cowboys from the SJ helped us fight them off. We figured Mendoza had given up." Bo shook his head. "Obviously, he hadn't. He just tried to take advantage of the confusion here in town, helped it explode into a riot by having Donnigan and McCreary killed, and then grabbed Miss Tolman and nearly carried her off."

Nodding, Dyson said, "I just saw her in the hotel, where she was reunited with the others. Thank God she was unharmed. Thank God none of them were hurt."

Scratch said, "Yeah, you got lucky, all right. A whole heap luckier than Donnigan and McCreary."

Dyson sighed. "Yes, they didn't deserve such a fate, especially after battling so hard against each other to win that competition. I suppose we'll have to declare the next man in line to be the winner."

"You're worried about that now?" Bo asked sharply. "I figured after this commotion, you'd call the whole thing off."

"Absolutely not!" Forbes Dyson snapped. "We're going to continue, if for no other reason than to honor the lives of the two men who were killed."

Bo wasn't sure how much of an honor that was, but Dyson had his mind made up. Anyway, it wasn't really any of his business, Bo told himself.

Dyson went on, "Jack, I want you to have this man locked up in that smokehouse down by the blacksmith shop. It's a sturdy building with no windows and only one door."

"You think the rest of his gang will come back and try to grab him?" Bouma asked.

"I don't know, but we'll keep a guard on the building. Are there any other prisoners?"

Bo and Scratch looked around. Scratch said, "I coldcocked a couple of 'em, but it looks like they must've come to and got out of town while the gettin' was good."

"I don't see the one I knocked out, either," Bo said.

"All right. We'll keep Mendoza locked up until we figure out what to do with him."

"I had a suggestion," Bouma said.

"Yes, I overheard what you said," Dyson replied. "We're not cutting off anyone's head, Jack. We're not barbarians, after all. Just lock him up for now."

Bouma shrugged and motioned for two of his men who had walked up to grab hold of Mendoza and take him down to the smokehouse. With that taken care of, Bo and Scratch headed for the hotel to check on the ladies.

* * *

Philip Armbruster sat on an old crate in an alley. His hands hung between his knees and he was breathing heavily, not so much because he needed the air, but more in reaction to everything that had happened over the past half hour.

He had seen men gunned down in cold blood right in front of him, men who had died without ever having any idea of the reason behind their deaths. He had been caught in a fear-crazed mob and almost trampled. He had been punched in the nose—by a woman!—and it still hurt, he thought as he lifted a hand and gingerly touched the injured member.

And he had fallen in love with that same woman after merely gazing into her eyes for a brief moment.

Such things happened in melodramatic novels, he supposed, but if anyone had asked him, he would have insisted that it was impossible in real life. He had firmly believed that . . . until now.

But even if it was true, what could he do about it? He was one man, and to be honest, not a very competent one at that. He couldn't hope to kidnap the woman who had captivated him and get away with it.

For that matter, he didn't *want* to kidnap her. He had always been a law-abiding man, until he started spending all his time with a group of Mexican bandits.

But if he was dressed in his real clothes again, if he was Philip Armbruster once more, and not some nameless peasant, would he stand a chance of winning her over? Had she gotten a good enough look at him that she would recognize him in his normal garb?

Armbruster felt his heart speed up with excitement as he pondered those questions. If he approached the young women as himself, no doubt those two self-appointed guardians would recognize him and tell the ladies that he had been with Mendoza's gang.

But he had an answer for that. He could explain that the bandits had *forced* him to go along with them, that he would have been killed if he hadn't done everything Mendoza told him to. He didn't know for a fact that that was true, but there was certainly a good chance of it. Good enough to be a reasonable explanation.

The more Armbruster thought about it, the more he believed it would work. He was free now, and he had to take advantage of that. He stood up and moved toward the far end of the alley, where his mule was tied. His clothes were in the saddlebags slung over the beast's back.

He hadn't reached the alley mouth when a man stepped into it. The figure, topped by a broad-brimmed, steeple-crowned sombrero, was familiar.

"Lupe," Armbruster said.

Guadalupe Sanchez, who had replaced Ernesto Reyes as Mendoza's second-in-command after Ernesto was killed, gave Armbruster a suspicious glower and said, "Were you running out on us, gringo?"

"What? Running . . . No! Certainly not. Where's Jaime?" Armbruster said, even though he knew perfectly well that Mendoza had been knocked unconscious and captured. Watching from a hiding place in the alley, he had seen men dragging Mendoza off toward the other end of the settlement a few minutes earlier. What they planned to do with him, Armbruster had no idea, but he was sure it wasn't anything pleasant.

"The gringos have him," Sanchez said, "but not for long." He draped a long apelike arm over Armbruster's shoulders. "Come with us now. Jaime trusted you, and because of that, the rest of us do, as well. Besides, you know the other gringos better than any of us do, so we will need your help rescuing him."

"R-rescuing him?"

"Of course! You did not think we were going to leave him here, did you? We will free him, and then we will have our vengeance on this town!"

So just like that, all the plans Armbruster had been forming evaporated. The bandits, for some unfathomable reason, still regarded him as one of them. And if he tried to back out of that alliance now . . . there was a good chance they would just go ahead and kill him.

Because he knew that, Armbruster summoned up a weak smile and said, "Of course, Lupe. Let's go. We have work to do."

Chapter 34

In the hotel, Rose threw her arms around Bo's neck, while Beth embraced Scratch. The young women had hurried to greet the Texans as soon as they came into the lobby.

"We thought you might have been killed!" Rose said as she clung to Bo.

Awkwardly, he patted her on the back as he said, "No, we're fine. Banged up a mite, but that's all."

Rose was a tall, firmly packed sterling example of young womanhood, and despite his age, Bo was well aware of that as she filled his arms and pressed against him. He wasn't so old that he couldn't appreciate such things, and for that reason, he thought it best to put his hands on Rose's shoulders and move her back a step.

If Scratch was thinking the same thing—and Bo knew he probably was—he wasn't quite as quick to act upon it. But then he disengaged from Beth's fervent embrace and said, "We just want to make sure none of you young ladies got hurt in that fracas."

"None of us were hurt," Cecilia said. "We owe that to the two of you."

"I especially do," Luella said. "I'd be a prisoner of those awful men right now if not for Bo and Scratch." She put a hand on Bo's upper arm and squeezed. "And don't try to use that just-doing-your-jobs excuse again."

"What about those two men who were shot?" Jean asked. "The ones in the contest? Are they badly hurt?"

"I'm afraid both of those fellas are dead, Miss Jean," Scratch told her as gently as he could.

Jean gasped and lifted a hand to her mouth. "That's terrible," she said. "I never dreamed that such a thing would . . . would take place right in front of us. I knew that the West isn't as civilized as it is back home, but this is just unbelievable."

"Does this sort of violent trouble happen all the time?" Rose asked.

"Hardly ever," Scratch said.

"Not really," Bo added. "Often enough that you need to keep your eyes open, though."

Forbes Dyson came into the hotel and headed directly for the group. He said, "You ladies don't have to worry about Mendoza anymore. He's locked up securely where he can't cause any more trouble."

"What about the rest of his men?" Cecilia asked. "Doesn't he have a large band of outlaws working with him?"

"He did," Scratch said, "but we whittled 'em down a mite out there on the trail. Remember?"

"I don't think I'll ever forget," Cecilia said.

"I daresay, none of us will," Jean said.

"You're calling off the other contests now, aren't you, Mr. Dyson?" Cecilia asked.

Dyson shook his head and said, "We were just discussing this outside. The competitions will continue. It's the only fair thing to do, since so many men invested their hard-earned money on entry fees."

"Just give them their money back," Cecilia suggested. "Surely, you have a record of who signed up for what."

"Of course. And we'll refund anyone's money who decides not to participate."

Bo said, "You could have quite a few of them asking for their dinero. After what happened out there to Donnigan and Mc-Creary . . ."

He didn't have to finish his comment. They all knew what he meant.

Dyson waved it off dismissively, though. He insisted, "Nothing like that is going to happen again. Without Mendoza to lead them, the few survivors of his gang don't represent any real threat."

"How can you be sure of that?" Scratch asked. "Some of those hombres might be ambitious and see this as a chance to take over the bunch."

"I'll post more guards around town," Dyson replied in a clipped, somewhat irritated tone. To the ladies, he went on in a more conciliating fashion, "As I said, you don't have to worry about anything like this happening again, I assure you."

"I hope you're right," Jean said. "I'm starting to regret that we ever agreed to go along with this."

"I've always regretted it," Cecilia said.

Before any of them could say anything else, the hotel doors opened and Rance Plummer came in. The lanky ranch foreman strode toward Bo, holding a familiar Colt, but not in a threatening manner.

"Saw this gun layin' outside and recognized it as yours, Creel," he said as he extended the revolver to Bo.

"Thanks," Bo said as he took the gun. "I was about to go look for it."

"You're lucky nobody walked off with it." Plummer grinned. "Reckon it helped that folks are just now startin' to come back out into the street after that little whoop-de-do. How come hell broke loose like that?"

"Shooting those two men was a distraction so Jaime Mendoza could try to kidnap Miss Tolman here," Bo replied as he nodded toward Luella. "That's the best way we can figure it."

"He wasn't after all five of the young ladies this time, like he was when he and his bunch jumped you on the way here?"

"Didn't appear to be," Bo said with a slight frown. "Nobody made a move toward them. They just went after Miss Tolman."

"You should feel special," Rose told Luella. "The big bad bandit only had eyes for you this time."

Luella shuddered and said, "Please. I don't even want to think about it."

Plummer pointed with a thumb and said to Bo and Scratch, "The boys and me were down the street, watchin' the contest. When things started poppin', we tried to get to where you two boys were. Figured we could lend you a hand again. But there were too many folks rushin' around and gettin' in the way. We never could manage it."

"We appreciate the effort," Bo told him. "How would you like a job, Rance?"

Plummer cocked a bushy eyebrow and said, "I already got one. Foreman of the SJ, remember?"

"This job would be temporary, just until all these competitions Mr. Dyson is putting on are over. Scratch and I could use somebody to help us keep an eye on the ladies."

"We sure could, Rance," Scratch added.

A grin stretched across Plummer's deeply tanned face. "Keepin' an eye on pretty girls ... Are you sure that ain't somethin' I should be paying you fellas for the chance to do?"

Bo chuckled and said, "I didn't say anything about pay. This is more in the nature of a volunteer job."

"In that case, I reckon I'm volunteerin'," Plummer said. "That is, if the ladies don't mind havin' another old pelican around."

"We're fine with that, Mr. Plummer," Cecilia said.

The others nodded.

The doors opened again, but this time they flew back and struck the walls hard. Hugh Craddock came in at a run and skidded to a halt as he looked around the lobby. When his eyes reached Cecilia, he exclaimed, "Miss Spaulding!" and rushed toward her.

Scratch got in his way. Bo and Plummer flanked the silver-haired Texan, and together, they made a formidable trio.

"Hold on there, mister," Scratch said as Craddock stopped again, but only a couple of feet away. The rancher's jaw jutted out angrily.

"Get out of my way, you old coots," he snapped. "I just want to make sure Miss Spaulding is all right."

"I'm fine," Cecilia said as she stepped up so she could look between Scratch and Rance Plummer. "Not that it's any of your business, Mr. Craddock."

"I'm making it my business."

"You've been trying to ever since we met in Fort Worth," Cecilia told him coolly. "It hasn't worked so far, has it?"

Craddock didn't like that, but he just glowered and didn't say anything else. Clearly, he was relieved to find that Cecilia was unhurt, even if she hadn't warmed up to him any.

Dyson said, "Ladies, I'm sure you're all shaken and upset about what happened, so why don't you go upstairs and rest for a while? We'll have supper here in the hotel dining room tonight and get a fresh start in the morning with the shooting competition."

"If you're bound and determined to go through with this," Bo said, "I don't reckon we can stop you."

Dyson summoned up a smile. "We're all going to put this tragedy behind us," he declared. "And tomorrow will be the biggest day in Silverhill's history."

Philip Armbruster, Guadalupe Sanchez, and two more members of Jaime Mendoza's band of thieves skulked through the darkness toward the smokehouse where Mendoza was locked up. It was very late, and Silverhill, despite being a boomtown, had gone to sleep for the most part.

Armbruster was no longer dressed as a Mexican peasant, but he didn't look like he normally did, either. He wore the trousers from his tweed suit, plus a white shirt, but no vest, tie, or hat. The shirt's sleeves were rolled up over his forearms. With a couple of days' worth of beard stubble on his chin and cheeks, he could pass as a laborer.

A half hour spent in one of Silverhill's more squalid saloons, eavesdropping on the conversations of the men who drank there, had provided quite a bit of information to Armbruster. He knew that Mendoza was locked up in a sturdy smokehouse next to the town's blacksmith shop, with armed men standing guard over him around the clock.

He had found out, as well, that the competitions staged by Forbes Dyson were slated to continue, beginning with a shooting contest the next morning, to be followed by a horse race in the afternoon and a boxing tournament that evening.

The boxing matches, as the culmination of the celebration, were bound to draw the biggest crowd. That was the time when the rest of Mendoza's men would make their move, storming the smokehouse to rescue their leader. Armbruster hoped to sneak up to the building, get Mendoza's attention somehow, and whisper the plan to him through the wall.

When they paused in a patch of darkness fifty yards from the back of the smokehouse, Armbruster said quietly to Sanchez, "You and the other two men stay here, Lupe."

"What makes you think you give the orders now, amigo?" Sanchez growled.

"If I'm seen around Jaime's prison, it won't be as suspicious," Armbruster pointed out. "I can pretend to be just a drunken gringo. There are plenty of them stumbling around Silverhill tonight."

"This is true, I suppose," Sanchez admitted grudgingly. "We will wait here. Try not to get caught."

"Believe me, that's my intention."

Armbruster moved like a phantom through the darkness. He felt a little like a dime-novel sleuth. At times in the past, when money was tight, he had given some thought to trying to write one of those lurid potboilers. He had read plenty of them to pass the time, and spewing out page after page of rambling, semiliterate drivel seemed easy enough.

The idea of an honest journalist writing something as sleazy and disreputable as fiction always put him off, though. He would stick with reporting the truth.

He reached the back of the smokehouse and carefully ran his hands over the thick beams of which it was constructed. He was trying to find a tiny chink so he could put his lips to it and hiss in an attempt to catch the prisoner's attention.

While he was doing that, Armbruster heard footsteps approaching the smokehouse. That didn't have to mean anything, but he stiffened in apprehension, anyway.

"Evening, boss," said one of the guards posted in front of the building.

"Any trouble?" That was Forbes Dyson's voice. Armbruster recognized it from Dyson's announcement to begin the strongman contest earlier in the day.

The thought of that event made Armbruster's stomach clench sickeningly for a moment. He'd had no idea that Mendoza's plans for kidnapping Luella Tolman included murdering two men in cold blood, including the big miner who had been friendly to Armbruster in the Silver King.

Since then, Armbruster had discovered that Sanchez, known to be a crack marksman, had been the hidden rifleman, shooting the two contestants from the roof of a building down the street.

But all that was over and done with, and there was nothing

Armbruster could do about it. Instead, he concentrated on the here and now.

"Everything's been peaceful," the guard replied to Dyson's question. "Nobody's been hanging around. I halfway thought some of the fellas might work themselves up into wanting to lynch that damn greaser."

"That's not going to happen," Dyson said. "I have a better use for Jaime Mendoza."

"Gonna collect the reward on him, eh?"

"Better than that." Armbruster heard Dyson chuckle. "He's going to help us all become rich men."

A frown creased Armbruster's forehead. What did Dyson mean by that?

Maybe instead of trying to rescue Mendoza, it would be better for Armbruster to wait and listen to what Forbes Dyson had in mind.

"Open the door," Dyson said. "I'm going to talk to Mendoza."

The guard sounded dubious as he began, "Boss, are you sure—"

"I said open the door."

Dyson's tone didn't leave any room for argument.

The shadows were still thick on the left side of the smokehouse. Armbruster pressed his back to the wall and slid toward the front of the building, still concealed but able to see and hear better.

He heard the rattle of a key in a padlock, and then a match rasped into flame. Yellow light from a lantern spilled on the ground. Hinges creaked as the smokehouse door opened.

"Don't try anything, Mendoza," Dyson warned. "These men have shotguns, and they won't hesitate to blow you to hell."

From inside the smokehouse, his voice slightly muffled, Jaime Mendoza said, "Why should I care, señor? A shotgun or a hangman's rope, I am still dead either way, no?"

"You don't have to be dead at all," Dyson snapped. "Just listen to me and cooperate, and you'll not only get out of here alive, but you'll also have some silver in your pockets . . . *and* that girl you tried so hard to carry off today."

Luella! Armbruster thought. Now that he had seen her, touched her, the thought of Mendoza's hands on her, with her completely in his power, sickened him even more than seeing those men shot down.

"Go on," Mendoza said to Dyson.

"Tomorrow evening, during the boxing matches, Jack Bouma and the rest of my men are going to blow open the safe in George McCallum's freight office and clean out the biggest shipment of silver ore this part of the country has ever seen. It's been building up for weeks now. The mine owners wanted it shipped all at once, and they've provided plenty of guards. But those guards are going to be distracted like everyone else in town tomorrow night, so that's when we'll hit the safe. At the same time, some of the other businesses in town are going to be robbed, including the Silver King. Since I'll be one of the victims, too, no one will suspect I was behind the whole thing. It'll just look like Bouma double-crossed me."

"An audacious plan," Mendoza murmured, so quietly Armbruster almost couldn't make out the words. "This is why you staged those contests to begin with?"

Dyson laughed and said, "Mostly. But I must admit, I've enjoyed seeing all the excitement in town, too. I want Silverhill to survive—and thrive—because I plan to own the whole place in due time, as well as all the mines in the mountains. This is just the first step in that plan."

"You are bold, señor, and it is said that fortune favors the bold." Armbruster could practically see Mendoza eloquently spreading his hands in the lantern light as the bandit went on, "But how does any of this enrich me?"

"Tomorrow evening," Dyson said, "you're going to escape

from this smokehouse. When you do, make for the boxing ring that'll be set up in the street. All the girls will be there, watching. The blast that blows open the safe will go off at the same time. You grab Miss Tolman. You'll be an added distraction to help make sure my men get away."

"It sounds as if this will be very dangerous for me, señor."

"Well," Dyson said, "a man never got his hands on anything worthwhile without taking a little risk, did he?"

"True," Mendoza admitted. "Then, after I make my escape with the señorita, you will send my share of the payoff from the robbery to me?"

"That's it exactly."

"And I must trust you to do this?"

"You know the truth about what's really going on," Dyson said. "I can't afford to double-cross you."

After a couple of seconds of silence, Mendoza said, "This is true. Not only will I have the ability to expose your villainy . . . if you betray me, but I will also kill you, Señor Dyson."

"We don't need to resort to threats," Dyson snapped. "We either understand each other or we don't, Mendoza."

"We understand each other," the bandit chief said. "And we have a bargain."

"Good. I wish I could offer you more comfortable accommodations in the meantime, but we have to keep up appearances."

"Of course. Throw a little extra in my share to make up for it, eh?"

Both men laughed at that, but Dyson didn't promise to go along with the suggestion.

"Be ready tomorrow night," Dyson said. Then the shadows shifted as he took the lantern and left the smokehouse.

Armbruster stayed where he was, his body motionless but his thoughts whirling madly, until Dyson's footsteps had faded into the darkness. Then he eased away from the smokehouse and hurried silently back to the spot where he had left Sanchez and the other bandits.

Sanchez reached out of the shadows and gripped his arm tightly.

"Did you talk to Jaime?" Sanchez asked in a harsh whisper.

"Yes," Armbruster lied, "and there's been a change of plan. Here's what we're supposed to do . . ."

Kenton O'Keefe wanted to light the cigar that was clamped between his teeth, but he suppressed the impulse. The smell of tobacco smoke, to say nothing of the flare of a match, might give away his presence in the darkened shed attached to the blacksmith shop.

Forbes Dyson needed to be far away from his mysterious meeting with the bandit Mendoza before O'Keefe ventured out from the shadows.

O'Keefe had been playing a hunch again when he followed Dyson from the Silver King down here to the far end of town. Dyson hadn't been moving furtively or anything like that. O'Keefe wasn't sure anyone with Dyson's ego was even capable of doing anything furtively.

But something about the saloon owner's manner had told O'Keefe that it might be worthwhile to trail him.

Since eavesdropping on that suspicious conversation between Dyson and Jack Bouma, O'Keefe had tried to figure out just what the two men were up to, but he hadn't been able to come up with a theory. He'd followed Dyson in the hope that the man's late-night jaunt might give him a clue.

Instead, it had only deepened the mystery. Dyson had paid a visit to Jaime Mendoza in the smokehouse. O'Keefe couldn't think of a reason for Dyson to do that . . . unless Dyson was trying to recruit the bandit for whatever scheme he and Bouma had cooked up.

The longer O'Keefe stood in the shadows and pondered that

possibility, the more likely it seemed. Mendoza would be a formidable ally, and no one would ever suspect that Dyson was working with him.

No one except Kenton O'Keefe, that is.

O'Keefe smiled in the darkness. He was a gambler, and if he wanted to claim a slice of whatever payoff Forbes Dyson had in the works . . .

Maybe it was time to run a bluff.

Chapter 35

By the next morning, Silverhill hadn't forgotten what had happened the day before, but after a night during which no further trouble had erupted, the town seemed to have drawn a deep breath and relaxed a little.

The atmosphere on the street was fairly calm as Bo stood on the hotel porch and looked up and down, but excitement was building. The shooting contest would take place at eleven o'clock. Men were already standing around talking about it and laying bets on the outcome.

Scratch and Rance Plummer were upstairs, waiting to escort the ladies down when they were ready to eat breakfast. Bo had ventured out to get a feel for the town. He didn't *see* anything wrong. . . .

Some instinct made the hair on the back of his neck stand up, though. Like the feeling in the air before one hell of a thunderstorm breaks loose.

Forbes Dyson strolled along the boardwalk with Jack Bouma, both men looking as self-satisfied as ever. They came up to Bo, and Dyson said, "How are our special guests this morning, Creel?"

"You mean the young ladies?"

Bouma sneered and said, "He sure as hell don't mean you, saddle tramp."

Bo ignored that and went on, "They're fine. I spoke briefly to each of them, and they assured me that they're still willing to carry on, if that's what you're worried about."

"I was more concerned with the ladies' well-being, but I won't deny I'm glad to hear that yesterday's unfortunate events didn't sour them on everything else."

"Unfortunate events," Bo repeated. "You mean two hombres getting gunned down and the riot that followed those killings?"

"I think it's a stretch to call what happened a riot. People were upset and frightened and trying to get out of harm's way, and understandably so."

"What's going to happen to Mendoza?"

"I've discussed it with the mine owners and the other leaders in the community, and we'll continue holding him in custody until all the festivities are over. Then Jack and some of his associates will take him under heavy guard to El Paso and turn him over to the authorities there."

"You worried about the reward, Creel?" Bouma drawled. "We'll tell the law it was you and that other old pelican who caught him, so you can claim the blood money."

Bo shook his head and said, "I don't care about the reward. I just don't want what's left of his gang showing up to bust him out—and putting innocent folks in danger in the process."

"I don't think that's going to happen," Dyson said. "There can't be enough of Mendoza's gang left to stage a real raid on the town, and nothing less than that would free him. No, I think it's more likely those bandits are south of the border by now."

"Let's hope you're right," Bo said. "For the town's sake."

"Now, if you'll excuse me . . ." Dyson's tone made it clear he didn't really give a damn whether Bo excused him or not. "I believe I'll go in and wait to say hello to the ladies when they come down for breakfast. I might even join them, if they're agreeable."

Dyson and Bouma went into the hotel. In one way, Bo was glad to see them go. Talking to those two was like trying to have a conversation with a couple of diamondback rattlesnakes.

On the other hand, it was usually better to keep a venomous serpent where you could see him . . . so you could blow the bastard's head off if he tried to strike.

With that thought in his brain, Bo went back into the hotel, too.

The shooting contest was staged in the street, like the strongman competition had been. Thick boards with paper targets tacked to them were set up. Even though complete misses were unlikely, the street was cleared beyond the targets. Spectators lined the boardwalks as the contestants got ready to shoot.

Bo, Scratch, Rance Plummer, and the five young women were on the hotel porch, as before.

Fourteen men had signed up for this event. Some of them looked a little nervous, Bo thought. That might be because they were eager to get started and hoped they would win, but some of the nerves probably stemmed from what had happened the day before. Those shots that had struck down Seamus Donnigan and Big Dog McCreary had been like bolts out of the blue, and nobody wanted that to happen again.

Dyson had sent men to check the roofs of all the buildings along the street, since it was thought that the killer had fired from one of them. As far as Bo knew, the searchers hadn't found anything.

Dyson got the contest under way, and the sound of gunfire and the tang of burned powder soon filled the air in Silverhill. Each round, the man farthest from the bull's-eye was eliminated, until only five contestants were left. From that point, each round consisted of five shots, with point values assigned to the rings on the targets. The lowest score went out each time.

When only two men were left, they each shot ten rounds, taking turns between each shot. The contest was extremely close, with the last man having to hit the bull's-eye on his last shot in order to win.

That competitor, a lanky hillbilly from the Ozarks, plunked a bullet right in the middle of the target. A thunderous cheer went up for the victor as the man thrust his rifle into the air over his head and did a little jig. His defeated rival just shook his head disgustedly.

Dyson brought the winner over to introduce him to the young women, who all smiled and nodded politely.

The man held his floppy-brimmed hat over his heart, grinned, and said with rough gallantry, "I'm shore pleased to meet you ladies, and I'm hopin' one of yuh will see yore way clear to lettin' me court yuh and maybe get hitched up one o' these days."

Now that this competition had gone off without a hitch, the town relaxed even more. The feeling in Silverhill was actually festive again.

The horse race that afternoon was another uproarious success. The course extended half a mile out of town, around a towering rock spire, and then back, with the starting line also serving as the finish line. One of the SJ cowboys won, with Rance Plummer whooping in excitement as he looked on from the hotel porch. Plummer waved his hat over his head wildly when the cowboy's mount thundered across the finish line first.

"That youngster is a fine lad," he told Cecilia and the others when he had recovered his composure. "I'll have a talk with him and make sure he's on his best behavior when you have your meetin' with him. From what I hear, all of you are gonna have dinner together tomorrow."

"That's what Mr. Dyson is planning," Cecilia said.

Rose, who had watched the young cowboy's victory with considerable interest, asked, "If one of us gets married to him, does that mean we'd have to go back to that ranch of yours and live there, Mr. Plummer?"

"Well, the ranch ain't exactly mine, and I reckon it'd be up to you and the lucky fella to work out where you'd live, but the SJ is a fine place, with some nice cabins for the married hands and their families. I think you'd be plumb happy there, Miss Rose."

"Living on a ranch *does* sound interesting . . . Would I actually get to work with the cattle? You know, ride the range with my husband?"

Plummer frowned and said, "Well, such things ain't normally done, but again . . . I reckon that'd be up to you and the lucky fella to figure out. I wouldn't run off anybody who made a good hand, whether they was male . . . or female."

Rose just nodded slowly, obviously deep in thought.

When Forbes Dyson came over to join them, Bo asked, "How's the poker tournament coming along?" He hadn't been back to the Silver King to check on the games.

"It's down to four players," Dyson replied. "All the others have busted or dropped out voluntarily. I think there's a good chance we'll have a winner by this evening."

Scratch asked, "How many fellas signed up for the boxin' matches?"

"Eight. Starting late this afternoon, we'll have four bouts of three rounds each, then this evening the semifinal matches of five rounds, if it takes that many, and then the finals, which will last until one man is knocked out or can't continue."

"It still sounds barbaric to me," Cecilia said.

"Some people claim that barbarism is the natural state of mankind," Dyson told her with a smile.

"That doesn't mean that we should aspire to it."

"Or that we can prevent its ultimate triumph." Dyson ticked

a finger against the brim of his hat as he went on, "I need to go check on that poker game, but I'll see you ladies later."

As Rance Plummer watched Dyson walk toward the saloon, he said, "Y'know, I just can't warm up to that fella."

"Me neither," Scratch said.

Bo didn't say anything, but he agreed with both his old and his new friend. Forbes Dyson rubbed him the wrong way and likely always would.

Professional gamblers had no interest in winning a bride. Most drifted around too much and didn't want the burden of having to drag a wife along with them. The professionals who had bought into this tournament had done so with the idea of cleaning up from some of the other players and then quitting while they were ahead.

One by one, that was what they had done, which meant the stakes in the final game weren't as high as they normally were in such a situation. The departure of the professionals had sucked most of the money out of the tournament.

The men who were left were playing for the chance of marrying a beautiful young woman. There were two middle-aged businessmen, both widowers, a mine superintendent who had never been married, and a railroad engineer who had taken time off from his work to come down to Silverhill and try to get himself a wife.

The mining man appeared to be winning as Dyson checked out the game. He didn't care who emerged as the victor. It didn't matter. None of the contests did. The money he would make from this venture was a drop in the bucket compared to what he would clean up from the silver robbery, not to mention the loot from the rest of the raid.

Best of all, because he would appear to be one of the victims, too, he would be in the clear, free to continue the work of buying out and taking over not only the businesses here in town but also the mining operations in the mountains. The idea of using the riches he was going to steal from those mines to turn around and buy them was particularly satisfying.

By the time he was finished, everything that turned a profit in this corner of the territory was going to belong to him.

With that pleasant prospect filling his thoughts, he never noticed Kenton O'Keefe until he was unlocking the door of his office on the second floor and the gambler hailed him from the top of the stairs.

"Can I talk to you for a minute, Dyson?"

With a grimace of annoyance, which he quickly concealed, Dyson asked, "What do you want, O'Keefe?"

"Just a few words. It won't take long."

Dyson didn't have anything he had to be doing right now. The town was waiting for the poker tournament to be over and the boxing matches to begin. So he shrugged, opened the door, and said, "Come on in."

O'Keefe followed him into the office. Dyson thought about offering him a drink, then decided not to. He had no desire to cultivate a friendship with a tinhorn gambler.

"What can I do for you?" he asked once the door was closed.

"You can let me in on what you and Jack Bouma and Jaime Mendoza are planning," O'Keefe said bluntly.

For a second, Forbes Dyson felt like he'd been punched in the gut. He recovered quickly, though, and put a frown on his face as he said, "I have no idea what you're talking about."

"Sure you do," O'Keefe said with an easy, confident smile. "I heard you and Bouma talking about it the other day, and then I saw you meeting with Mendoza last night to discuss his part in the plan."

Dyson stiffened, and O'Keefe must have seen the reaction, because he held up a hand, palm out.

"No need to get upset," he said. "I think it's a very smart move on your part, and it's going to be quite lucrative. I'd be a fool to try to ruin that for you . . . especially since you're going to cut me in on it."

"Is that what you think?"

"You're a smart man, Forbes," O'Keefe said, the familiarity annoying Dyson just that much more. "You know it's going to be well worth it to pay me, say, five thousand dollars to keep my mouth shut about the whole thing."

"Five thousand dollars," Dyson repeated slowly. "How do I know you won't ask for more later on?"

"Why, I'm a man of my word." O'Keefe tried to sound offended, Dyson thought, but with the self-satisfied smirk on his face, he couldn't quite pull it off. "I plan to just take my share of the money and move on."

"Your share . . . You haven't done a damned thing to earn a share."

O'Keefe's expression hardened. He hooked his thumbs in his vest pockets and went on, "Let's not argue, Forbes. You're a practical man. You know it wouldn't look good if people found out you've been having middle of the night meetings with a notorious Mexican bandit."

The way O'Keefe returned to that detail but didn't provide any others struck Dyson as odd, and suddenly he realized the gambler was running a bluff. O'Keefe had seen him down at the smokehouse, talking to Mendoza, but other than that, he didn't know a blasted thing.

Still, O'Keefe had a point. The little bit he *did* know could still prove damaging to Dyson's plans.

Dyson wasn't going to allow that.

"Five thousand dollars, you said." He went behind the desk and opened the middle drawer.

"That's right." Greed made O'Keefe's eyes widen. His tongue came out and licked his lips in anticipation, like that of a hungry man sitting down to a feast.

Dyson reached into the drawer and took out a stack of

greenbacks with a string tied around it. The bills didn't add up to five thousand; a thousand was more like it. But O'Keefe couldn't tell that without counting them.

Dyson dropped the money at the front edge of the desk and said, "There you go."

The sight of the greenbacks made O'Keefe less cautious than he normally would have been. He stepped forward and leaned over the desk slightly as he reached down to pick up the bills.

Dyson leaned forward, too. His left hand shot out and grabbed O'Keefe's shirt. He yanked the gambler toward him.

At the same time, Dyson's right hand plucked a loaded derringer out of the desk drawer. It was a .41-caliber single-shot weapon, but that lone bullet was enough as Dyson rammed the barrel against O'Keefe's chest and fired it into the gambler's heart.

O'Keefe's body muffled the shot, so it wasn't any louder than a handclap. He lurched and gasped. He had gotten the money in his hand, but the little bundle slipped out of his fingers and fell back to the desk. As he stared in shock at Dyson, he tried to fumble something out from under his coat. A pistol of his own, more than likely, Dyson knew. He drew back his hand and slammed the derringer against O'Keefe's left temple. O'Keefe gasped again as his knees buckled. Dyson let him fold up on the floor in front of the desk.

Dyson went quickly around the desk and saw to his satisfaction that O'Keefe had fallen on his back. That meant the blood welling from the hole in the gambler's chest wasn't going to get on the rug.

"You cheap tinhorn chiseler," Dyson said, getting the insult in before the life faded completely from O'Keefe's eyes. "I'm going to own an empire down here. Did you really think I'd let a worm like you stand in the way of that?"

Dyson didn't expect an answer, and he wasn't going to get one. O'Keefe stared sightlessly at the ceiling now.

Dyson put the money back in the drawer, then reloaded the derringer and replaced it, as well. Bouma would be somewhere close by, he thought. He'd get the gunman to clean up this mess.

And when that was done, he would join the ladies for supper. The last supper before all his plans came to fruition . . .

Chapter 36

Sam Calloway, who owned a successful hardware store in Silverhill, emerged victorious in the poker tournament late that afternoon. He was a soft-spoken man with thinning brown hair and a mustache. He was rather tongue-tied when Forbes Dyson introduced him to the ladies, but after he had left the hotel, Jean commented, "He seems nice. A very stable gentleman."

"Stable?" Rose scoffed. "Try boring."

Jean sniffed and said, "Not every woman wants some wild, reckless cowboy who's liable to get killed in a gunfight or fall off his horse and break his neck."

"That's right," Beth said, but her sly smile belied her words. "There's something to be said for dying in bed of old age."

"You and Rose go ahead and run after young hellions," Jean told her.

Off to one side of the hotel lobby, Scratch nudged Bo with an elbow and said quietly, "You and me are old hellions, I reckon."

"Yeah, I figured that out a long time ago," Bo said.

Hugh Craddock came into the hotel. Bo was a little surprised he hadn't seen Craddock all day. He'd expected the rancher to enter either the shooting contest or the horse race.

Craddock had stated that he didn't believe he should have to compete to win Cecilia's affections, though, and evidently, he had stuck to that.

Craddock had traded his trail clothes for a suit, a clean white shirt, and a string tie. He looked freshly barbered and shaved, and he smelled a little of bay rum as he approached Cecilia with hat in hand.

"Miss Spaulding," he said, "I've come to beg your pardon."

"I'm sure there is an abundance of reasons for you to do such a thing," she told him coolly, "but what in particular are you begging my pardon for, Mr. Craddock?"

"Acting like a jackass," he said.

"Again, you're going to have to be more specific."

Anger flared in Craddock's eyes for a second, but he remained calm as he said, "I had no right to just bull my way in, declare that I was going to marry you, and expect you to go along with it."

Cecilia nodded and said, "I'm glad you understand that."

"But you have to understand this," he went on. "That's the way I've been used to dealing with problems for most of my life. When you're trying to carve a ranch out of a wild stretch of Texas, you've got to go at it hard and fast, without ever taking no for an answer. I want you to know, though, that I never meant any offense to you or any of these other ladies. I just, uh, let my mouth get ahead of my brain."

For a moment, Cecilia regarded him intently; then she nodded again. "I appreciate your apology, Mr. Craddock, and I appreciate your honesty, as well, even though you express it in a rather blunt fashion."

"I always found it saved time to be plainspoken."

"In that case . . . what do you want?"

Craddock turned the hat in his hands and said, "Have dinner with me. I'm told that restaurant, Harbinson's, is a nice place."

"Wait just a minute," Forbes Dyson said. "The ladies' company is spoken for."

"Not yet," Cecilia said. "We promised to sit down with the men who won those competitions, but that's not until tomorrow."

Craddock said, "Then you *will* have dinner with me?"

"I didn't say that." Cecilia glanced at Bo and Scratch. "What do you gentlemen think?"

"We ain't your uncles," Scratch said. "It's up to you what you do, Miss Cecilia."

"Scratch is right," Bo added. "You'll have to make up your own mind how much you want to have to do with Craddock here . . . as long as he's planning to keep you safe."

"Nothing will hurt a hair on this lady's head," Craddock declared emphatically. "Not while I'm around."

Bo shrugged and said, "I believe him."

"So do I," Cecilia said. "Very well, Mr. Craddock. I'll have dinner with you."

A grin spread across the rancher's face. "Right now?" he asked.

"Why not? It's late enough."

As if something had just occurred to him, Craddock turned quickly toward Rose, Beth, Luella, and Jean.

"You ladies are welcome to join us, of course—"

"No, thanks," Rose said. "This is Cecilia's engagement, not ours."

Cecilia began, "I wouldn't call it an—"

"A dinner engagement," Rose went on.

"Well . . . all right." Cecilia offered her arm to Craddock. "Shall we go?"

Still grinning, he linked his arm with hers and led her out of the hotel.

"She forgave him mighty quick," Scratch commented. "Quicker'n I expected her to."

"Cecilia has a stern nature," Jean said, "but she's also compassionate. Most people just don't ever see that side of her."

"And she hasn't necessarily forgiven him," Luella pointed out. "She's just giving him a chance."

Forbes Dyson said, "Why don't we all go on in the dining room, ladies? We'll meet Miss Spaulding later at the boxing ring."

"Do we really have to watch that?" Jean asked. "Sweaty men, stripped to the waist indecently, beating on each other . . . It sounds terrible."

"Speak for yourself," Rose said.

Philip Armbruster wore his Mexican peasant's garb again so he could blend in with the crowd. He was getting used to not wearing his pince-nez. Maybe his eyes were actually improving in this climate, far away from the irritating smoke and stench of New York City.

Guadalupe Sanchez and the remaining handful of bandits were scattered through the crowd, ready to follow the plan Armbruster had laid out. They believed they were supposed to kidnap Luella Tolman and rendezvous with Jaime Mendoza outside of Silverhill, well south of the settlement.

Mendoza knew nothing about that, so no matter what happened to him once he "escaped" from captivity in the smokehouse, he wouldn't show up at the meeting place. Sanchez and the others would believe Mendoza had been killed or recaptured in the fracas, and at Armbruster's subtle urging, they would withdraw below the border, taking Luella with them.

After that, it would be up to Armbruster to find a way to get her away from the bandits. She would be so grateful to him that she would fall in love with him. He was sure of it.

The boxing ring, a raised square platform covered with canvas, had been built in an open area at the far end of town from the freight office where the silver shipment was cached in the safe. A dozen blazing torches on posts surrounded it. Most of the population of Silverhill, permanent and temporary alike, was gathered around the ring, watching as two of the boxers pummeled each other.

This was the second semifinal. One of the contestants for the final battle had already been determined and would face whoever won this match. So there was still a little time to wait, Armbruster knew. Dyson's men wouldn't strike until the final bout was going on.

That couldn't happen soon enough to please Armbruster. His nerves were drawn painfully tight. He wasn't cut out for a life of crime.

But he was learning.

After supper in the hotel dining room, Bo, Scratch, and Rance Plummer escorted Rose, Beth, Luella, and Jean down the street to the area where the boxing matches were being held. Scratch linked arms with Rose and Beth and clearly enjoyed being flanked by the two beauties. Bo took Luella's arm, while Plummer walked with Jean. No one bothered them, but the ladies garnered cheers and applause from the crowd when they walked up.

Cecilia and Hugh Craddock were already on hand. While there was no air of intimacy between the two of them, they weren't glaring at each other, either, and they stood fairly close together, so Bo figured the meal at Harbinson's must have gone all right.

The thudding of fists against flesh and bone, as well as shouts of encouragement from the crowd, filled the air as the spectators watched the two men battle in the ring. Blood was always spilled in a bare-knuckles fight, and that was the case here, as crimson spurted from cuts and spattered the members of the crowd in the front rows. That just increased their frenzy.

"Like I said, barbaric." Jean raised her voice to be heard over the tumult.

The bell rang, signaling the end of the round. As the fighters went to their corners, the noise level subsided a little, so Bo had no trouble hearing the female voice that said from behind them, "So there you are, Mr. Craddock!"

Hugh Craddock turned, his eyes widening in surprise. Seeing that reaction made Bo glance over his own shoulder, and when he did, he saw that a woman had emerged from the crowd to stand there glaring at the rancher.

The sight of her was a shock to Bo, too.

The last time he had seen her was on the platform of a railroad car, as they shared a few minutes of pleasant conversation on the way to El Paso.

"Miss Hampshire!" Craddock exclaimed.

Bo's thoughts raced back to his previous meeting with the woman and then on to Fort Worth and things that had been said there. She had told him her name was Susan but hadn't mentioned a last name. However, Bo recalled that the woman who had traveled west to marry Craddock, only to be rejected by him, was named Hampshire. Could they be one and the same?

Craddock had called his prospective bride "old" and had acted like she was some sort of crone. This woman who confronted him now was not exactly young, but she was still in the prime of life and every bit as attractive as Bo remembered her from their brief encounter.

Given all that evidence, Bo could reach only one conclusion.

Hugh Craddock was a damned fool.

Susan Hampshire said, "It's nice to know that you remember my name, at least."

"Mr. Craddock, who is this woman?" Cecilia asked.

Susan didn't give Craddock time to answer the question. She said, "I'm the lady to whom he proposed marriage and then backed out like a scoundrel."

Cecilia turned her head and gave Craddock a look that would have wilted flowers like a blue norther blowing through.

"Now, wait just a minute," Craddock said, looking more nervous and less sure of himself than Bo had ever seen him. "That's not the whole story. You lied to me, Miss Hampshire."

"I did no such thing!" she objected.

"You sent a photograph taken years ago and claimed that's what you looked like."

"I told you that was not a recent picture."

"Yeah, but you said you hadn't changed much."

"That's a matter of perspective, I think," she said.

Bo had seen that photograph, and while it was true that Susan Hampshire had changed some since it was taken, the resemblance was still strong enough that he thought he should have recognized her when he met her on the train. He hadn't been expecting to ever meet the woman, though, and his brain just hadn't put it all together.

Despite all that, Craddock's objection about her being too old for him was ridiculous. The two of them were about the same age. They would have been a good match, Bo thought—if Craddock hadn't been such a jackass.

Cecilia said, "Mr. Craddock, if you need to speak with this woman—"

"I don't," he interrupted. "We don't have anything to talk about."

"But if you promised to marry her—"

"A man's got a right to change his mind!" Craddock took off his hat and scrubbed a hand over his face in frustration. "Doesn't he? Hell, any fella can get cold feet!"

In a chilly tone, Cecilia said, "That doesn't exactly make you appeal to me as marriage material."

Susan laughed and said, "Now he's after *you*, dear? Be careful. He's not a man of his word."

"Damn it, I am, too!" Craddock jammed his hat back on his head. "Look, Miss Hampshire, I apologize for the way things worked out. I reckon you have to see, though, that it was better to break things off between us before we got married, instead of waiting until it was too late. We wouldn't have been happy together."

"You never gave us a chance to find out, did you?" Susan said. Her eyes still glittered with anger, but Bo saw a little tremble in her bottom lip, too. Maybe some tears were mixed with that anger in her eyes. Craddock's rejection of her had to have hurt.

"I don't know what to say." Craddock spread his hands and shook his head. He looked over at Cecilia, but she turned away, and so did the other ladies who had been listening to the conversation. When he looked back at Susan Hampshire, she sniffed and turned her back on him, too. She started to move off through the crowd, which was getting impatient for the next round of the boxing match to begin.

Craddock's problems were his own lookout. Bo said to Scratch, "Keep an eye on the girls," then hurried to intercept Susan Hampshire.

She stopped short as he stepped in front of her and took off his hat.

"Pardon me—" she began, then said, "Wait. I know you, don't I?"

"We met on the train from Fort Worth to El Paso," he said. "I'm Bo Creel."

"Bo! Of course. I remember you now." She shook her head in confusion. "What are you doing here?"

"It's a long story. How'd you get to Silverhill?"

"By stagecoach, earlier today."

With everything else that had been going on, Bo hadn't even noticed that the stage from El Paso had rolled into town. After getting off the train there, Susan must have gotten a hotel room and waited for the next stagecoach to Silverhill.

"You came all the way out here just to follow Craddock?"

"Wait a moment. You know Mr. Craddock?"

"Yeah, I'm afraid our trails have crossed a few times. It's all part of that long story I mentioned. I could tell you all about it . . . over a late supper tonight, maybe?"

What the hell? How had those words come out of his mouth? He didn't go chasing after women. At least, he hadn't for a long time.

"To answer your first question," Susan said, "yes, I followed Mr. Craddock. I wanted him to have to look me in the eye and reject me in person. I was going to demand an explanation, as well, but I see now that's not necessary. Mr. Craddock is a shallow, narrow-minded . . ."

"Fool," Bo suggested.

"Yes. A fool. And that's all the explanation his actions require." Her chin lifted. "Now I can go back home with some self-respect still intact."

"But not just yet," Bo said. "You've come all this way. You might as well stay a few days. Come to think of it, you'll have to, since the stagecoach has probably left already and you'll have to wait for it to come again before you can go back to El Paso."

"That's true," she admitted. "Were you thinking that you might be willing to keep me company while I'm waiting?"

"That's sort of what I had in mind," Bo said.

She seemed to think about it, but only for a moment, before nodding. "All right. We can begin with that late supper you mentioned."

The bell rang to signal the start of the next round.

"But first," Susan went on, "at least you can tell me what in the world is going on here!"

Chapter 37

The second semifinal bout ended with a knockout in the next round. After a half-hour break, the final match would begin.

During that interval, Bo and Susan Hampshire had coffee in the dining room of the Territorial House, and he explained to her about the competitions Forbes Dyson had staged.

"I'm surprised that Mr. Keegan would have gone along with such a thing," Susan commented. "He seemed like a very honorable man."

"Cyrus didn't know about it," Bo said. "Dyson fooled him."

Susan cocked a finely arched eyebrow and said, "The same way I fooled Mr. Keegan and Mr. Craddock?"

Bo shook his head. "You didn't try to fool anybody," he told her. "You told the truth."

"Well . . . there's such a thing as a lie of omission, I suppose." She sighed. "I could have been more forthcoming. I was angry at Mr. Craddock—"

"And you had every right to be."

"But some portion of the blame for the misunderstanding lies with me," Susan went on. "Perhaps I owe him an apology . . ."

"I don't think so." Bo smiled. "But if you decide you do, you ought to wait before you deliver it. Let him stew awhile first."

Susan laughed and said, "Now, *that* I could certainly do."

They rejoined the others outside before the final boxing match got under way. Susan talked and laughed with the five young women. Her presence made Hugh Craddock visibly uncomfortable, but that didn't bother anyone except him.

Scratch said quietly to Bo, "You and that Miss Hampshire seem to be gettin' along mighty fine."

"She's a nice lady," Bo said. "We met on the train between Fort Worth and El Paso."

"Yeah, I got that idea."

"Don't make it out to be any more than it is, though," Bo cautioned. "Craddock may be loco enough to think she's too old for him, but she's a heap younger than me."

"She wouldn't be the first gal who ain't bothered by that." Scratch grinned. "As I recollect, you've had some nice young fillies chasin' after you in the past."

"And none of them have caught me, have they?"

"There's an old sayin' about how there's a first time for everything," Scratch reminded him as one eyelid drooped in a wink.

Forbes Dyson climbed into the ring and raised his voice to announce the beginning of the final bout. He introduced the two contestants, a miner from the mountains and Silverhill's blacksmith; and then the referee, who had been brought in from El Paso especially for this event, stepped in and got the round started.

The two fighters circled each other warily and then began throwing punches, but they were just feeling each other out at this point. They had seen each other in action during the earlier rounds, and each probably had some plan of attack in mind, but they didn't launch into it right away.

Then the blacksmith feinted, the miner bit on it, and the blacksmith's right fist slammed into the miner's jaw, knocking him back against the ropes. The miner bounced off, ducked under an attempted follow-up by the blacksmith, and hooked a left-right combination into the blacksmith's midsection.

They were fighting in earnest now, slugging away at each other with more power and determination than real skill.

That fierce exchange got the crowd even more excited, and once again, the shouts were like thunder.

But even over that sound, Bo and everyone else heard the boom of an explosion somewhere else in town, followed instantly by crashing gunshots and terrified screams.

Philip Armbruster had worked his way up close behind where the mail-order brides stood. As he heard the blast, he lunged toward Luella. At the same time, Sanchez and the other men opened fire. Armbruster had instructed them—supposedly on behalf of Jaime Mendoza—to shoot over the heads of the crowd, with the goal of stampeding them, not actually hurting anyone.

Armbruster hoped it would work out that way. He wasn't sure just how careful Sanchez and the others would be, but he had done what he could to try to prevent bloodshed.

It was more important that he get Luella and take her away from here, to some place where she could get to know him and fall in love with him.

As he grabbed her from behind, she writhed and fought, of course, but with so many people lunging around wildly, he was able to separate her from her companions without too much trouble. Now to reach the horses and get out of Silverhill . . .

The smokehouse door swung open, and Jaime Mendoza stepped out into the night. The two guards had alerted him a moment earlier that they were about to let him "escape." Now he was free again.

"Give me a gun," he said to one of the men.

"The boss didn't say nothin' about that," the guard responded. "He just told us to let you out of here when we got the signal. We just saw a light in one of the second-floor windows in the saloon, and that was it."

"So you can just light a shuck, greaser," the second man said. "We'll come up with a story about how you managed to get out."

"Or perhaps you won't have to worry about that," Mendoza murmured.

"What's that?"

The explosion shook the ground under their feet. The two guards instinctively turned toward it. As fast as a striking snake, Mendoza's hand closed around the butt of a gun holstered on the closest man's hip. He yanked the gun out and in the same motion lifted it and blasted a round through the side of the man's head.

The second guard tried to swing his shotgun around, but with blinding speed, Mendoza shot him in the head, too, and his corpse dropped to the ground next to the body of his dead companion. Mendoza bent over, pulled the second guard's Colt from its holster, and then with irons in both hands, he headed toward the middle of town.

The thought that this was another distraction staged by Jaime Mendoza's gang to rescue their leader and kidnap the young women flashed into Bo's mind as soon as he heard the explosion. He turned swiftly toward them, in time to see a Mexican grab Luella and drag her into the crowd. It was like the killings at the strongman competition all over again. He drew his gun, but he couldn't risk a shot, and in the blink of an eye, Luella and her captor were gone.

"Get to the hotel!" he told Susan Hampshire. "You ought to be safe there! Scratch! Rance! Guard the ladies!"

With that, he went after Luella and the man who had snatched her.

The guards at the freight office had been grumbling earlier in the evening about not being able to go and watch the boxing matches.

Now they lay crumpled in death, dark pools spreading around them as blood flowed from their slashed throats. Smoke from the blast curled out the door and windows of the office.

Jack Bouma stood in front of the building, gun in hand, as Dyson's men carried crates full of silver ingots out of the office and loaded them in two wagons.

Farther up the street, chaos reigned. Nobody was coming in this direction, though. The panicked crowd fled away from where the explosion had taken place. That situation probably wouldn't last long, but Bouma and his crew needed only a few more minutes to finish cleaning out the safe.

Then two struggling figures emerged from the melee and stumbled toward the freight office. A man and a woman, Bouma saw. From what he could make out in the edges of the glare from the multitude of torches that surrounded the boxing ring, a Mexican and one of those mail-order brides.

Neither represented a threat to the robbery that Bouma and Dyson were trying to pull off.

But then, running after them, came another man, and this one Bouma recognized as Bo Creel. He didn't like Creel, had known with his gunman's instincts that Creel was a problem as soon as he met the old pelican. Bouma's mouth twisted in a snarl as he brought up his gun, aimed past the Mexican and the girl, and pulled the trigger.

* * *

"Hey!" a man yelled behind Armbruster and Luella.

Armbruster twisted his head to look around, and that caused him to veer to his right. At that same instant, Luella twisted her body to the left and almost got loose, but Armbruster clamped his left hand on her right arm just in time to prevent her escape.

A split second later, something slammed into his right shoulder with sledgehammer force. Pain and shock filled his entire being as he spun around, losing his hold on Luella in the process, and crumpled to the ground.

For an instant, Bo thought Luella was hit, but then he saw her stumble away and the Mexican sprawled in the street. He'd seen the Colt flame as it bloomed into a crimson flower in the darkness in front of the freight office. Now he spotted the wagons and the men loading crates into them and knew immediately what was going on.

And there in the street in front of the building, the lean figure of Jack Bouma, gun in hand. Another spurt of orange from the muzzle, the wind-rip of a bullet past his ear, and then Bo was down on one knee, the Colt thrust out in front of him, bucking and roaring as he fired twice.

Bouma took a couple of stumbling steps backward as the bullets smashed into his chest. His mouth opened and closed like that of a fish out of water. He triggered one more shot, but it was just nerves spasming as they died, and the slug went into the dirt a few feet in front of him. He fell to his knees, bent far backward, and then toppled over to lie in a motionless heap.

Bo went into a roll as some of the other men stopped what they were doing and opened fire on him. Bullets kicked up dirt where he had been a heartbeat earlier. He came to a stop on his belly and triggered three times, spraying lead among the silver thieves. Two of the outlaws went down.

Bo's Colt was empty now, though, and he didn't figure the others would be in any mood to let him reload.

He didn't have to, because at that moment Rance Plummer and several of the SJ cowboys charged along the street, guns blazing. The silver thieves were concentrating on Bo and didn't see this new threat until a couple of them had already gone down, filled with bullet holes.

For ten seconds that seemed longer, a storm of lead swept back and forth along the street as Bo sprawled underneath it, and when it ended, the outlaws were all either already dead or kicking out their lives. Some of the SJ crew were wounded, but all were still on their feet.

Plummer helped Bo up and asked, "You all right, Creel?"

"Yeah, thanks to you and those other hombres." Swiftly, Bo started thumbing fresh cartridges from his shell belt into his Colt. "Where's Scratch?"

"In the hotel, with the ladies. They all made it safe and sound. They ought to be all right if they stay there. Hell's poppin' all over town. Owlhoots are raidin' some of the businesses, but it looks like folks have stopped panickin' and are fightin' back."

"What about Forbes Dyson? Have you seen him?"

"He's in the hotel, too, pitchin' a fit because they're robbin' his saloon and he can't get back there to help run 'em off."

Bo didn't believe for a second that Dyson's reaction was genuine. Bouma wasn't smart enough to have come up with this plan on his own. Dyson was neck-deep in it, too, and the pieces of the puzzle fit together well enough in Bo's mind to form a coherent picture.

Just as he snapped the Colt's loading gate closed, Luella rushed up to him and flung her arms around him.

"Mr. Creel! Thank God you came for me. That man—" Her voice choked off as she turned to look at the spot where her captor had fallen when Bouma shot him. Bo turned his gaze in that direction, too.

The man was gone.

Bo grimaced. He didn't know how badly the Mexican was hit or what his connection was to Jaime Mendoza, but right now none of that mattered. He said to Plummer, "Keep Miss Tolman safe but stay away from the hotel for now."

"How come?"

"Because that's where I'm headed," Bo said, "and there's liable to be more shooting."

Chapter 38

The dining room in the Territorial House didn't have any windows, so that was where Scratch had had the ladies take cover. The building's adobe walls were stout enough to stop anything short of a cannonball.

Scratch had hustled Susan Hampshire into the dining room with them. He knew that was what Bo would want him to do.

The young women were consumed with fear over what might have happened to Luella. Scratch told them, "Bo went after her, and I ain't ever known Bo to fail when he set out to do somethin'. He'll bring her back safe. You wait and see."

"But it sounds like a war out there," Cecilia said.

"Nobody's going to hurt you," Hugh Craddock assured her. He had made it into the hotel with them. "I'll make sure of that."

"I'm not worried about myself," Cecilia snapped. "I'm worried about Luella."

"I sent my boys to look for Creel and help him—" Craddock began.

Forbes Dyson strode through the arched opening between

the lobby and the dining room, wearing a harassed, angry look on his face.

"It sounds like the shooting is starting to die down out there," he said. "Maybe this disaster will be over soon."

"What happened?" Cecilia asked. "Did every bandit gang in the territory decide to raid Silverhill tonight?"

Dyson sighed wearily and said, "That's what it looked and sounded like. I should have known there are bad men out there who might use the big celebration as distraction for a raid, but in my enthusiasm to promote the town, the thought never crossed my mind."

"What was that explosion?" Craddock asked.

"I don't know," Dyson replied with a shake of his head. "I know there was a silver shipment in the safe down at the freight office, and they may have gone after that, but right now I can't be sure." He grimaced. "I'm pretty certain they've cleaned out all the cash in *my* safe at the Silver King, though."

"We have guns," Rose said. "We should have stayed out there and fought the outlaws, too."

Jean stared at her, aghast, and said, "Have you lost your mind, Rose? We would have all been killed!"

"Sometimes you've got to stand up and fight," Rose said stubbornly.

"You're right," Beth agreed with her. "If we're going to be frontierswomen, we have to learn how to . . . to stomp our own snakes!"

"Miss Beth," Scratch said, "if I was forty years younger, I reckon I'd court you myself!"

Muzzle flashes still split the night here and there, but for the most part, the battle appeared to be over as Bo approached the Territorial House. He knew from what Rance Plummer had told him that Scratch had gotten the ladies to safety, but he'd feel better about things when he saw that with his own eyes.

He had just stepped up onto the porch when a man slid out of the shadows of the alley at the other end of the building and climbed onto the porch, as well.

For a split second, they faced each other there. Jaime Mendoza had guns in both hands, and they came up spitting fire, as that impasse had lasted only a shaved heartbeat of time.

Bo felt a bullet pluck at his coat. Another sizzled past his ear on the other side. He centered his Colt on Mendoza's chest and triggered three shots. The gun barrel came up a little with each round, so the three bullets marched up the bandit chief's breastbone, shattering it on their way to smashing his spine. Mendoza went down.

Bo rushed along the porch and kicked the fallen revolvers out of Mendoza's reach, just in case. Mendoza was too far gone to be much of a threat, though. He would be dead within seconds.

But not before he rasped out, "Dyson! He was . . . behind it all! Promised to . . . free me . . . if I helped him rob the town . . . blind."

Bo hunkered beside the dying bandit and said, "Why are you telling me this, Mendoza?"

Blood leaked from both corners of Mendoza's mouth as he smiled.

"Because if I die . . . tonight . . . I want Dyson to suffer . . . along with me. He cannot . . . get away with . . ."

Mendoza's final breath rattled from his throat.

Bo stood up. He figured Forbes Dyson was in the hotel. As soon as he had reloaded the Colt, he went inside.

Several of the ladies exclaimed in relief when he entered the dining room.

Scratch came toward him and said, "Bo, are you all right?"

"Yeah. Came close a few times, but I managed to dodge the reaper again."

"He's a nimble ol' son of a gun, ain't he?" Scratch said with a grin. "But we're faster."

Bo spotted Dyson on the other side of the room. The saloon man's clothes were disheveled, and his hair was awry. This had been a rough night for him.

It was about to get rougher.

"Scratch, Craddock, move the ladies over there by the wall," Bo said.

Scratch knew his trail partner well enough to be aware instantly that something was wrong. He also knew Bo wouldn't give an order like that unless it was important, so he turned immediately and said, "Ladies, move back over there."

"Creel, what's going on?" Craddock demanded.

Bo nodded toward Dyson, who was staring at him in apparent confusion. "There's the man responsible for all hell breaking loose in Silverhill tonight."

"What?" Dyson said. "What in blazes are you talking about, Creel?"

"I ran into Jaime Mendoza outside," Bo said, his voice flat and hard. "You probably heard the shots. Mendoza confirmed something I already suspected. You planned this whole thing, Dyson."

"The . . . the competition for the mail-order brides? I never made any secret of that—"

"No, I mean getting the town all stirred up and using that as a cover for Bouma and his men to rob the freight office of that silver shipment. Bouma's dead, in case you're wondering, and nobody got away with the silver. Some of the other businesses probably got cleaned out, but at least now you won't be able to swoop in and take them over. That's what you were planning to do, isn't it? Turn Silverhill and this corner of the territory into your own private kingdom?"

Dyson sneered at him and said, "You can't prove any of that! You'd take the word of a . . . a filthy greaser bandit? Anyway, you said he's dead and Bouma's dead. There's nobody to back up your crazy story, Creel."

Bo smiled and shook his head slowly. "I never said Mendoza

was dead, just that Bouma is. And I think Mendoza is kind of bitter about the whole thing."

It was a lie, but it worked. Dyson stiffened, ripped out a curse, and clawed under his coat. Bo had pouched his iron when he came in, but he drew now as Dyson yanked out a pistol. Bo summoned all the speed he possessed because he didn't want Dyson even getting off a shot. In a room crowded with innocents like this one, there was no telling where a stray slug might land.

Bo's Colt roared, and Dyson's head snapped back, with a red-rimmed hole in the middle of the forehead. The bullet had drilled cleanly into his brain. He folded up, his dreams blasted out of his head, along with a good-sized chunk from the back of his skull.

Now the battle of Silverhill really was over.

The next day, Bo and Scratch were taking it easy on the hotel porch when Rance Plummer rode up, along with the cowboys from the SJ spread.

The Texans stood up and moved to the railing.

Bo said, "Are you headed back to the ranch?"

"Somebody's got to run the place," Plummer answered with a grin. "We might could stay another day or two, though, if you need any help cleanin' up the mess around here."

"No, you go ahead," Bo told him. "Everybody's pitching in. Silverhill will be back to normal in a few days, I expect."

"Except there's nobody to run the biggest saloon in town," Plummer pointed out.

"I guess that'll be up to Dyson's heirs, if he's got any. One of the lawyers over in El Paso who works for the mine owners will be looking into that."

"Until then," Scratch said, "I reckon the other saloons in town will just have to take up the slack."

Plummer rested his hands on the saddle horn and leaned forward.

"What about the young ladies? Steve, here, won the horse race, you know." Plummer nodded toward one of the cowboys. "He don't want to leave if he's got a claim on a bride."

"Aw, I, uh, I never said it quite like that," the young puncher stumbled, clearly embarrassed.

"All that's been set aside," Bo said. "Dyson never acted in good faith. But the ladies have agreed to stay here awhile and maybe meet some of the fellas and see what happens." Bo shrugged. "You never know when there might be some courting going on."

"See?" Plummer said to the young cowboy called Steve. "Maybe you can ride back over here sometime and find out how things stand."

With that, the foreman turned his horse, lifted a hand in farewell, and urged his mount into motion.

Scratch called, "So long, Rance!" as the crew from the SJ rode away.

"You didn't tell him that Craddock is bein' stubborn enough to hang around and try to convince Cecilia to marry him," Scratch commented.

"He didn't ask," Bo said.

"One more thing I been wonderin' about . . . What's Miss Hampshire gonna do? She ain't said nothin' else about goin' home, leastways not that I've heard."

"She has to wait here for the next stagecoach."

"You think she's gonna be on it when it rolls out?"

"I don't know," Bo said as he thought about Susan Hampshire. "It'll be sort of interesting to see."

On a rise a mile south of Silverhill, half a dozen men sat on horseback and looked toward the settlement.

Guadalupe Sanchez said, "Jaime is dead. What are we going to do now?"

"We could still raid the town," another bandit suggested.

"And get killed for our trouble?" Philip Armbruster said. "There are too many good fighting men there. Those two old Texans are there, and they seem to be worth a dozen men each."

Armbruster no longer wore the peasant garb. His wounded shoulder was bandaged, and his right arm was in a makeshift sling. Sanchez had found some trousers for him, with embroidery down the legs, and he wore a loose white shirt and a serape thrown over his shoulders. A gray sombrero was on his head.

One of the men, a wizened old-timer named Tomas, had a lot of experience patching up bullet wounds, and he had assured Armbruster that his shoulder would heal. No bones were broken. The bullet had passed cleanly through muscle. For now, he wouldn't be able to write, but that would come back to him.

He might even start learning how to use a gun.

Becoming aware that the bandits were all looking at him, Armbruster realized they were waiting for him to tell them what to do. Officially, Sanchez might be their leader now, but the man was rather dull mentally and would be open to suggestions.

"Why don't we head back south of the border?" Armbruster said. "We can lie low for a bit and make plans, perhaps recruit a few more men. Jaime wanted to lead a rebellion against the oppressive government in Mexico City, didn't he?"

"He always *said* that he did," Sanchez replied, "but I think mostly he wanted to steal and have the señoritas think he was a big hero."

Armbruster mused for a moment. It was a shame about Luella, but for now, he had to put his feelings for her aside. Bigger ideas had come to him.

"Maybe we'll do it for real."

Sanchez stared at him and said, "A revolution? You mean it?"

"Why not? We should give it a try, anyway." With that,

Armbruster turned his horse toward the south and added, "*Andale!*"

As they spurred away, he thought about all the bizarre twists of fate that had left him, a gringo reporter, as the de facto leader of a gang of Mexican bandidos and would-be revolutionaries. It was almost beyond belief. . . .

But what a book this was going to make!